ROGER
WILLIAMS
IN AN
ELEVATOR

To Lottie,
May your best
dreams become
reality!,

Karen Petit

ROGER WILLIAMS
IN AN
ELEVATOR

KAREN PETIT

TATE PUBLISHING
AND ENTERPRISES, LLC

Published by Tate Publishing & Enterprises, LLC
127 E. Trade Center Terrace | Mustang, Oklahoma 73064 USA
1.888.361.9473 | www.tatepublishing.com

Tate Publishing is committed to excellence in the publishing industry. The company reflects the philosophy established by the founders, based on Psalm 68:11,
"The Lord gave the word and great was the company of those who published it."

Book design copyright © 2016 by Tate Publishing, LLC. All rights reserved.
Cover design by Albert Ceasar Compay
Interior design by Richell Balansag
In this novel, two of the photos of Roger Williams statues were taken at Roger Williams University, Bristol, R.I.
Creator of Roger Williams statues at Roger Williams University: Armand Lamontagne
Use of Photos: Courtesy of Roger Williams University

Published in the United States of America

ISBN: 978-1-68254-428-0
Fiction / Christian / Suspense
15.12.17

ACKNOWLEDGMENTS

My family has been very loving and helpful throughout my life. My thanks are extended to my children: Chris (my son), Cathy (my daughter), and Chris (my stepson). I am also thanking my brothers and sisters for their loving support: Ray, Rick, Margaret, Carl, Sam, Bill, Dan, and Anne.

My many friends at Phillips Memorial Baptist Church, the Fitness Studio, and the Dancin' Feelin' have also been very supportive. I am very thankful for their continuous help and for the never-ending joys they have added into my life.

I have many other helpful friends from my past and present positions at various educational institutions. My thanks go out to the students, faculty, and staff members at the following colleges: the Community College of Rhode Island, Bristol Community College, Bryant University, Massasoit Community College, New England Institute of Technology, Quinsigamond Community College, Rhode Island College, Roger Williams University, the University of Massachusetts at Dartmouth, the University of Rhode Island, and Worcester State University.

My thanks also are extended to my fellow authors in the Association of Rhode Island Authors and to the helpful employees at Tate Publishing. The people in both of these places have helped me to appreciate my writing, editing, and marketing skills.

Finally, I am most thankful to my Lord and Savior for his continuing love and guidance. He not only has created my life, but has also made it into a very joyful one. He has made my best dreams become my reality.

CONTENTS

PREFACE

———————◉———————

*R*oger *Williams in an Elevator* is a fictional novel with accurate historic information about Roger Williams and the seventeenth-century culture. This historic novel explores freedom while making connections between Roger Williams's beliefs and our current society.

When Roger Williams left the Massachusetts Bay Colony during January 1636, he fled into a New England blizzard to avoid being arrested. He soon established his new home at Providence Plantations; he "created a second New World—a modern society where the ideals of religious liberty, independence of thought and freedom of speech would take root in American soil." [1] His beliefs, writings, and actions helped to inject religious and other freedoms into the structure of our society.

Like different groups of Pilgrims, many of the fictional characters in *Roger Williams in an Elevator* develop their own new worlds when they become stuck in elevators. The elevator communities—yelling, accounting, liberty, watery, fiery, falling, sharing, and hidden—determine their own rules and freedoms based on their current beliefs, past experiences, future expectations, individual personalities, and cultural settings. The eight elevators show different kinds of freedom, as well as varying reactions to a loss of freedom.

The religious freedom that Roger Williams systematized in our society is currently a part of many people's lives. However, for some people, religious freedom is still just a dream, rather than being an integral part of their reality. We need to cherish our freedom, help those who lack freedom, and use our freedom responsibly. Then we will be able to choose correct paths for ourselves, our communities, and our connections to God.

ILLUSTRATIONS

———◉———

Roger Williams Timeline

Dates	Events in the Life of Roger Williams
1603	Born in London
1627	Graduated from Pembroke College, Cambridge
12/1630	Left England on the *Lyon* with his wife, Mary Barnard
2/5/1631	Arrived in Boston after 57 days on the Atlantic Ocean
8/1633	Birth of 1st child: Mary Williams; his later children were Freeborn, Providence, Mercy, Daniel, & Joseph
7/8/1635	Was warned by the General Court to behave.
10/9/1635	Was banished, had 6 weeks to leave, told not to preach
1/1636	To avoid arrest, fled his home in a blizzard; left family behind; in the Spring, founded Providence
1638	Started First Baptist Church in Providence
1643	Published *A Key into the Language of America*
1644	Obtained patent for Providence; published *The Bloudy Tenent of Persecution for Cause of Conscience.*
1651-54	With John Clarke, tried to get Providence charter; John Clarke received the charter on July 8, 1663.
3/29/1676	House was burned during King Phillip's War.
1679-83	Wrote "A Brief Reply" in the margins of a book
1683	Death and home-going to be with God

Roger Williams Timeline

Roger Williams Statue in Roger Williams
State Park, Providence, Rhode Island

SHIFTING TERRITORY

K ate sat down on the edge of her bed and frowned as she
looked at the note on her bedside table: "Lucid dream
about my new office and the elevators."

Her facial expression showed her lack of desire to follow her
own directions. She then said out loud, "No, I'm too tired. I just
want to relax. I'm not going to try any lucid-dreaming techniques.
Tomorrow, I'll figure out some other way of dealing with that
awful building." She crinkled up the paper and threw it into the
trash. After lying down on her bed, she quickly fell asleep. For
most of the night, she was unaware of the content in her dreams.

When it was nearly time to wake up, she found herself inside
the bank where she used to work. She immediately began to move
everything into its proper place. She put a pen on the counter
back into its holder and then twisted it, so the pen's chain fell
vertically straight down along the side of its holder. She lined up
the piles of deposit and withdrawal tickets, so they fit perfectly
into their tiny cubicles beneath the countertops. When she tried
to go into the bank vault to fix the stacks of money, the door
closed before she could enter. A police officer came up to her and
said, "You're not supposed to be here anymore."

"You're right. I should be in the new office. I must have made
a mistake."

"Did you get here by going the wrong way on a one-way street?"

"No, I haven't done that mistake in at least a year."

"You're lying."

"No, I'm not."

"Just last week, you left a parking lot by exiting through the entrance lane."

"Driving in a wrong lane is different from driving the wrong way on a one-way street."

Instead of listening to her, the police officer was writing on a piece of paper.

"What are you writing? You're not giving me a ticket, are you?"

"Yes, I am."

Kate said, "I think I'm just dreaming, and that ticket is not real. I'm going to try a reality check." She looked down at her feet. Her right foot was wearing a brand-new, lace-covered white shoe with a four-inch heel. Her left foot was wearing an ugly old slipper; strings of dirty yarn were hanging off both its sides, so it looked like a spider with dirty legs.

The officer asked, "Why are you dressed so funny?"

"I'm dreaming, so some things are a little strange. In my reality, I would never dress in such a weird fashion. Everything would match perfectly and be correctly ironed. I'm too well organized to be wearing this kind of confusing clothing." Kate looked up at the officer. He had a pair of handcuffs on top of his head. She added, "This is a lucid dream."

"What's that?"

"I consciously realize that I'm dreaming, and I can sometimes change a part of my dream."

"Really? Can you change this?" The officer took out his gun.

Kate waved her hand, and the gun disappeared. She waved her hand again, and the officer disappeared. The traffic ticket, however, remained behind. As Kate watched, the ticket changed into a hundred-dollar bill. When she tried to pick it up, it flew away.

Harry, her old boss, suddenly was standing in front of her. He was a lot taller than normal, and Kate found herself looking down at his formal black shoes. The laces were tied into knots, rather than in bows. Harry grew even taller as he said, "This branch office is closing down. I want you to fire all the bank tellers."

Kate's mouth flew open, but no words came out. She jumped backward and then said, "Wait a minute—I'm already backward in time. I need to jump forward in time."

She looked at Harry's knees. He was standing too close to her; she couldn't jump forward without bumping into him.

"Are we in an elevator?" she asked.

Harry ignored her question and said, "You need to fire everyone." His eyebrows then moved upward; he looked like he wanted Kate to say something.

"You're kidding, right?"

He laughed. "Why would I kid about something like this?"

"What about me? Am I fired too after I'm done firing everyone else?"

"No, you have a promotion. You're being transferred to the main office in Providence, Rhode Island."

"Can other people in this branch also be transferred?"

"Well, you can tell them that, if you want to."

"Will I be lying?"

"Definitely!"

"How about if I say that I'll help them with their resumes, and a few of them might be hired in the Providence office?"

Harry thought for a moment before replying, "Okay. You can say that. It'll make them happier, and at least one of them might even be transferred to the main office."

"Will that be true?"

"Maybe." His eyes looked past Kate. He was trying to avoid eye contact with her.

Kate looked beyond Harry and saw other bank employees. She slowly walked up to each one and said, "You're fired." Every employee's face became bright red, looking as if it was on fire. Each person got so mad at her that her other words were not even heard: "I'll help you with your resume for a possible job in the Providence office."

Harry walked into his office and was looking at friendly faces on Facebook as Kate was looking at the angry faces of ten just-fired employees. The tellers formed a circle around her. She said loudly, "I'll try to help all of you."

"How?" Lisa, one of the tellers, asked her.

"I'll try to get you jobs in the main branch of our bank."

Harry left his office and walked up to the circle of employees. "You're lying, Kate." He looked at the circle of tellers and said, "Kate's been promoted, but there are not enough jobs for everyone else."

"Oh, so Kate still has a job?" Lisa asked with a surprised look on her face.

Kate said, "I'd rather stay here where we've all been working together for years. I hate that giant building with the main office in it, and I really hate its elevators." She sighed and then added, "I'm also going to miss everyone so much."

Lisa said, "I'm going to miss everyone too." She looked around at the other people in the circle. "We'll probably all wind up working for different companies."

Another teller said, "We'll have to get together every month or two and have a party."

Lisa said, "Definitely. We're all friends on Facebook, so we can do something like that."

"Yeah." Kate's smile became frozen as she looked around at the circle of people who were frowning back at her.

One of the tellers in the circle said, "I know someone who's about to be unfriended by a lot of people."

Laughter broke out. Kate looked at their faces. She could no longer recognize any of them. They had already unfriended her. Even though this was a lucid dream, she was unable to make them happy again. She could only change some of the things in her dreams.

The tellers in the circle were still staring angrily at Kate. She asked, "Why are you all mad at me, instead of at Harry?"

They started yelling at her.

"You can't fire us!"

"You can only lay us off!"

"You can't fire good workers!"

"I was nearly killed during a bank robbery here."

"We'll still file for unemployment!"

"And we'll get unemployment!"

"If we have to, we'll hire one lawyer who will help all of us together."

"Today's the day! We need to steal money from our teller drawers!"

"Better yet, we could have a money war."

"What's a money war?"

"We'll use money as a weapon and throw it at someone."

"Yeah, there's someone here who's getting a raise."

"She'll be getting a lot more money, and we'll be getting a lot less."

All eyes turned toward Kate. After a few seconds of silence, the tellers ran over to their stations and began grabbing money out of their teller drawers. Even though Kate tried to hide by putting her hands over her face, money began to fly across the room in her direction. Most of the bills fluttered to the floor, but the coins kept on hitting her. Suddenly, the bank vault became noisy. Kate's mouth flew open when she saw the large number of bills and coins that were leaving the vault and coming toward her. The bills were tied together in stacks, so most of them were now hitting her, rather than fluttering to the floor. Even so, they weren't too painful. However, the coins were leaving red marks and scars on her hands, arms, and head.

Kate began to cry and then said, "I have to focus on what's positive. I can live with these bills and coins. At least there are no longer any heavy bars of gold in that vault." Suddenly, golden bars started to fly from the vault toward her. She ran and hid behind a desk. She could still hear the noises of bills, coins, and bars as they were thrown down to where she had been standing just a moment earlier.

Suddenly, the bank was quiet. Kate peered up from behind the desk. All of the bank's money was in the middle of the room. A circle of tellers had formed around the money. Kate said, "I like money, but not like this. A money war is all wrong." For some reason, the bills, coins, and bars listened to her; they flew into the bank vault and stacked themselves up neatly into piles.

Kate said, "Oh, the money did what I wanted it to. My real money never listens to me. I must be getting better at lucid dreaming techniques." She looked at the faces of her colleagues. They appeared sorry for what they had done.

One of the tellers said, "We told the bars, bills, and coins to go back into their correct places."

Kate said, "Thanks so much for understanding. I'm not the one who decided to fire all of you."

The faces of her colleagues began to look upset again.

Kate said, "Oh, no! Even riding on an elevator will be better than going through that money war again." She tried to open her eyes, but she couldn't wake herself up. She then tried to change the content of her dream by concentrating on walking toward the door of the bank. After a few missteps, her walking worked! She suddenly found herself outside the bank and moving toward a different building. Taking a few more steps forward, she entered the front door of the new building and looked around inside the first floor of a too-tall building. In front of her was an endless row of elevators. She said out loud, "There are too many elevators here. I don't see any space left for offices."

Two of the elevators disappeared, and a bank lobby took their place. The remaining elevators turned toward the bank lobby and loudly began to open and close their doors. The bank lobby was scared; it became smaller and smaller until it disappeared. Only the elevators remained.

Kate said, "Why are you kicking the lobby out of your building?"

A voice inside of the center elevator said, "If you come in here, I'll tell you all about this building."

"No, I can't go in there," Kate said in a too-loud response.

"Why not?"

"I hate elevators!"

The elevator's doors opened, bent outward, pulled Kate into the elevator, and then closed with a thundering noise. Even though she pressed the "open door" button multiple times, the doors remained closed.

A voice from the elevator's speaker said, "Since you're the only one here, you have your own personal space. You should like being in this elevator."

"No, I hate the changing motions in an elevator. I can't do anything to make it move according to how I want it to move."

"You can push the different buttons."

"Then other people push the elevator's buttons, and everything keeps on changing. The elevator goes fast when I think it should be stopping. It moves too slowly when I expect it to be going fast."

Kate concentrated on trying to make the elevator's doors open. The elevator's metal doors bent forward and backward; they then began to twist into different shapes. Finally, they changed into a set of stairs. The silver metal stairs moved sideways and connected to the other elevators, which also changed into stairs. Finally, the whole building became a giant set of stairs, extending upward for hundreds of feet.

Kate yelled, "I hate walking up stairs in tall buildings. It's too tiring."

One of the stairs shifted forward, so it looked like a slide. Other stairs joined in until they made a giant slide. A ladder, railing, and top area were added to the slide. Water began flowing down the slide, which became a waterslide that moved out of the front doors of the office building. It stopped moving in the middle of a quiet street.

Kate slowly climbed up the waterslide's slippery ladder. When she was near the top of the slide, it began to move with every motion of hers. Her feet froze. She looked over the right side of the slide, which tilted slightly to the right. She then looked to the left, and the slide shifted to the left. The slide began to shake from one side to the other. With each motion, it was increasing the speed and severity of its movements.

Kate gripped the railing as she asked, "Is this an earthquake?" The slide responded, "No, you're just trying to change the shape of this slide into your own idea of a slide. You can't do that."

"This is my lucid dream. Why can't I change things?"

"You can't change me. You can only change yourself."

"But slides aren't supposed to move like this." Kate grabbed more tightly onto the ladder's railings. Hidden snakes in both the railings began to hiss. When one of the snakes bit her, Kate moved both her hands backward and held onto the railings with the tips of her fingers. The cold metal railings stretched themselves out, becoming larger and larger until they were giant rectangular sheets of black metal. She was now inside an elevator again. Its walls moved in closer and closer until she could no longer move and was having problems breathing inside the metal walls.

Kate pressed her hands against the walls, but was unable to push them away from her. "Please move," she said to the walls.

The elevator said, "Okay." It then moved upward with erratic and shaking movements.

Kate tried to calm herself down. She deeply inhaled and exhaled, but her still-fast breathing showed her continuing anxiety. She stretched out and then relaxed her hands, but she was still shaking. Finally, she said, "You can't keep on going upward. This building only has forty floors, not four thousand."

"Because I'm in your dream, this building does have four thousand floors."

"Please stop and let me out."

"Okay." While still moving upward, the elevator opened up its doors and tilted forward until Kate fell out into a dark night sky. As she was falling downward, she suddenly woke up. She found herself to be curled up in the middle of her own bed. Her arms were hugging her knees, and her head was curled downward and touching her knees. She slowly extended her arms and legs outward. After stretching for a minute, she said out loud, "Even though I have to go to work today, at least I'll have more freedom to control things than I did in that dream."

*Roger Williams Statue in the Visitor Center
of the Roger Williams National Memorial*

Wellcurb in the Hahn Memorial at the Roger Williams National Memorial

A NEW OFFICE

---●---

Kate looked over at her bedside clock. As usual, she had woken up before the clock's alarm could make any noise. She turned the alarm's switch off before running out of her bedroom and showering. She then ate some cereal while getting dressed in a blue skirt, matching jacket, and a plaid blouse. Her feet slid themselves into two-inch high heels. All her movements were very fast, while also being jittery, showing her anxiety about the upcoming day.

When Kate began to put on her makeup, her movements slowed down. She rubbed moisturizer on her face and neck. Pausing to look at her face in the mirror, she sighed at the brightness of her freckles. She then rubbed the skin of her face with both her hands. Her movements were unsuccessful in removing any of the freckles. She partially covered them up with foundation. After putting on the rest of her makeup, Kate glanced down at her watch and smiled. It was 7:01. She said out loud, "Yes, I'll be at my new job at least fifteen minutes early!"

Kate walked briskly out the front door of her home. She was holding onto her keys, her lunch bag, and her purse. Pausing briefly, she looked at the tires of her car, and then at the edges of her driveway. Her smile showed her satisfaction that her car was parked perfectly in the center of the driveway.

Out on route 95, the traffic was moving fairly quickly. Then suddenly, all the vehicles slowed down and soon came to a complete halt. Kate looked at the clock in the dashboard of her car and sighed. She then kept changing the channels on her radio until one of them had some news about the traffic: "An accident just happened on route 95 North, right after the Thurbers Avenue curve. Only one lane is open."

"Which one? Should I move to the left lane, where the traffic seems to be moving slightly faster?"

The radio announcer didn't respond to Kate's question, but instead announced the next song as being "Couldn't Get It Right" by the Climax Blues Band. After a few seconds, the beginning line was heard: "Time was drifting."[2]

Kate glanced at her watch and said, "I can't be late for my new job." She then heard another line of the song: "I started searching for a better way."[3]

After looking in all her mirrors, she said, "Finding a better way would be a great idea. The only problem is there's nowhere else to go. I'm completely locked into this one lane."

Kate switched channels on her radio, but she couldn't find any other news about the traffic jam. Five minutes later, the traffic began moving faster, but it was still only going about twenty miles an hour. After another ten minutes, the traffic sped up. Kate moved into the high-speed lane and then switched into the far right lane right before the State Offices exit. She turned off the highway and was soon driving on the hill above the statehouse. As she sped down a one-way street, a blue car suddenly turned onto the road in front of her. She slammed on her brakes and yelled out, "You stole my spot!" The driver of the blue car ignored her; he kept on driving very slowly, and his eyes moved to the left, to the right, and then up the hill. He was possibly looking for the Roger Williams statue or some other landmark.

Kate pressed down on her gas pedal until she was only four feet behind the blue car. She beeped her horn and turned on her high-beam headlights, but her actions did not make the slow car move any faster.

A minute later, Kate found herself in a line of stopped traffic. At least thirty cars were in front of her. She arched her head upward until she saw flashing lights from several police cars. She then glanced at the clock in the dashboard and finally at her watch. It was already seven forty-five.

After slowly driving up the street and passing the police cars, Kate turned into the parking lot for the Pilgrim office building. She parked her car, glanced down at her watch, and walked quickly up to the front door of the building. Once she was inside, her eyes moved back and forth between the stairs and the elevators. She looked at her watch again and then went up to one of the elevators.

Several other people were also waiting. When the doors opened, Kate walked hesitantly up to the doors of the elevator and then stopped. A person standing behind her asked, "Are you okay?"

"Yeah, I'm just tired, and I don't like elevators."

"Well, these are really good ones."

"Thanks for trying to cheer me up."

Kate walked through the doors and quickly found herself pushed into the back of the elevator; at least eight people were squeezed into the small space around her. She blinked her eyes a couple of times and then asked, "Can someone please press the button for the twenty-first floor?"

"That one's already been hit."

"Thanks."

As the elevator's doors closed, Kate took in a deep breath and closed her eyes. When the elevator moved upward, her breathing speeded up. Every time the doors opened and closed, she sighed.

Finally, a man said, "We're at twenty-one."

Kate opened her eyes and smiled at the faces that were staring at her. Several drops of sweat were moving down her face, falling onto her neck, and landing in the collar of her suit.

She quickly exited the elevator and walked down the corridor toward the main office of the New World Bank. Before reaching the doorway, she took a Kleenex out of her purse and wiped the sweat off her face and neck. She then knocked on the door, glanced at her watch, and saw that she was thirty seconds early. A lady inside the bank came up to the glass door, opened it up, and asked, "You're Kate, right?"

"Yeah, I am. How did you know?"

"We have a picture of your driver's license."

Kate laughed. "Of course you do. I didn't even think of that."

"Come on in," the lady said as she held open the door.

"If your name tag's correct, you're Carol."

"Yeah, I am." Carol locked the door of the bank again before showing Kate around to the different sections of the bank. The front section was for customers and bank tellers. The middle section had ten cubicles, including one for Kate. The back section had offices for the president and other upper-level management personnel. There was also a meeting room with a large round table, chairs, a coat closet, and a refrigerator. Kate hung her coat in the closet and moved some of the hangers, so they each had the same amount of space.

Carol showed Kate where her desk was while saying, "Joe told me to give you these training materials."

"I already had training when I worked at the Warwick branch of the New World Bank."

"I know. You've probably seen all these things, but you're still supposed to read them."

"Okay. Are there some forms in here?"

"Yeah."

Kate glanced briefly at a stack of ten folders; each one had multiple papers inside it. "I guess I know what I'll be doing for the next day or two."

Carol laughed. "I'll also be setting you up with a teller drawer."

"I thought I was just going to be doing loan applications and other office work."

"Most of the time, yes, but when we need an extra teller, you'll be out front at a teller station."

"I'm okay with that."

Carol frowned. "I'm surprised no one told you."

"I don't think my old boss knew too much about this job." Kate paused before adding, "Anyway, I'm really happy doing a variety of jobs. Then I won't get bored."

"That's great." Carol looked out the window. "Do you know what happened this morning in the building next door? There were at least five police cars and a fire engine."

"I saw several police cars, but I didn't notice a fire engine. Were there really that many police cars?"

"Yeah. One of the officers had a dog."

"What kind of a dog?"

"I don't know. It could have been a drug-sniffing or a bomb-sniffing dog."

"At least you saw a dog. You already know more than I do."

Carol laughed. "Thanks, but I don't know very much at all. I'll just keep on asking as people come in. Maybe someone will know something." She turned around and went back to her desk.

Kate looked at the papers in the first folder. There were a few forms that she had to fill out. Sighing, she grabbed a pen from her purse and began filling in the first form.

Before she was finished with the first form, her new boss, Joe, walked into the office. He looked at her and said, "I'm glad you're here on time. The traffic today was so bad."

"Yeah, it was." Kate shook her head, stood up, and smiled.

"After you have a chance to read some of the folders, I'll check with you about any questions you might have."

"Thanks, Joe. I'm so happy to have this new job in the main office."

"Well, you've been doing a great job in the Warwick branch. There's no way we could let you go to work for some other company."

"Thanks."

Joe waved good-bye before walking to his office.

Right before nine o'clock, Carol went up to Kate's desk and said, "I'll be opening the front door in a minute. Would you like to come and see how everything's being done?"

"Definitely." Kate followed Carol into the front section of the bank. The first ten minutes were fairly quiet. Then a short, skinny man wearing a hood walked through the front door. He went over to one of the walls, put his ear close to it, and then hit the wall several times while listening to the sounds. Kate walked over to him, noticed that he was wearing sunglasses, and asked, "What are you doing?"

He moved his head downward, so it was difficult to see any part of his face. He just ignored Kate's question, moved over to the other side of the bank, and again knocked on the wall. He then took several pictures of the bank's interior.

Carol went over to Kate and whispered, "Please go tell Joe what's happening."

"Okay." Kate went to Joe's office; he immediately came out to the front of the bank, but the hooded man had already left.

"Do you know who that guy was?" Joe asked Carol.

"No, I don't think I ever saw him before."

"Maybe Kate knows him." Carol looked at Kate and added, "I've heard that she has a great memory."

"People keep on saying that, but my memory's only average."

"Have you ever seen that guy before?" Joe asked.

"No, I don't think so."

"Did he do any transactions? Then we might have his name."

"No, he didn't cash any checks or make any deposits. All he did was listen to the walls and take some pictures. Then he went into the corridor, and I saw the flash going off some more."

"So he's not just taking pictures of our bank—he's taking pictures of other locations too."

"Yeah. Do you want me to look around the building and try to find him?" Carol asked.

"I don't know if you'd be safe doing that," Joe said. "I'll contact security and send through whatever photos our cameras took of him."

"He was wearing a hood and sunglasses," Carol said.

"People can't do that in a bank."

"I know. That's partially why Kate went to tell you about him."

"Okay. I'll talk to security, and you can both go back to doing your jobs."

Kate asked, "Should I help the tellers out front or go back to my desk?"

"You can just work with those folders on your desk, unless Carol thinks she needs you out here." Joe looked at Carol. She waved her hand, indicating that she didn't need any extra help. Kate went back to her desk and began to read more papers, as well as filling in some forms.

A little after twelve o'clock, Carol came up to Kate's desk. "Are you eating lunch here or going to the cafeteria?"

"I didn't know there was a cafeteria."

"There's one on the second floor. I usually bring my lunch, like I did today. Occasionally, though, I eat in the cafeteria."

"I brought my lunch today too." Kate opened one of her desk drawers and took out her lunch tote bag.

"Do you want to join me for lunch in the meeting room, or are you in the middle of something?"

"I can finish this paperwork later." Kate closed a folder and followed Carol into the conference room.

Carol opened up the refrigerator and said, "We can have any of the sodas or bottled waters in here."

"That's really nice. Who buys the soda?"

"The president does." As Carol reached her hand into the refrigerator, she asked, "Would you like one?"

"Yes, please. Bottled water would be great."

Carol handed Kate some water; another lady then came into the room. She walked over to Kate and said, "Hi, I'm Sue."

"I recognize your voice. You're Susan Sayles, right?"

"Yeah, I am."

"This is great! It's so nice to finally meet you."

"I feel the same way."

"How do you two know each other?" Carol asked.

Sue said, "For years, we've been talking on the phone about customer account problems."

The three ladies sat down at the table and opened up their lunch tote bags. Kate asked, "Has anyone found out about what happened next door?"

"I did," Carol said. "One of the customers told me about it."

Kate asked, "So what happened?"

"Over night, someone made holes in a bunch of the walls. The cops were kidding about it being a 'hacker'—someone who was hacking into the walls of the building."

Kate laughed before responding, "Did they hack into the computers too or just the walls?"

"I'm guessing it was just the walls."

"Yeah, it would have been faster to steal the computers, rather than to hack into them."

"Also, a lock on a circuit box was broken, and one of the fire alarms went off."

"They were hacking circuit boxes too not just the walls."

"Did they steal anything, like computers?"

"I don't know," Carol said. She looked at Sue, "Did you hear anything else about what happened—or why it happened?"

"You both know my boyfriend's a cop." Sue smiled before adding, "He told me that nothing was stolen."

Kate looked at Carol and asked, "What about that guy this morning who was listening to the walls?"

"Was someone really listening to the walls?" The upward motion of Sue's eyebrows showed her surprise.

"Yeah," Carol said. "He also took pictures and tried to hide his face."

"I'll tell Joe and have him call the police." Sue stood up.

"Joe already called them. A police officer actually came in and asked me a few questions, but he didn't mention the building next door." Carol thought for a few seconds and then added, "The police will surely make a connection between the broken walls next door and this guy listening to our walls, right?"

Sue said, "Just to be safe, one of us should still tell the police. We shouldn't be assuming things."

Kate said, "Different officers could be working on the two different cases."

"Because of the close locations of the two buildings, even if there are different officers on each case, they'll still be communicating with each other." Sue put the rest of her lunch into her tote bag. "I'll go talk to Joe right now. He'll make certain the police are called again."

"Thanks," Kate said.

As Sue was leaving the room, she smiled and said, "I'll also call my boyfriend, Charles. He'll want to double-check everything in order to keep us safe."

After a moment of silence, Carol asked Kate, "What do you think about all this?"

"I don't know."

"I'm guessing a few people might call in *sick* tomorrow."

"There's no way I'd do that."

"Really?"

Kate said, "In my whole life, I've never called in sick, not even once."

"What have you done when you've gotten the flu? If you went into work, especially working in a bank, you could have made other people sick."

"I've always been careful to cough and sneeze into my elbow. Plus, I wash my hands a lot."

"I guess going into work when you're sick can be helpful in some ways, but please let me know if you're ever sick. I'll then just try to stay away from your desk and teller station."

"Okay." Kate laughed. "I think you're right, though, about a few people calling in sick tomorrow."

"In the building next door, the hackers did their crimes during the night. We should be safe here during the daytime."

"It doesn't make sense that someone would hack a wall or a computer during the daytime. That's when there are lots of people around who would notice things."

Carol said, "If anything happens, it'll be at night."

"You weren't really thinking of calling in sick tomorrow, were you?"

"No, I wouldn't do that, but other people might."

"Then maybe a teller window should be set up for me this afternoon, so I'll be able to fill in as a teller tomorrow."

"Definitely. I'll check with Joe about this."

After lunch, Carol helped Kate to set up a teller window. Because Kate had experience at a different office of the bank, she already knew about the process.

At four o'clock, the front doors of the bank were locked. The last customer had already exited the bank. Joe immediately called everyone together for a meeting. He began by talking about several possible security problems related to the wall-hackers of the building next door. He then asked, "Does anyone here have experience with lucid-dreaming techniques?"

Kate said, "Yeah, I do. Sometimes, I can lucid dream. I just wish I could control them better."

Sue said, "My dreams are occasionally really great with bright colors and lots of interesting activities. Does that mean they're lucid?"

"I don't know," Carol said. "Joe, what is a lucid dream?"

"Lucid dreaming is knowing that you're dreaming while you're dreaming." He then read from a *Wall Street Journal* article: "Some lucid dreamers are able to control elements of their dreams once they realize they're dreaming...Others use the technique to solve problems, spur creativity, overcome nightmares, or practice a physical skill."[4]

Kate said, "This morning, right before waking up to come to work, I had a nightmare."

Carol asked, "What was it about?"

"Elevators."

Sue laughed. "I think everyone has nightmares about elevators, especially in this building."

Joe asked, "Kate, were you able to lucid dream within your nightmare?"

"Yeah, I did. I was able to control a few things in the dream."

"Did you walk up twenty-one flights of stairs, rather than taking an elevator this morning?"

Kate said, "I was running late, so I took the elevator. I think more practice being in elevators will help me to be a little less nervous."

Joe looked at Sue and Carol, who both said the word "elevator" at the same time. He then said, "According to the article that I just read that quote from, lucid dreaming can help people to overcome problems. In fact, another article that I read had information about a survey of 684 lucid dreamers. About 30 percent of the people used their lucid dreams to solve problems.[5]"

Kate said, "I think my nightmare about elevators helped me to be a little less fearful this morning."

Joe shook his head in agreement. "Thinking about a problem can sometimes help us to deal with it. Lucid dreaming can help."

Sue asked Joe, "Why are you telling us about lucid dreaming?"

"I'd like us all to try to lucid dream tonight. After what happened in the building next door, we need to think of creative ways to improve our security."

Kate said, "Trying to dream about security measures may result in nightmares about bank robberies."

Joe pointed to a part of one of the articles, passed it over to Kate, and said, "Lucid dreaming can also help us to cope with nightmares. If we try to control a nightmare, even if we're unsuccessful while sleeping, we might get ideas to help us when we're awake."

Kate squeezed her hands as her eyes moved down to look at her feet. She remained silent, but Sue said, "Joe, how in the world can we all dream about our bank's security? You're saying we can all dream about the same thing. That's not logical."

Several other employees shook their heads in agreement.

Joe smiled. "I have a third article here. It has information about lucid-dreaming methods. Perhaps its most interesting suggestion is to set 'your alarm for an hour before you would usually wake up. When it goes off, try to remember your dreams. Then get out of bed, and only head back under the blankets an hour later, focusing on trying to have a lucid dream.'[6]"

Sue opened her mouth, closed it, and then opened it again. "Are you telling us to come into work at least an hour late tomorrow morning?"

"No, of course not. I think we could all just try doing something similar. We can set our alarms an hour or two early, get up for a few minutes, and then try to lucid dream as we go back to sleep."

The employees looked at each other; they all had sad or angry expressions on their faces.

Joe then said, "Everyone who tries to lucid dream tonight and comes into work tomorrow will get paid for two hours of overtime."

Sue's sad face turned into a happy one. "That's very generous of you, Joe." She paused and then added, "I think trying to dream about the bank's security will make our reality a little less anxious. We'll at least be thinking about security a little more."

Kate sighed. "You're right, Sue. Even if some of us have nightmares, a nightmare is better than something bad happening in reality."

Joe let everyone look at the articles; he then said "good night" and left the conference room.

While standing together in one corner of the room, Kate and Sue started to talk softly together. Kate asked, "What do you really think about this? Can our boss actually tell us what to dream about?"

"Well, he's paying us overtime to try to dream." Sue smiled. "I also think it will be an easy way to earn a few extra dollars."

"I do need some more money, but I also want my dreams to be for me, not for my job or my boss."

"In a way, I think you're right. I want to be free to dream about whatever I want to." Sue paused and then added, "However, I often dream about work anyway. Plus, we will be getting overtime pay—two hours of time and a half."

"Even though I like the overtime idea, I don't want to have any nightmares."

"Maybe you can think of a positive focus for a lucid dream about security."

"Actually, that's a good idea. I'll try to dream about police officers, rather than criminals, in the bank."

Sue laughed. "I'm completely in love with your suggestion. I'm going to dream about police officers, too, but my dream will be about one specific police officer: my boyfriend Charles."

"You probably dream about that police officer every single night."

"I don't remember most of my dreams, but I've had a few nice ones about Charles."

They both smiled. Kate then asked, "Are you seeing Charles tonight?"

"Yeah, I definitely will."

"If you find out anything about what happened in the building next door, can you let me know?"

"Yes, I will."

"Do you still have my cell phone number, so you can call me at home tonight?"

"Yes, I still have your phone number, but I might have to wait until we're at work before I can tell you about anything."

"That's okay."

The other employees were leaving the conference room. Kate and Sue followed them out of the room and into a hallway. Within half an hour, everything was locked up, and all the employees walked through the bank's front doors to go home.

With Carol on her right side and Sue on her left side, Kate went into the corridor; they walked close to an elevator. Two people from another office were standing there, and the "down" button already had been pressed. Kate's eyes moved to the end of the corridor and then stared at an exit sign outside of a stairway. When she heard the sound of the elevator doors opening up, she looked back at the elevator. Eight people were already inside. The eight people repositioned themselves backward and sideways. The two people from the other office got into the elevator. There was enough space for only one more person. Kate tried to take a step backward, but Carol and Sue gently pushed against her back, indicating that she should get into the elevator.

Carol said, "Go ahead, Kate. You need the practice."

Kate had no choice but to move forward into the one remaining space. The doors closed while she smiled blandly at the faces closest to hers. She then turned around and looked at the silver metal doors. She closed her eyes, breathed deeply a few times, and opened her eyes up again. The doors were still there, but they now seemed to be almost like mirrors. She noticed partial reflections of some of the people in the elevator. One lady was wearing red, and at least one of the men was wearing a formal suit and tie. While Kate was still looking at the doors, she said, "Elevator culture is interesting."

A stranger's voice said, "Yeah, it is."

"I meant to say 'thank you' for making room for three more people in here."

"You're welcome. I'm sure you also are always doing the same kind of thing."

The elevator suddenly stopped; the doors began to open. Kate looked upward to a rectangular screen. The elevator was only on the fourteenth floor.

When the doors were completely open, Kate saw a group of at least ten people; all of them just stared at her and the already-filled elevator. Then one of the men in the group took a step closer to Kate while saying, "There's always room for one more, right?"

Kate tried to move to her left and then to her right. Both times, she found herself only pushing at people who were refusing to move. The lady on her right said, "This elevator is already a little bit too overcrowded."

Kate turned sideways and gestured at the man who wanted to get onto the crowded elevator. He frowned, waved his hand, and stepped backward, moving away from the elevator. The metal doors closed as Kate turned around to face forward again. She then sighed before saying, "Well, we tried to make room for one more."

"Yeah, we all tried, but not everything's possible. Plus, that guy was too pushy."

Kate's eyes lit up. Her mouth softly whispered, "Only with God's help is everything possible."

The lady standing next to Kate asked, "What did you say?"

"I thought I was just talking to myself. Did you hear what I said?" Kate looked at the lady's face.

The lady looked down at her feet and said, "No, I didn't hear anything at all." The last few words in her statement sounded wobbly; this change in the tone of her voice suggested that she was lying.

Kate looked back at the closed metal door. After thinking for a few seconds, she moved her lips slightly while saying softly, "Lord, if someone else wants to get onto this elevator, please help the person to be able to do so. I really need practice to overcome my fear of crowded elevators. In Jesus's name I pray, Amen."

On the ninth floor, the elevator doors opened again. There were three people waiting beyond the metal doors. Kate turned sideways again and gestured toward the three people to come forward into the elevator. Not one of them moved. Then the other elevator people also turned sideways, moved around, and waved at the three people to get onto the elevator. The three people stepped forward into the elevator. Kate smiled and said softly, "Thank you, Lord."

One of the new elevator people asked Kate, "What did you say?"

Kate swallowed and then said, "Oh, I was just thinking out loud."

"I thought you said, 'Thank you.'" The lady paused and then added, "I should be thanking you."

"You're so welcome."

"Yes, I feel really welcome now. I had a bad day at work, so having some elevator people sharing a small amount of space with me is a complete blessing."

Tears filled Kate's eyes as she said, "Oh, you're a blessing to me too. I was really scared of crowded elevators until this one trip."

"Were you really?"

"Yes, I was. However, when you first got into this elevator, I was actually thanking God."

"Were you thankful for a crowded elevator?"

"No, I've always hated crowded places. I was actually thankful for all these wonderful people. They shared a small amount of space with some other people." Kate looked around and smiled at the faces of other people in the elevator. Several of them smiled back at her.

The elevator lady who had had a bad day at work also looked at the other elevator people. She said, "Thanks." Several people responded to her by saying, "You're welcome." She then turned back to look at Kate, who also said, "You're welcome!"

Kate and the thankful lady were standing so close together that they were touching each other. They even looked like they were hugging. Now, their tightened arm muscles showed that they really were hugging.

The elevator doors opened again. The people behind Kate and her new elevator friend moved sideways, walked around them, and then exited. Some of the people smiled, and some of them had blank faces. One person's face looked mean. Kate and her new friend were the last ones to exit the elevator. Once they walked out into the hallway, Kate turned to her new friend and said, "I'm Kate Odyssey."

"I'm Phebe Robinson."

"What was so bad about your day at work?"

"I just had to multitask too much. Then I spilled my coffee all over my desk. It messed up some paperwork, made my keyboard all sticky, and even drizzled onto my legs." She looked down at her slacks before adding, "I probably still smell like coffee."

"There's nothing wrong with smelling like coffee. I've done the same thing before, and I really loved smelling the coffee all day."

"Thanks." Phebe sighed. "There was a really mean customer too. She kept yelling at me for something someone else did."

"I know what that's like." Kate took out a piece of paper and a pen from her purse. After writing on the paper, she gave it to Phebe. "Here's my cell phone number and e-mail address. We'll have to eat lunch together some day."

"We'll have to drink coffee with our lunch."

Kate laughed. "Definitely, I love coffee."

Phebe put the piece of paper with Kate's phone number on it into the billfold in her purse and then said, "I can usually only take a long lunch break on Fridays, but I'll send you an e-mail before then."

Phebe and Kate hugged each other; they then walked out to the parking lot, waved good-bye, and got into their cars.

Kate drove up to the Roger Williams National Memorial, parked her car, and went over to the visitor center. When she walked in the door, she turned to her right and looked at the seven-foot tall statue of Roger Williams. Its head was nearly hitting the ceiling. The statue's right hand was holding onto a book.

Kate said, "Roger Williams wrote multiple books."

"He also wrote letters and other kinds of responses to different people's writings."

"My mom told me that this Roger Williams statue was originally made for the Roger Williams Savings and Loan Association in 1960."

"Yeah, it was. Then on July 10, 1984, it was given to the Roger Williams National Memorial."

"That's a really nice statue."

"Yeah, everyone loves it."

"I also love seeing the United States flag standing right next to this statue."

"Would you like to see the Roger Williams video?"

"No, thanks. I've already seen it several times." Kate reached into her purse, pulled out an envelope, and gave it to the lady. "My mom asked me to drop this off."

"What is it?" the lady asked.

"The envelope has some pictures that my mom took. There's also a letter with permission for their usage by several state organizations. Several people's names are listed here on the front of the envelope. You can send the photos to whoever needs them the most."

The lady took some pictures out of the envelope. They all showed parts of the Roger Williams National Memorial.

Kate said, "Those photos were taken by my mom in August when there wasn't any snow. I actually haven't even had the chance to look at these photos yet."

"They're really nice. I especially like this one of the Hahn Memorial with the well curb in it." The lady showed Kate one of the photos.

"What's the Hahn Memorial?"

"It's a part of the Roger Williams National Memorial. Judge Jacob Hahn donated the area to Providence with the intent of memorializing his father, Isaac Hahn."

"Who was Isaac Hahn?"

"He was 'the first person of Jewish faith to be elected to public office from Providence.'[7]"

"It's so wonderful that Jewish people helped with the memorial of a Christian minister. This kindness shows people of different religions connecting with each other."

"In his *Bloudy Tenent of Persecution* book, Williams showed that he respected people's diversity. Just because people were different, he didn't think they had to be at war with each other. He said, 'true civility and Christianity may both flourish in a state or kingdom, notwithstanding the permission of divers and contrary consciences, either Jew or Gentile.'[8]"

Kate looked at the picture again and asked, "Is the well curb that octagon structure in the picture?"

"Yeah, the octagon looks like a limestone well. It's where the Roger Williams Spring was located."

Kate and the lady both looked at the photo. Kate then said, "My mom can send electronic versions of the photos too. I think she says that in her letter."

The lady read the letter and said "thanks."

Kate waved good-bye and then left the visitor center. By the time she got home, she was already yawning, but she still called

43

her mom. After saying "hi," Kate told her mom about dropping off the letter and photos to the lady in the visitor center. Then she started to talk about her first day in her new office: "You know how much I hate elevators, Mom."

"Yeah, I know. Even when you were little, you hated them."

"I really hate the crowded space and feeling unsteady."

"Did you have to take an elevator this morning, or could you have taken the stairs?"

"I was running a little late because of the traffic, so I had to take one of the elevators."

"That's too bad. Were you okay?"

"Yeah, I was. It wasn't as bad as I thought it would be. I even took the elevator more than once today."

"That's great!"

"With practice, I might even get used to elevators."

"Other than the elevators, did you like the new office?"

Kate told her mom about the office and her new boss. She then asked, "Mom, is the weather forecast still predicting snow for tomorrow?"

"Yeah, we'll be getting at least six inches."

"Winter's really tough this year."

"I know. So far, we've had a lot more snow than we've had in quite a few years."

"Even so, I might enjoy the snow a little bit tomorrow."

"Really?"

"Yeah, I drive past the Roger Williams National Memorial on the way to work, and lately, I've been thinking of Roger Williams every time it snows."

"Then you must know why he called his colony *Providence*."

"Yeah, I do. I remember you told me a month or two ago about Roger Williams being forced out of his home during a blizzard. Williams then said that he called his colony by the name of Providence because of 'God's merciful providence until me in my distress.'[9]"

"I think we'll both be thanking God because we have our cars to travel in during snowstorms."

"You're right, Mom. Even if our cars break down, we have our cell phones and can call each other for help. During that 1635–36 winter, Roger Williams was all by himself; he was forced to leave his family behind and run for his life."

"Initially, he was all by himself, but then he spent the winter in Massasoit's village."

"It was so wonderful that the natives helped him out by giving him food and shelter."

"I know. In the spring of 1636, the natives also let Williams's family and a few of his friends stay in their village."

Kate paused to think for a few seconds before saying, "I don't think I would have run away into a blizzard like Roger Williams did."

"He really didn't have any choice. Winthrop warned him about his upcoming arrest. If Williams didn't run away immediately, he would have been captured, transported to England, and put into prison, where he probably would have died."

"The prisons in the seventeenth century must have been really bad."

"Yes, Kate, they really were. The prisoners even had to pay for their own expenses, like food and rent."

"What happened if they had no money?"

"Then their friends and family members would have to pay their bills."

"I know you will always help me out, Mom, whenever I need it."

"Of course I will. You'll also always help me and your dad."

"I definitely will, Mom. Tomorrow, with the amount of snow we're getting, will you need help shoveling your driveway?"

"No, thanks, Kate. You know that your dad and I like to do our own shoveling. That way, we'll both get in a little bit of exercise."

"Well, if you need my help tomorrow, Mom, please call me."

"Yes, I will, Kate. You too should call me if you have any problems with the snow."

"I will, Mom. Have a good night."

"Thanks. I'll call you tomorrow."

Kate said good-bye to her mom and hung up her phone. She next called her dad, who was in New York for a few days, and told him about her new job. She then cooked a microwave meal for her dinner. After watching two of her favorite TV shows, she got ready for bed. She said a prayer and reset her alarm for five o'clock. As soon as her head hit her pillow, she fell asleep.

POLICING AN ELEVATOR

W hen the alarm clock went off at five o'clock, Kate woke up, quickly reset the alarm for six o'clock, and then went back to sleep. She immediately found herself to be in a lucid dream.

She was inside of her new office building, standing on the ground floor and waiting for an elevator. The furthest one to the left suddenly opened its doors. By the time Kate walked over to the elevator, its doors had closed up again. She waited for another elevator to arrive. The one that was furthest to her right now opened its doors. Kate ran as fast as possible, but she was still too slow. The doors closed before she was even halfway there. She then put her hands in front of her face, trying to hide herself from the elevators. It worked! They all opened up, so Kate had the freedom to choose which one she liked.

Several of the elevators contained some nice clothing, shoes, and boots. Another elevator had an office desk and chair. The elevator closest to Kate had a rocking recliner. The next elevator had a TV set on one of its walls. Kate asked, "Why can't the recliner and TV both fit into the same elevator?"

The rocking recliner started to rock back and forth. It went forward, came outside of its elevator, and moved into the TV's elevator.

"Okay, that's perfect." Kate walked into the perfect elevator, sat down in the recliner, and picked up a remote control. Before she could turn on the TV, a police officer walked into the elevator and stood in front of her. He looked at the elevator's control panel and then at Kate's hand that was still holding onto the remote control.

"Why are you watching TV? Aren't you supposed to be at work right now?"

"No, I'm dreaming. It's time for me to relax, not to work."

The officer looked at his watch before saying, "It really is time for you to be at work."

"This is a lucid dream, so I can find out the real time by doing a reality check."

"Okay, what time do you think it is?"

"It's just after five o'clock in the morning. I'm still at home and sleeping."

He looked at his watch again. "That's the correct time, but aren't you being paid to do a lucid dream about the bank's security?"

Kate sat up straight, put down the remote control, and said, "You're right. Even though I am not actually at work, I am being paid to dream this dream."

Kate suddenly found her recliner changing into an office chair. The TV disappeared, and a desk stood up in front of her. One of its drawers opened up, and a stack of papers flew out of the drawer and onto the desktop. The letters and numbers were so small that Kate couldn't read them. Some glasses attached themselves to her face. Kate tried to pull the glasses off, but they would not move. She looked at the first paper in the stack, which was now readable. It said, "They were drawing a map of the building."

"Who was drawing a map?"

The paper did not answer Kate's question. She lifted the top piece of paper off the stack; the next piece of paper was blank. She looked at all the other papers. They were also blank.

After Kate set aside the map paper and put all the blank papers into the recycling bin, she looked down at the desktop. A compass was there. "Where did you come from?" she asked.

The compass slid a few inches until it landed on top of the map paper. "Oh, you're trying to say something about a location on a map."

The compass spun around quickly. As it turned in circles, the paper beneath it changed from a paper with writing on it into a paper with a map of the Pilgrim office building.

Kate said, "Okay, so you're trying to tell me something about my office building." She tried to stand up, but she was chained onto the office chair. She then asked the police officer, "Can you please push the twenty-one on the elevator's control panel?"

The officer asked her, "Are you really twenty-one?"

"No, I'm twenty-nine."

"Can I see your driver's license?"

"Yeah, it's in my purse."

The officer found her license, carefully looked at the front and back of it, and then said, "Okay. I now believe that you're truly twenty-nine."

The officer pressed twenty-nine. The elevator immediately closed its doors and then stayed still. It did not move upward or downward.

"Did you break the elevator?" Kate asked him.

"No, of course not. Look up there on the ceiling."

A smile appeared under the ceiling's light. The officer said, "See? The elevator is just very happy to have people inside." The smile on the ceiling changed into a series of prison bars. "The elevator now wants to act like a prison."

"I didn't do anything wrong."

"Yes, you did. You got into the wrong elevator. Instead of a desk and a chair, you chose a TV and recliner."

The prison bars stretched out from the ceiling and covered the elevator's walls. When the doors opened up on the twenty-ninth floor, the prison bars were still there, barring entry out of the elevator. Kate tried to get up out of her chair, but she could not. The police officer took a box out his pocket. He used a key on his key chain to open up the box. Inside were at least ten more keys. He used one of the keys to unlock the bars that were blocking the elevator's door. He then put the keys and the box back into his pocket. Finally, he stepped outside into a hallway. When Kate didn't follow him, he turned around, looked at her, and asked, "Why aren't you coming with me to your office?"

"I'm still chained into this chair."

The officer took the box of keys out of his pocket again. He unlocked the box, took one of the keys out, and then unlocked Kate's chains.

"Thanks. That box of yours reminds me of Roger Williams and his keys."

"Did Roger Williams really have keys?"

"I don't know if he had actual metal keys, but in his 'Introduction' to his book, *A Key into the Language of America,* he said, 'A little Key may open a box, where lies a bunch of Keys.'[10]"

"How do you know he wasn't just talking about a key to open up a box or a door?"

"Roger Williams often used metaphors. I think his use of the word 'key' showed that he was trying to unlock knowledge about culture, as well as about language."

"Did he translate words from the natives?"

"Yes, he did, but he was also telling everyone about their culture. For example, at the end of a section called 'Of Salutations,' Roger Williams discusses the courteous nature of the natives. A part of his commentary says: 'From these courteous Salutations Observe in general: There is a favour of civility and coutesie.'[11] He was obviously commenting on how courteous and polite the natives were."

"I guess the words of a language do say something about the people. A courteous person might refer to a female as a 'lady.' A noncourteous person might call the same female something else."

"On the title page of *A Key into the Language of America,* Roger Williams said that his book included 'briefe Observations of the Customes, Manners and Worships' of the natives.[12] He obviously talked about their language, but he also talked about their customs, manners, and religion."

The police officer waved at Kate's chair and said, "Now you're free from your office chair, so you can escape from this prison and go unlock some other things."

50

"My office isn't a prison. I like my job."

"Why then do you have your desk and chair inside an elevator?"

"Okay, this is the first time that my office has been a prison. I'm only thinking this way because I was told what to dream about."

"You've now already dreamed about your office, so you're free to dream about whatever you want to."

"You're right. Now I'm free." Kate was still inside the elevator. She looked at the control panel. Even though no one was touching its buttons, many of them were lighting up.

The officer looked at the panel and then at Kate. "Where are you really going?"

Kate was watching the elevator's control panel as now only six different numbers lit up. "I don't know what to dream about. There are so many different possibilities."

"I think you'll have to choose just one."

"Why must I choose only one floor? Maybe I'll check out all six of these."

Suddenly, a siren started to sound. She asked, "What's happening?"

"I think you're lying about something. Perhaps you're looking at all the wrong floors."

"No, I'm not. I just don't know where to go."

"If you keep jumping around onto different floors, people will think you're doing something wrong."

Kate said, "You're so right. I'll have to choose only one of these floors, at least for right now." She pressed the button for the twenty-first floor, but the siren kept on making its loud noise.

Kate stepped outside the elevator and then realized that she was now standing in her bedroom at home. She looked over at her alarm clock, which was going off. She asked, "Are you in my dream?"

When the clock still kept making its loud noise, she realized that—outside her dream—her real alarm clock was ringing. She turned it off.

*Statue of Roger Williams with Clio and Betsey Williams's
Home in Roger Williams State Park, Rhode Island*

WALLS WITHIN WALLS

A fter Kate turned off her alarm clock, she immediately wrote down some of the details from her lucid dream. She looked at her own handwriting and said out loud, "When I write too fast, my handwriting looks even worse than seventeenth-century shorthand."

Quickly, Kate got ready for work and then drove to the Pilgrim building. Once inside, she paused in front of the elevators. Her eyes went back and forth between the stairway and the elevators. A familiar voice said, "Are you waiting for me?"

Kate turned around, saw Phebe, and smiled as she said, "Yes, I was waiting for you, and I'm so glad to meet you again! Yesterday, you made my trip in the elevator so wonderful."

"You made my trip really great too! You cheered me up after a tough day at work."

One of the elevators opened its doors. Kate followed Phebe into its metal interior. Phebe pressed the number nine and then looked expectantly at Kate.

"Twenty-one."

Phebe pressed the correct number into the control panel. The doors closed, and the elevator started moving upward. "So, Kate, are you ready for the snow we're supposed to get today?"

"Yeah, I'm used to our New England winters. How about you?"

"My van is an all-wheel drive vehicle, so I'll be okay."

"I've never been in a car accident, but some of the bad drivers out there are even worse on slippery roads." Kate moved her foot back and forth a few inches on the elevator's floor.

"I know." Phebe looked at Kate, smiled, and said, "You take care driving home tonight."

"You too be careful out there." Kate and Phebe hugged; the elevator doors then opened up onto the ninth floor. Phebe stepped out onto her floor; as the doors were closing again, she and Kate waved good-bye to each other.

Kate was now all by herself in the elevator. She moved her purse and lunch bag to her other shoulder. She then tried to relax by slowly inhaling and exhaling. She stretched out both her arms before moving her purse and lunch bag again. Her breathing was still slightly faster than normal. When the metal doors opened up onto the twenty-first floor, she quickly jumped out and walked down the corridor to the New World Bank. Carol immediately opened up the bank's front door and let her into the lobby area.

Kate asked, "Were you waiting for me?"

"No, I wasn't really waiting for you. I was actually looking for Sue." Carol laughed, so Kate was uncertain about whether Carol was just kidding or if she was telling the truth.

"Carol, is anything going on? Did anyone break into the building next door again?"

"I don't know about that building. Our building, though, might have had some criminals in it last night."

"How do you know that?"

"When I was in the elevator, one of the librarians told me about a closet in the library; it had a broken lock."

"Was anything stolen?"

"I don't really know." Carol frowned.

"Sue might have some more information."

"Yeah, she might also know if other areas were broken into."

"If she doesn't know, she can check with her police officer boyfriend."

Carol was silent as she looked over at the front door. Sue was standing there, waiting to be let into the bank's lobby. Carol quickly let her in and then asked, "Did you hear about the library's closet having a broken lock?"

"Yeah, I did. When I was driving to work this morning, Charles left me a text message."

"Did anything else happen overnight in our building?"

Sue hesitated and then said, "I guess you'll both hear about this eventually. At least four different offices in this building had broken locks."

"Was anything stolen?"

"People are still checking out their inventories, but according to Charles's message, nothing yet has been reported as stolen."

The front door of the bank opened, and their boss stepped inside. He smiled at Kate, Sue, and Carol. "Are we having a meeting or something out here?"

Sue laughed. "No, I don't think so, Joe. Carol just let me and Kate come inside." Carol began to walk toward her teller window.

Joe said, "Before it's time to open the front doors to customers, let's have a meeting. Right now would be a good time."

Everyone followed him into the conference room. Carol had already made some coffee, so they each grabbed some before sitting down around the table.

Joe asked Sue, "Is there anything new that I need to know about?"

"You got my text message that I sent this morning, right?"

"Yes, I did. Thanks for letting me know about problems in our building." Joe inhaled and then looked at everyone seated around the table. "How many of you tried to lucid dream last night?"

All the hands went up into the air.

"That's so great. Let's share what we dreamed about."

Sue laughed. "I'll tell you a little bit about my dream, but Charles was in it, so I can't tell you about everything."

Joe said, "Okay. What can you tell us?"

"I began trying to do a lucid dream by thinking about the lobby of our bank. I noticed a lot of customers in line at one of the teller windows. Charles then came in. He told me that thieves often try to do things when there are a lot of customers around. That way, the people working in the bank would be distracted by all the activity."

"That's right." Joe paused and then said, "We should be watching for problems around lunchtime. Is there anything else you want to add?"

Sue thought for a few seconds and then said, "No. The only other thing is that Charles and I are getting married someday."

"Has he proposed yet?"

"No, he hasn't. But I think he's planning something. He wanted to know what my ring size was."

Everyone at the table congratulated Sue. Then Joe asked, "Did anyone else have a lucid dream last night?"

Kate said, "My lucid dream had me pressing different buttons in the elevator. It might be a good idea to install more cameras in and near the elevators. If people are getting off at multiple floors, they might be doing something wrong."

"Installing more cameras is something we've already decided to do. It's a good idea, though, for us to watch out for people who are getting on and off at different floors."

"There was also something in my dream about a map."

"What about a map?"

"I think I was trying to tell myself that the pictures being taken might have to do with a map of our building."

"That could be." After checking to see if there were any more ideas, Joe told everyone to go to their desks and teller windows.

Because a couple of people had called in sick, Kate worked as a teller for the whole day. When she took a quick break to have lunch in the conference room, Sue joined her.

Kate asked, "Have you heard anything new?"

"No, I haven't heard anything yet." Sue took a soda out of the refrigerator before asking, "Did anyone in our office tell you about the stolen jewelry?"

"No one's told me anything. We haven't had too much time to talk."

"Well, over fifty years ago, when this building was in its original structure, one of the earliest stores sold jewelry. There was a robbery, and two of the robbers were killed."

"Were there more than two thieves?"

"There might have been. Everyone assumed the thieves hid the jewelry somewhere and were then killed."

"Was the jewelry ever found?"

"No, it wasn't. My boyfriend Charles was wondering if it was hidden inside this building or in some other nearby place."

"How much was the stolen jewelry worth?"

"Back then, it was only worth a hundred thousand dollars. But now, the gold alone would sell for quite a bit more."

Sue went back to work, and Kate quickly finished her lunch. She then went over to her teller window. The afternoon was fairly quiet. Because snow had started to fall, not too many customers came into the bank.

Kate left work about four thirty. The snow was still falling. It was dark enough for her car's headlights to be turned on, but there was still enough light for her to see most of her surroundings. As she drove close to the Roger Williams National Memorial on North Main Street, the traffic became worse. The cars in front of her slowed down and then stopped. When Kate also stopped, she turned her head to the left to try and see the Roger Williams statue. It was too faraway. When the traffic started moving again, Kate drove up a hill for a few blocks until she saw the statue. Snowflakes were fluttering around the concrete canopy; some of the flakes flew under the canopy and onto Roger Williams. His outstretched hand kept melting the snow into a non-icy dampness. Kate said out loud, "It looks like Roger Williams is fighting snow and melting ice."

Kate drove down the hill and out to Interstate 95. The roads had been plowed and sanded, so they were not slippery. The traffic, though, was moving slower than usual. When Kate reached route 10, the traffic slowed down even more. By the time she reached Park Avenue, the snow was heavier; the roads had some snow-covered and icy spots. Near Roger Williams Park, the trees were completely covered in snow. While she was driving at only ten miles per hour, her car suddenly jumped. She had hit something. Slowing down, Kate pulled over to the right side of the road, got out of her car, and looked backward. In the middle of the road was a slowly crawling animal that suddenly stopped its motion. Kate got into her car and backed up. When she got out, she noticed two men who were standing near a gray minivan. They were a short distance from the place where the animal had been lying. One of the men was wearing a coat with a hood, and the other one had long straggling hair. Kate slowly walked up to where the animal should have been. There were tracks that looked like paw marks in the snow on the roadside, but the animal was nowhere to be seen.

Even though music was playing from the gray minivan, Kate could still partially hear the two men's words.

"Yeah, thanks for e-mailing those maps and pictures to me."

"You're welcome."

"Here's a compass."

"Do you have one too?"

"Yeah, I do."

"These may help."

"Yeah, they should."

"The people leaving work will be a nice distraction for the first responders."

Kate opened her mouth to say something, but then stopped herself. She had already made a gasping noise, though. Both of the men turned around and looked at her.

The man with the hood asked, "What are you...?" His voice trailed off, so Kate could not hear the end of his question.

"What did you say?"

"What are you doing here?" The voice sounded funny, like a hand or a scarf was masking its sound.

Kate looked closely at the man, but it was too dark for her to see anything, except for the snow that had accumulated on the top of his hood. She stuttered as she replied, "I hope it's okay."

"You hope what's okay?"

"I think I hit an animal with my car, but it's no longer here."

"If it's healthy enough to run away from you, especially in this weather, then it must be okay," the man said as he moved his hood further down over his forehead. Some of the snow flew off his hood and fluttered down to the ground. He pulled at his hood some more, stretching the cloth so that his eyes were covered. He was obviously trying to hide his face.

"I really hope the animal's okay. I think it's a small dog," Kate said. She blinked her eyes a couple of times and then asked, "Do I know you from somewhere?"

The man didn't respond to Kate's question, but instead turned around and started to walk toward the gray minivan. The other man with the straggly long hair turned around and followed him.

Kate's eyes closed for a few seconds as she whispered, "I don't just hope the animal's okay, but I also pray that it's okay." When she opened her eyes, the men were talking to each other inside their van. They were both looking at Kate. After a few seconds, they got out of their van and began to walk toward her.

Kate ran back to her car and got quickly inside. Even though her hand was quivering, she managed to put the keys into the ignition, turn on the engine, and start moving forward. After realizing that snow was covering her windshield, she turned on her windshield wipers. The sound of a bullet striking metal made her right foot press down harder on the gas pedal as she drove into the entrance to Roger Williams State Park. She turned to the left and soon was driving past the Roger Williams statue. The statue's left arm was curved around a book with the words "soul" and "liberty" carved into its surface. Below the Roger Williams statue, at the top of the stairs, was a smaller statue of Clio, the history muse. Clio was writing "Roger Williams" and "1636" onto the monument. The cottage of Betsey Williams (the great-great-great-granddaughter of Roger Williams) was a short distance to the left of the Roger Williams statue.

Kate continued to move further into the center of the park. Her car skidded, slid off the road, and stopped in a field. She looked up and down the street. There were no other cars around, but she still hesitated about moving her car back onto the street. She instead jumped out of her car and ran over a bridge. She paused for a few seconds and looked at her footprints in the snow. Sighing, she ran over to a river, went through some slush, and then stepped into the water. After walking in the shallow water for about forty feet, Kate noticed a large bush near the edge of the river. She stepped onto the shore, being careful to slide her feet and hide her footprints. She then sat down against a tree while inhaling and exhaling deeply and trying to slow down her heavy breathing. She put her hands together and asked God for his help. She then kept her hands clutched together as she tried to stop shivering while seated against the snow-covered tree.

Ten minutes later, Kate saw the gray minivan with its high-beam headlights on; it was being driven very slowly down the nearby road. When the slow-moving van got close to Kate's car, it pulled over to the side of the road. The two men got out and started walking over to her car. Before they got too close to her car, another vehicle drove past them. Thirty seconds later, a blue Toyota went down the road. The two men talked to each other, and then walked back to their van and drove away.

Kate sighed deeply, but she still did not leave her spot against the tree. Her fingertips were turning numb, and her lips were chapped. Finally, after another fifteen minutes of quivering in the snow, Kate got up and slowly walked back to her car. Her toes were numb; she felt weak and unbalanced. After every few steps, she paused and carefully listened for any noises. The two men were nowhere to be seen or heard, so she got into her car and began to drive. A few minutes later, she said out loud, "Thank you, Lord, for the warmth of my car."

When she arrived at her house, she looked at her car for any damage. A small hole was visible in the back bumper. She then went inside and changed into warm, dry clothing. Her fingers and toes were still cold and numb as she used her cell phone to call her mom. She explained to her mom what had happened with the two men.

Her mother asked, "Did you call the cops yet?"

"No, but as soon as we're done talking, I'll call them."

"Are you sure a gun was fired at you? Maybe the noise you heard was something else."

"Just a few minutes ago, when I got out of my car, I saw the damage that was done to my car's rear bumper. "It had to be a gun."

"Could the damage have been done by someone throwing a rock at your car's bumper?"

Kate paused before answering, "I don't know. In a situation like that one, almost anything's possible."

"Are you sure you're okay? Running around outside in this weather is not a great idea."

"I'm fine, Mom. At least I didn't have to stay out in the cold for a long time, like Roger Williams had to."

"Did you see his statue while you were running around in Roger Williams Park?"

"Yeah, I did. I'm actually curious now about his experience running around outside in the middle of the winter. I'm planning on reading about him again tonight."

"Do you still have that book about Roger Williams?"

"Yes, I'm sure I do, Mom. You've given me so many wonderful books."

"I'm talking about Perry Miller's book: *Roger Williams: His Contribution to the American Tradition.* You might want to read about the banishment of Roger Williams and how he lived through his winter in the wilderness."

"Yeah, I'd love to read some of Miller's book, especially now that I know how awful it feels to be scared, alone, and outside in the middle of a New England snowstorm."

"Keep yourself warm tonight."

"Yes, I will. You and dad also need to stay warm and safe."

"We will."

"Thanks so much for the book about Roger Williams."

"You're welcome." Kate's mom sighed. "It's really nice to know that we're some of his many descendants."

After saying good-bye to her mom, Kate talked to her dad for a few minutes. She then called the police. While waiting for the police officer to arrive, she looked at her fingers and toes. They looked and felt normal again.

When an officer arrived at Kate's house, he talked to her for a few minutes about what had happened. He then said, "It's too bad you don't have a license plate number, but at least we have a minivan description and a little bit of information about the suspects."

Kate blinked her eyes and smiled.

The officer went outside to take pictures of her car while she filled in a couple of forms. When he came back inside, he said, "You could have been frostbitten. Can I take you to the hospital for a short visit?"

"No, thanks, I'm okay. My fingers and toes were feeling numb and really cold, but they're fine now."

"Are you sure about that?"

Kate waved her hands at the officer. She then took off her slippers and wiggled her toes in front of the officer. "See? My fingers and toes are fine."

"Okay. Stay warm, and we'll call you if we find out more information about those two men." The police officer left.

Kate was finally able to sit down and relax in front of her TV while she had some hot soup and a microwaved pizza. She then read about Roger Williams before going to sleep. The final item that she read was about how Roger Williams felt concerning the difficulties he suffered during his banishment into a New England winter: He "suffered tortures that winter of flight, but he never thereafter let anybody forget them...The experience deepened his pessimism about this life, and his letters abound with longings for 'the Alpha and Omega of all blessedness,' for escape from the body of this death, where men are but 'poor grasshoppers, hopping and skipping from branch to twig in this vale of tears.'"[13]

*Phillips Memorial Baptist Church's "The Roger Williams Window,"
created by W.P. Jack from Whittemore Associates, Boston, MA*

A Grasshopper's
Branches and Twigs

———————⬥———————

At four thirty in the morning, Kate woke up. After glancing briefly at her alarm clock, she closed her eyes and went back to sleep. The noise of a ringing bell woke her up again. She opened her eyes and found herself to be standing inside a building. The lights were not turned on, but a single candle on a small round table was partially lighting up a part of the building. A Bible was open on the table next to the candle.

Kate asked, "Is anyone here?"

When no one answered, she asked, "Is this my church?"

Again, no voices were heard. To her right, near the back of the building, Kate looked for the stained glass window picturing Roger Williams talking to some natives. It was nowhere to be seen. Instead, there was an unpainted wooden wall with a small window in it. The window's glass seemed really thick.

Kate walked around in a circle, looking at the interior of a single room. There was no separate sanctuary. The front of the church was missing the large stained glass window of Jesus praying at Gethsemane. Only a single podium was visible. The floor had no carpeting, and the ceiling had no chandelier.

Kate sat down on one of the benches. They were older and less comfortable than the ones in her church. Phillips Memorial Baptist Church had cushions on its benches; this church only had old wooden benches with no cushions on them.

Kate looked at her watch. It said the year was 2015; the numbers next moved backward to 1603. The year then changed to other dates in the seventeenth and twenty-first centuries. For several minutes, the tiny hands on her watch kept jumping around onto different numbers on its face. The watch's hands then ran into each other, turned green, and took on the form of a grasshopper.

Kate laughed. "This must be a lucid dream, so maybe I can make the grasshopper get off of my wrist."

The grasshopper jumped off her wrist, onto her bench, and then onto a different bench. On the new bench, a twig and some paper appeared next to the grasshopper; the green insect picked up the twig and started writing on the paper.

"What are you writing?" Kate asked.

"I'm taking notes about what the minister is saying."

Kate looked at the podium. A preacher was now standing there and reading a Bible verse: "It is he who sits above the circle of the earth, and its inhabitants are like grasshoppers; who stretches out the heavens like a curtain, and spreads them out like a tent to live in" (Isa. 40:22, RSV).

Kate said to the grasshopper, "He's talking about God being above the earth with lots of people who are like grasshoppers. Back in the seventeenth century, Roger Williams wrote down that he thought people were like grasshoppers too. Perhaps Williams's idea about people being like grasshoppers was a reference to that Bible verse."

"I think Roger Williams was also talking about people jumping around to different locations in a sad world," the grasshopper said while still taking notes.

"You're taking notes like Roger Williams used to do."

"Yeah, I am. Pretty soon, I'll even get really good at using seventeenth-century shorthand."

"Do you think you're Roger Williams?"

"Possibly, I'm jumping around like he used to do."

"You'll be going to Pembroke College in Cambridge."

The grasshopper jumped onto a different bench.

"After you become a minister, you'll have to leave England to avoid being put into jail."

The grasshopper jumped onto the church's floor and hid under one of the benches.

"You and your wife, Mary, will go across the ocean on a ship called the *Lyon*."

The grasshopper flew out from under the bench and landed on another bench. A second grasshopper appeared next to him. This second grasshopper had a different-looking abdomen.

"Are you a female?" Kate asked.

"Yes, I am."

Kate glanced down at her watch. It said, "December 1631." She looked up at the bench. Its wooden boards shifted until they took on the form of a boat. The word "Lyon" appeared on its side. The boat started to shift up and down as it moved across water. The grasshoppers jumped around to different places on the ship's decks. When a storm appeared, they stopped jumping and instead clung onto a rope. Finally, the ship finished its journey across the Atlantic Ocean. Its wooden boards shifted around until they had formed themselves back into a bench. The grasshoppers sat together in the middle of the bench.

Kate mentioned different places where Roger Williams went, including cities in England (London, Cambridge, Essex, and Bristol) and New England (Nantasket, Boston, Salem, and Plymouth). The male grasshopper jumped onto a new bench for every city. Sometimes his wife joined him; sometimes she remained behind on a different bench.

Kate then said, "Providence." The grasshopper left his wife behind on a wooden bench as he flew crazily through the church's front door. Kate got up and followed him outside. The winds and snow of a blizzard flew onto the grasshopper and then onto Kate. She turned around, trying to go back inside the church, but the building was no longer there. Only a cold New England wilderness was present.

The grasshopper flew up onto the thickest branch of a nearby leafless tree. When the wind started to blow even harder, the grasshopper pressed onto its rear legs. It looked like it was trying to stay in the same spot while the wind was forcing its wings to open up. Without even understanding what was happening, the grasshopper jumped off the branch and flew away with a gust of the wind. After arriving at a river, the grasshopper slowed down. The wind had lost its strength and now released the grasshopper's wings. The still-green insect landed on a wet twig that was lying on the river's bank. The grasshopper hopped multiple times from one wet twig to another one. With each hop, bits of cold moisture, looking like a vale of tears, flew away from its head, body, and feet.

Kate asked, "Are you still Roger Williams?"

The grasshopper was shivering and only shook its head.

"Are you saying yes or no?"

The grasshopper's face looked wrinkled, as if it was thinking of an answer. However, it still remained silent.

"Are you a man looking like a grasshopper or a grasshopper looking like a grasshopper?"

After another few seconds of silence, it said, "I'm a man looking like a grasshopper, or maybe I'm just trying to look like you."

"You're all green. I'm only wearing green pajamas."

The grasshopper rubbed its antennae together, making a noise that sounded like a laugh. "You're also wearing a green blanket; it has pictures of green flowers, green grass, and green leaves all over the place."

"Even so, I'm not one of those poor grasshopper people about whom Roger Williams was talking. I'm not 'hopping and skipping from branch to twig in this vale of tears.'[14] I'm rather having a lucid dream in the twenty-first century."

"Doesn't *vale of tears* have something to do with a valley of sadness?"

Kate thought for a moment and then said, "Okay, I just left an old job and started a new job, so I am sort of in a valley between two hills."

"You've also been crying a lot."

"Yeah, but I'm starting to feel better."

"How are you feeling better?"

"I'm not as scared of the elevators."

"If you think you're okay, tell me about the sorrows of Roger Williams, and then tell me how you're different."

"Roger Williams grew up in a really sad environment. He lived close to where people had been burned at the stake. On the Internet, the Roger Williams Family Association said, 'While a young man, he must have been aware of the numerous burnings at the stake that had taken place at nearby Smithfield of so-called Puritans or heretics.'[15]"

"Is your neighborhood better?"

"I think so." Kate paused for a moment and then added, "Well, there's a criminal who lives a few houses away from me. Plus, in my neighborhood, there have been break-ins and thefts of household items. I do get scared a lot."

"Is everyone else in your neighborhood okay? Do most of them go to church every Sunday, which is what happened in Roger Williams's neighborhood?"

"I don't know if my neighbors go to church. However, I think most of them still believe in God."

"If they don't go to church, how do you know they believe in God?"

"A 2013 Harris Poll showed that 74 percent of Americans do believe in God."[16]

"So does that mean your neighborhood is good or bad?"

"I don't know." Kate thought for a minute and then said, "Even if my neighborhood isn't the greatest, at least my house is better than Roger Williams's was. It has electricity, an air conditioner, a better heating system, hot water, and lots of wonderful appliances."

"Okay, your house is a lot better than a seventeenth-century house."

"Plus, the last time I had to stay outside in the cold, I was outside for less than an hour. I was then able to go to my nice, warm house and have some wonderful food. Roger Williams was stuck without a home for months in a New England winter. Also, his family couldn't join him until the spring."

The female grasshopper flew onto one of the twigs next to the male grasshopper. Then six small grasshoppers appeared.

The male grasshopper said, "I know how tough the winters are in Rhode Island and Massachusetts." Several flakes of snow fell onto his head as he said, "I'm glad I'm a human, rather than a grasshopper."

His wife said, "You're a grasshopper."

"No, I must be a human. Most grasshoppers die in the winter, but I'm still alive, and so are you."

Kate said, "You're alive because you're in my dream."

"I can understand how dreams can be very creative, but this is the first time I've heard of a dream creating a life." The grasshopper looked at the other grasshoppers standing near him. "Actually, your dream has created more than one life."

"I don't think you and your family are really alive. However, it's possible that you've survived somehow by finding shelter in a warm house."

"Are you saying we might really be alive somewhere, besides just being inside a fictional house in your mind?"

"It's possible. In reality, some grasshoppers will still be alive somewhere."

"Maybe I'm in your house."

"There must be some kind of connection between me and your reality for you to appear in my dream." Kate thought for a few seconds before adding, "I might have possibly seen you in my house, or maybe I read a Roger Williams quote about grasshoppers."

"So what happened to Roger Williams?"

"In October 1635, he was banished."

"What does *banished* mean?"

"After a court hearing, he was told where he couldn't go. It was sort of like a restraining order today."

"Did Roger Williams listen to what the court told him to do?"

"No, he didn't."

"Was he sent to jail?"

"He almost was. In January 1636, some officers were going to capture him and send him to England, where he would have been tried and put into prison. He probably would have died there. One of his friends, Governor Winthrop, warned him about the officers who were coming. Roger Williams then had to run away during the night into the middle of a snowstorm."

"Did he have any food?"

"He didn't have much food."

"What did he have?"

"He took some dried corn paste that he managed to throw into his pocket as he was running out of his house." Kate paused and then added, "He had to leave his wife and two kids behind."

"His family was left behind?" The grasshopper frowned before looking over at the other grasshoppers.

"Yeah, Roger Williams had to leave without his family. His wife had just had their second child, and a young baby really shouldn't be outside in the middle of a snowstorm. Roger Williams wanted his family to live through the winter. Luckily, one of Roger Williams's friends, Mr. Winslow, went to the Williams's house and put a piece of gold into Mary Williams's hand. This obviously helped her and the children to live through that tough winter by themselves."

"How did Roger Williams survive?"

"The natives helped him. Otherwise, I don't know how he would have made it through that winter. In a letter that Williams wrote in 1670, he said, 'And surely betweene those my Friends of the Bay and Plymmouth I was sorely tost for one 14 weekes (in a bitter Winter Season) not knowing what Bread or Bed did meane.'[17]"

"Even if he didn't have a bed, he had to sleep somewhere."

"Yeah. At least on some nights, he slept in the hollowed-out trunk of a tree."

"A tree trunk would be a little bit different from a bed."

"Yeah, it was. Roger Williams said that he had no bed because he wasn't sleeping in a bed like the other Pilgrims were. When he was outside, sleeping in a tree trunk might have helped him to stay alive. He also was sometimes sleeping in native people's homes."

"Did they sleep in tree trunks or on the floor?"

"If there were too many people in one native's home, some of them might have slept on the floor. However, against the walls of their homes were benches made out of tree branches. That's where a lot of people normally slept. They also had canoes made of tree trunks, so it's possible that Roger Williams slept in a tree trunk inside or outside of a native's home."

"Did the natives give Roger Williams any food?"

"Yeah, even if he had no bread, he would have been given some other kinds of food. He would have eaten cornmeal, for example."

"I'm all of a sudden hungry." The grasshopper looked around at the nearby ground. A small piece of a dried-up leaf was near its left foot. The grasshopper jumped closer to the chunk of leaf and stuffed it into its mouth. "Did Roger Williams also eat leaves?"

"I don't know. He might have. The Pilgrims and natives ate things like pieces of bark, berries, walnuts, mussels, clams, fish, birds, ducks, chickens, turkeys, deer, and fish."

"Winter is always a tough season, especially for those of us who don't have homes." The grasshopper's huge eyes looked down at the ground; an inch of snow was quivering on the soil's frozen surface. The huge pair of eyes glazed over; they appeared to be covered in a thin sheet of ice.

"Even though that first winter of banishment was really tough for Roger Williams, the beginning of one of his poems in his book *A Key into the Language of America* shows how he depended on God for help: 'God makes a Path, provides a Guide, / And feeds in Wildernesse!'[18]" Kate looked at the grasshopper's frozen appearance and added, "God is always with us. A part of what Jesus says in the last verse of the book of Matthew is: 'I am with you always, to the end of the age'" (Matt. 28:20, RSV).

"Yes, I know God will help me." The grasshopper's eyes looked slightly less icy as it said, "So God turned the bitter winter for Roger Williams into something sweet."

"Yes, God helped him. The ending of that poem by Roger Williams tells us about God's sweetness: 'No Cup so bitter, but's made sweet, / When God shall Sweetning be.'[19]"

"God makes bitter things sweet."

"Yes, he does. Even though we sometimes have to deal with bitter things, God helps us. Decades after that winter of banishment, Roger Williams still remembered the horrors of that bitter winter, but he also was thankful to God for helping him survive."

The grasshopper moved its antennae toward each other and then closed them around each other. It appeared to be praying.

Kate said, "I also am praying. May God help you to get through this bitter winter in our century."

"Thanks."

"I can actually help you out right now. Let's find a warm building." Kate looked at the snowy wilderness around them. She rubbed her head while staring at one of the trees; it immediately grew wider and wider until it took on the form of her house. Kate ran over to her home, and the grasshoppers followed her. Once they were all inside, Kate sat in her rocking recliner, folded her hands together, and tried to make her fingertips warmer. The grasshoppers jumped up onto the coffee table in front of her. They now looked warmer and more alive.

Kate said, "After Roger Williams lived through that first winter, he started a new colony in Seekonk. Some houses were built, and gardens were started. The governor of Plymouth then told Williams that he had to move to the other side of the Seekonk River."

All the grasshoppers on Kate's coffee table jumped over to one of the end tables.

Kate laughed as she rocked her chair forward and backward several times. She then said, "Roger Williams next purchased land from the Narragansett tribe. In June 1636, he moved across the Seekonk River into the area that would soon be called Providence. Williams said that his friendship with the local natives is how he bought the land from them."

"Really?" The grasshoppers moved closer to each other and then looked at Kate for more explanation.

"According to the exact words of Roger Williams, 'It was not price nor money that could have purchased Rhode Island. Rhode Island was purchased by love.'[20]"

"Was Rhode Island really purchased with love?"

"Yeah, it was."

"That's really interesting."

"It is. I wish I could just go to a real estate agent, become friends, and get a free piece of land."

"Could we all live with you?" the grasshopper asked as he looked at his family members.

"Of course you can." Kate smiled and then added, "Canonicus, one of the chiefs of the Narragansett tribe, loved Roger Williams 'as a son.'[21]"

"It's so nice to know at least one person loved Roger Williams."

"A lot of people back then loved him. Some of them just disagreed with his beliefs. William Bradford, who was the governor of Plymouth for over thirty years, liked Roger Williams. In *Of Plymouth Plantation*, Bradford called him 'a godly and zealous man, with many rare qualities but a very unstable judgment.'[22]"

I think a lot of people in the seventeenth century felt the same way: they admired his personality and love for God, but they also disagreed with some of his ideas."

"What was so wrong with his ideas?"

"Some of his ideas were different, such as his belief about separation of church and state. The Puritans were trying to establish their own colony, so they could worship God in their own way. They were persecuted in England and wanted the freedom of being themselves in the New World. They were trying to create their own colony based on their own beliefs."

"Roger Williams was too different from them?"

"Initially, they thought he believed the same way as they did. Then things started to change." Kate made her rocker recliner move around in a circle. When her chair stopped moving, Kate's arms were holding onto the arms of her chair, rather than resting in her lap.

"You look different now," one of the grasshoppers said.

"I'm the same. You just think I look different because my position changed a little bit." Kate paused and then added, "The same thing happened to Roger Williams. When he came over to the New World, he was in a new location. There were different rules, which affected how people thought about him."

The grasshoppers all jumped to different areas of the room. One of them asked, "What did Roger Williams do after moving to Rhode Island?"

"He made his new colony legal by first getting a patent and later helping to attain the 1663 charter from England. He also achieved separation of church and state through the wording that was used in the patent and charter."

All the grasshoppers jumped back onto the coffee table. One of them said, "So he didn't just establish a colony. He worked to make it a good colony."

"Yeah, he did. Roger Williams published letters and books. In his written works, he debated different ideas with other New

England people, such as John Cotton. He also helped with communication between the natives and other New England colonies. He was a minister, a debater, a writer, and a diplomat."

"As a minister, did he do anything religious?"

"In 1638, he established the first Baptist Church in America. Four months later, he left the church 'because he began to have doubts about the validity of baptism by immersion as the true basis of church order.'[23] He then became a 'seeker.'"

"What's a seeker?"

"A seeker was defined in a biography about Roger Williams as 'someone who accepted no creed but believed in the fundamental truth of Christianity.'[24]" Kate paused and then added, "I think a seeker is someone who is trying to find the true Christian God."

"A minister should definitely be trying to find the truth about God."

"We all can look at God's truth. The Bible tells us what we need to know about God."

"I can't read."

"I know you can listen, though. Earlier today, you were taking some excellent notes."

"Thanks." The grasshopper looked down at its feet. There were ink stains from its note-taking activities. "Did Roger Williams do anything else?"

"He established a trading post near Wickford, so New Englanders could trade with the natives."

The grasshoppers jumped again. "What did they trade?"

"They traded a lot of things, like clothing, furs, food, seeds, potteries, baskets, metal utensils, and tools. This trading post helped him to connect not only with natives but also with traders in the different colonies, so he made a lot of friends."

The grasshoppers jumped up onto the wall, where a clock was hanging. They kept on jumping on the clock, which remained silent. No chiming noises were made. Kate opened up her eyes and saw that she was in her bedroom. Her alarm clock was not making any noises yet; it would be going off in another fifteen minutes. She sat up and stretched before getting out of bed and turning off the alarm clock.

Armand Lamontagne's Roger Williams Statue at
Roger Williams University, Photo Usage Courtesy
of Roger Williams University, Bristol, R.I.

*Armand Lamontagne's Roger Williams Statue in the
Library at Roger Williams University, Photo Usage
Courtesy of Roger Williams University, Bristol, R.I.*

BROKEN ELEVATORS

O n Wednesday morning, Kate looked out the window of her bedroom. Her car was covered in four inches of snow. Sighing, she began to get ready for work. She grabbed one sweater, frowned at its light weight, and then exchanged it for a thicker one. In a similar fashion, she chose the warmest slacks, socks, and boots from her closet and bureau. Her cell phone rang. She put it up to her ear and said, "Hi, Mom."

"Are you feeling okay?"

"Yeah, I'm fine. But after yesterday's walk in the snow, today I'm wearing the warmest clothing that I own."

Her mother laughed, which made Kate smile before asking, "How are you, Mom?"

"I'm okay, too, especially since I can work from home today."

"I hate driving in the winter. Whenever I lose control of my car, even if it's only for a second, it really bothers me."

"Can't you stay home today?"

"I don't think the roads will be bad enough for me to stay home. I'm also in a new office, so I really have to be at work on time every day, at least for the first few months."

"I don't want to make you late. I'll call you later."

"You're so great! I love you, Mom. Good-bye for now."

"I love you too, honey."

Kate turned off her cell and placed it in her purse. Instead of eating breakfast, she put a few cereal bars into her purse and went outside to clear the snow and ice off her car. In less than ten minutes, she was driving to work.

Most of the main roads had been salted, so Kate only encountered a few slick areas. For each slippery spot in the road, she gripped the steering wheel very tightly and gritted her teeth together. As she drove close to the Roger Williams statue at Prospect Terrace Park, the roads were clear, but the cars in front of her stopped. Kate also had to stop. She glanced over to her right, but she was too faraway from the statue to see it. The cars started moving again, so she also began to move forward.

In another minute, Kate was pulling up into the parking lot of her office building. About twenty cars were there already; she moved her car into a parking spot beneath a tree at the end of the second row of cars. Slowly, she walked on the slippery sidewalk and then went inside the big front doors. When she went up to the elevators, another lady was there and had already pressed the "up" button.

Kate introduced herself and said, "This is my first week working in this building. I'm at the New World Bank."

The lady said, "I'm Nancy—one of the librarians."

"I love libraries! When I was a kid, my mom used to bring me to the library at least once a week."

"Do you still go to the same library?"

"Yeah, I usually go to the Cranston Public Library, but now I want to check out the one in this building."

"Do you read a lot?"

"Yes, I do. Just last night, I was reading a book about Roger Williams. Its title is *Roger Williams His Contribution to the American Tradition*," Kate said.

"The author of that book is Perry Miller, right?"

"Yeah, it is. Have you ever read it?"

"Not yet, but I was planning on reading it sometime soon," Nancy said.

"Do you just like to read history books?"

"My husband is a descendant of one of the Pilgrims, William Bradford, so I like to read about the early history of our country."

Kate smiled as she said, "I'm a descendant of Roger Williams."

Nancy and Kate shook hands with each other. Nancy then took a book out of her large purse. "I was just reading too about Roger Williams. Here's the book that I finished yesterday." Nancy showed the book to Kate. Its author was Edwin S. Gaustad, and its title was *Roger Williams: Lives and Legacies*.

"I haven't read that one yet."

"It has a lot of nice information, comments, and quotations." Nancy opened the book and then added, "Here's one of my favorite comments: 'In 1860, the president of Brown University, Francis Wayland, said that "the Pilgrims and Puritans sought religious liberty for themselves; Roger Williams sought it 'for humanity.'"'"[25]

Kate silently read the quotation a couple of times before saying, "That's a nice summary of the legacy of Roger Williams."

"Yeah, it is. He wanted people to have the freedom to worship God in their own way, rather than in some way dictated to them by politicians."

"That's why he thought separation of church and state was so important." Kate flipped through a few pages of the book before asking, "Can I borrow this book from the library?"

"Definitely, I'll reserve it for you."

A ringing sound and a red light indicated that one of the elevators was on their floor. When its doors opened, Kate followed Nancy into the silver metal interior. Nancy pressed the button for the twenty-second floor and asked, "What floor, Kate?"

"Twenty-one would be perfect."

A young man wearing a baseball cap walked through the elevator's still-open doors, turned around, and stood between Kate and Nancy as he said, "Fifteen." Nancy moved closer to the control panel while Kate stepped backward into the left rear corner of the elevator.

Before the elevator's doors could close, eight more people entered the six by eight foot interior. The doors almost closed; then a man in the hallway placed his hand between the two metal doors, making them open up automatically. When the man in the hallway saw how many people were already on the elevator, he still walked forward and bumped into people. They moved out of the way and let him squeeze in between them. A lady standing in the corridor behind the man looked at all the people inside of the elevator, waved at them, stepped backward, and said, "I'll get on the next one."

As the elevator started moving upward, a squeaky noise was heard several times. A tall man with gray hair was standing near the elevator's control panel. As he turned to look at the panel, his arm brushed against the lady standing next to him. "Sorry," he said.

The lady moved backward; she didn't notice when her purse bumped into Kate's elbow. Hoping that the lady would hear her, Kate cleared her throat. The lady just moved closer to Kate. Her purse was now pressing tightly into Kate's right arm.

Kate moved sideways and slightly backward. Once she stopped moving, her own purse, which was hanging on her left shoulder, started to press into her left arm. Kate looked to her left. A lady in a gray hat was glaring at her.

Kate said, "I'm sorry, but there's nowhere else for me to move."

The lady purposefully shoved her purse against Kate's purse. Kate pulled tightly onto her own purse, looking as if she was worried that the glaring lady would steal it or break it.

A very loud squeaking noise made the tall man near the control panel grunt. He then said, "I think this elevator's belts are getting old."

A passenger in the elevator's right corner said, "Well, this whole building has to be at least fifty years old."

Nancy said, "It's over forty years old, but renovations were done a few years ago."

The right-corner passenger asked, "Weren't the renovations just carpeting and paint?"

Nancy replied, "You're partially right. New carpeting and paint were put all over the place. Then some new walls were added. Something was also done to the elevators."

When the elevator stopped at the tenth floor, the right-corner passenger pushed past other passengers to get out.

The doors closed, and the elevator began moving again. Kate looked at a document on the silver metal wall, raised her hand, pointed to it, and said, "Whether this elevator's new or old, it must be okay. Three months ago, it was inspected."

"Do any of us believe that piece of paper means anything at all?" the tall passenger asked.

Several of the passengers laughed. The elevator slowed down and then stopped. Its doors opened again; three passengers left. The remaining people rearranged themselves. Kate moved to her right and sighed; her left hand relaxed and was now just holding onto her purse, rather than gripping it tightly.

By the time the elevator reached the twenty-first floor, there were only four passengers remaining; each passenger should have had a quarter of the elevator's space. However, the tall man was standing too close to the center of the elevator. When the elevator doors opened, Kate said, "Excuse me."

The tall man did not move, so she turned sideways and walked around him. While standing in the doorway, Kate paused, looked backward at Nancy, and said, "I'll stop at the library and get the Roger Williams book during my lunch."

"That sounds great. Depending on the time, I might be able to join you for lunch."

"I'd love to have lunch with you. What's a good time?"

The tall man said, "Hey, some of us have to get to work. Can't you two talk later or at least move out of the way, so the elevator's doors can close?"

Kate smiled at him. "Sorry." She then turned to Nancy and said, "I'll call you later to find out when you can leave for lunch."

"Anytime between twelve and one should be okay. If your name is already in the library's system, I can check out that book for you and bring it to the cafeteria with me."

"I think I'm already in the library's system." Kate opened up her purse and began to look through a stack of cards.

Nancy noticed the angry face of the tall man and said, "Kate, don't worry about finding your library card right now. When you call me later, you can give me your information over the phone."

Kate moved past the elevator doors into the hallway, looked at Nancy, and said, "Thanks so much. I'm guessing I'll be able to leave around twelve. I'll call you before then."

As the elevator doors closed, Kate waved to Nancy and then walked quickly up to the door of the First World Bank. Carol immediately opened the front door and let Kate into the bank's lobby.

"How are you today?" Carol asked.

"I'm fine." Kate paused and then added, "Actually, I'm not really feeling too great."

"What's wrong?"

"I'm just cold. I had to run around Roger Williams Park last night."

"It was freezing last night."

"It was worse than freezing. The temperature was below twenty degrees." Kate took off her gloves and unfastened her coat. She looked at her fingers. "I think it's all just in my head. My fingers don't really look frostbitten or anything." Kate moved her right hand forward, showing it to Carol.

"Your fingers look a little bit red."

"I think that's just normal. Your fingers look just the same as mine do."

Carol turned her hands upward and looked at her own fingers. "You're right. Either we're both frostbitten, or we're both normal."

Kate laughed. "I've never in my whole life been even close to normal." She looked down at her hands again. "I'm still feeling cold though. I didn't even bring my lunch today. I'm hoping it's okay if I eat something hot in the cafeteria."

"That should be fine. I'm sure Joe won't mind. He'll hopefully be acting like a happy boss today."

"Why?"

"I think he'll just be happy because most of us are here again today."

"I'll check with him before going to the cafeteria." Kate paused before adding, "One of the librarians, Nancy, said that she can probably have lunch with me at noon, but you can join us too if you want."

Carol thought for a few seconds before saying, "Since one person called in sick today, it's probably better if I eat lunch up here. That way, I can run into the bank's lobby and help out if things suddenly get too busy."

Someone was knocking on the bank's glass front door. Kate turned around and saw Sue standing there. She let her in, went over to her own desk, and placed her coat on the back of her chair.

Sue walked up to her. "Are you trying to be ready to leave quickly? People usually hang their coats in the conference room."

"That room's also called the *break room*, right?"

"Yeah, it is." Sue looked at her coat.

"I'm just cold today. Last night, I was outside while a couple of weird men followed me."

"Did they hurt you?"

Kate explained what had happened and then said, "I even filed a police report."

"Do you or the cops know who they are?"

"I don't think so. However, it was dark out, so I couldn't see their faces or hear their voices too well."

Joe walked in and asked, "Are you sure you're okay now?"

"I'm fine. Thanks for asking, Joe." Kate smiled and then asked, "Is it all right if I go to the cafeteria to eat something hot for lunch today?"

"Definitely, especially if you bring me back some pizza."

"Okay. What kind of pizza would you like?"

Joe said "pepperoni" as he reached into his wallet, took out a ten-dollar bill, and handed it to Kate. He then waved and walked away from her desk toward his office. Several minutes later, Carol came up to her and suggested that she get a teller drawer ready.

Right after Kate had set up her teller station, the bank's front door was opened. Several customers came inside. One man was wearing sunglasses and a sweatshirt with a hood pulled up over his hair. A compass was in his right hand. After he took five steps into the interior of the lobby, he stopped and turned to his right. He watched his compass while he took another five steps. Then without saying a single word, he turned around and left the bank lobby.

Kate walked over to Carol. "Did you see that man with the compass?"

"Yeah. I was going to ring the robbery button to get the cops over here, but he left too quickly."

"He looked sort of like the hooded man who was in here yesterday."

"He was wearing a different sweatshirt though. I think his glasses were also different."

"Even so, he looked like he was about the same height and weight."

"Did you notice if either one of them was wearing the same sneakers as the guy who was here yesterday?"

"I think both men were wearing black boots, but I could be wrong."

"With all the snow around right now, they both must have been wearing boots." Sue paused for a few seconds before adding, "I'll call my boyfriend Charles and tell Joe, in case he needs to talk with the cops again."

"Okay. I'll stay out here, so I can help any customers who come in."

Sue left the room for about ten minutes. When she returned, Kate went back to her own desk and kept busy by reading the contents of several file folders. About twenty minutes before noon, she checked with Joe and other people in the office to see if anyone wanted some hot food from the cafeteria. After taking a couple of orders for pizza, she called Nancy in the library. "Can you still join me for lunch at around noontime?"

"Yeah, I can," Nancy said. "I'll even bring that Roger Williams book for you."

Kate gave Nancy her full name and library card number. Nancy then said, "I'll be leaving the library a little after noon. I'll be in the cafeteria five or ten minutes later."

"If I get there first, I'll try to save us a table."

"Okay. I'll see you then."

At noon, Kate left her office. She paused to look at the doorway leading to the stairs. She looked at her watch and then walked over to the elevator. Sighing, she pushed the elevator's down button. Another three people walked up to the hallway and waited near the elevator with her. After a moment, one of the other people said, "This elevator's taking forever."

Kate shook her head in agreement. "I'd take the stairs, but I think that would really take forever."

The elevator's doors suddenly opened up. Kate and the three other people walked into the elevator's space; Kate pressed the button for two. The elevator stopped several more times, and more people filled the elevator. On the third floor, a lady in a gray sweater got into the elevator. She put her index finger up to the "open door" button and kept it there.

One of the other passengers, who had a blue cap on, asked, "What are you doing?"

The gray-sweatered lady said, "It'll just be a minute."

The blue-capped man said, "I think we're all trying to go to lunch. We also have to get back to work again. We can't just stand here all day."

"It'll just be a minute. My friend was right behind me."

"Why don't you and your friend take the stairs? You'd only have to go down one or two flights of stairs."

"Since you're in such a hurry, you should take the stairs."

"I was on the seventeenth floor. That's a long walk down the stairs."

"Well, you're on the third floor now, so you can get out and go for a walk down the stairs."

The blue-capped man frowned as he moved his hand toward the elevator's control panel. He pressed on the "close door" button while the gray-sweatered lady was still holding onto the "open door" button. The elevator just remained where it was with its doors still wide open.

Kate said, "If you two keep on doing stuff like this, you're going to break the elevator. Then a lot of people will have to take the stairs."

The two index fingers were still both pressing on the two different buttons on the control panel. Kate sighed and took a step forward toward the open elevator doors. Before she could step out of the elevator, the gray-sweatered lady's friend was outside the doors. Kate took a step backward, and the lady's friend entered. The elevator's buttons were suddenly free, and the doors closed. After a few seconds, the doors opened again for the second floor, and everyone in the elevator left. Kate followed them all down the hallway and then turned right into the cafeteria. She sat down at one of the small round tables and looked up at the menu that was printed on the wall.

After only a minute of waiting, Kate noticed that Nancy was standing next to the other chair at her table. Kate smiled, stood up, and followed her over to the food line. They filled their plates with food. When they arrived at the dessert section, they both looked at the brownies.

Kate said, "I'm trying to watch my weight, so I can only eat a half of one of those. Would you like the other half?"

"You read my mind, Kate. I too should only eat a half of a brownie."

After they choose a brownie and paid for everything, they sat down. Kate cut the brownie in half and put one of the pieces on Nancy's plate.

"Thanks."

"You're welcome."

"This food smells so good."

"It really does. It also looks like it's hot without being too hot." Kate took a bite of her turkey and smiled. "It's perfect."

After tasting her chicken, Nancy shook her head in agreement.

A minute later, Kate asked, "Were any locks broken today in the library?"

"I didn't hear of any. Were there any broken locks in the bank where you work?"

Kate laughed. "The security setup is a little better in a bank."

"Even so, was everything okay?"

"Nothing was broken, but someone in sunglasses and a hood came into the bank. He had a compass."

"That's strange."

"Yeah, it was. He was probably trying to do something related to maps."

"If anything's going to happen, it might be in the next few days." Nancy paused and then asked, "Did anyone call in sick at the bank today?"

"Yeah, but only two people claimed they were sick, and maybe they really were sick."

"In my library, three people were supposedly 'sick' today."

"It's not right for people to be absent during tough times."

"I agree with you. That's why I'm at work today."

After a few seconds of silence, Kate said, "Anything's possible in our strange world, but I keep on telling myself to just do my job and to let the police do their jobs."

"I really like my job too."

"I think I like my new job, but it'll be a few weeks before I know for sure."

"If you liked working in the other office of the bank, you should also like this one."

"I really loved working in the Warwick branch of the bank, but I'm not entirely certain about this one. Even though I'm working for the same bank, the job that I'm doing now is a little bit different. Plus, I don't like the elevators."

Nancy laughed. "I don't think anyone likes elevators."

"I keep telling myself that I can always take the stairs, but twenty-one levels are a little too much."

"I know." Nancy shook her head in agreement and then opened up her purse. "Before I forget, I'll give you that book by Gaustad." Nancy removed the book from her purse and gave it to Kate. "It's due back in two weeks. Inside the book is a piece of paper with a list of interesting quotations and books about Roger Williams."

"Did you create the list?"

"Yes, I did."

"Thanks. I've been having so much fun learning about my ancestors."

"Roger Williams liked books too."

"Did he really?"

"Yeah, in December of 1631, when he left England and traveled over to New England on the *Lyon*, he brought a part of his library with him."

"That's interesting."

"Most statues of Roger Williams depict him holding onto a book."

"Is that true of his statue in the United States Capitol Building?"

"Yes, it is. Franklin Simmons created that marble statue of Roger Williams. The statue was then given by the state of Rhode Island to the National Statuary Hall Collection in 1872."

"There are a lot of statues of Roger Williams."

"You're right. There's even a well-known statue of him in Europe."

"Is there really?"

"Yes, his statue is at the University of Geneva in Switzerland. The Roger Williams statue is lined up on a wall with other protestant reformation statues. The monument is called the International Monument to the Reformation." Nancy looked for a picture of the statue on her iPad. When she found a picture, she showed it to Kate.

"Thanks. I love seeing his statues."

Nancy put her iPad back into her purse before saying, "One of my favorite statues is the one at Roger Williams University in Bristol, Rhode Island. This statue, like most of his statues, is holding a book. The book's front cover is even engraved with the date '1636' and the words 'soul' and 'liberty.'"

"I've seen that statue many times. I've just never noticed what was engraved on the book. The statue's facial features though always look familiar to me."

"That may be because the face of Ted Williams was used for the statue."

"Was it really?"

"Yes, no one in our time frame knows what Roger Williams really looked like, so the face of Ted Williams, the famous Boston Red Sox player, was used to create that statue."

"Having a statue of Roger Williams in a university that's named after him is really nice."

"What's also nice is the other statue of Roger Williams at Roger Williams University."

"What other statue is that?"

"The library has a painted statue of Roger Williams."

"It's so great that he's connected to education through his presence in a library at a university."

"The Pilgrims thought education was important. They educated their kids by doing things like teaching them to read the Bible. They had a lot of books too."

"Did they really?"

"In Massachusetts, in the seventeenth century, Governor John Winthrop had a huge library with a thousand books in it."

"Was he the one with the apple and pear orchards?"

"No, he wasn't. The historians talk about Endicott as the one with the orchards." Nancy smiled before adding, "Roses, as well as the apple and pear trees, were brought over from England."

"I heard that Roger Williams also brought his wife over on the *Lyon*."

"Yeah, he did. Mary Barnard came with him."

"Did any of their children come over on the *Lyon*?"

"No, their first child, Mary, was born in 1633. Then their next few children actually had really interesting names."

"Really?"

"Freeborn was born on October 4, 1635, right before Roger Williams was banished. Then Providence was founded in the spring of 1636, and Providence Williams was born in September 1638. Mercy, Daniel, and Joseph Williams were born in later years."

"Did the *Lyon* have a lot of passengers on it, like the *Mayflower* did?"

"No, only about twenty other passengers came over with Roger and Mary Williams. The ship was mostly needed to bring some food and other supplies for the Massachusetts Bay Colony. People were starving. Governor John Winthrop actually declared a day of thanksgiving when the *Lyon* arrived on February 5, 1631."

Kate looked down at her plate. "It's so neat to be talking about Thanksgiving while eating turkey."

"Eating chicken is also nice." Nancy looked over at the food being sold at the far end of the cafeteria. "It's even nicer to not be starving."

"I'm so thankful that we have a lot of food to eat."

Nancy shook her head in agreement. "The first Thanksgiving was a three-day celebration in the fall of 1621."

"The Pilgrims had that celebration with the natives."

"The Pilgrims had multiple other times of Thanksgiving, such as when the food and supplies arrived with Roger Williams on the *Lyon*."

"George Washington declared a day of Thanksgiving too."

"Yeah, he did," Nancy said. "It was on November 26, 1789."

"When did Thanksgiving become one of our once-a-year holidays?"

"In 1863, Thanksgiving as a national holiday was begun by Abraham Lincoln. He said American citizens should, on the last Thursday in November, observe 'a day of thanksgiving and praise to our beneficent Father who dwelleth in the heavens.'[26]"

"I thought Thanksgiving was the fourth Thursday in November."

"In 1941, President Franklin Roosevelt changed the Thanksgiving date to the fourth Thursday in November."

"Well, I'm thankful for a lot of things." Kate paused and then added, "I miss my old job and my old friends, but I'm glad that I have a new job." Kate looked at Nancy and smiled. "I'm also so glad to be making some new friends here."

"Thanks, Kate. I like you as a new friend too. We'll have to 'friend' each other on Facebook."

"Definitely, I'll look for you on Facebook tonight."

A man's voice behind Kate asked, "Who's your new friend, Nancy?"

Kate turned around and looked up into the face of a man who was standing behind her. He had short brown hair and an inquisitive look on this face. His sparkling light blue eyes appeared larger than average as he stared back at Kate.

"I'm Kate Odyssey," she said as she stood up.

The man shook hands with her. He then said, "I'm Thomas Hart, but people call me Tom." His eyes glanced at Kate's left hand. When he saw no rings were on her ring finger, he smiled. Kate looked at his left hand and also smiled.

While Kate and Tom stared at each other, Nancy said, "Tom, please join us."

"I'd love to." He stood there in the same spot, still looking at Kate as she stared back at him.

Nancy stood up, pulled another chair over to the table, and asked, "Would you like me to get you some food, Tom?"

"No, that's okay. I can grab some food really fast." After hesitating for a few seconds, he let go of Kate's hand, waved, and then moved toward the short line of people at the cafeteria's food counter. As he walked, his shoulders shifted slightly. When his left foot moved forward, his right shoulder also moved slightly forward. When his right foot stepped forward, his left shoulder shifted.

Kate said to Nancy, "His handshake seemed really strong while also being sweet."

"He's a firefighter, so he works out a lot."

"How do you know him?"

"He goes to my gym."

Kate looked at Nancy's face as she asked, "Are you two dating each other?"

Nancy laughed. "No, I'm a little too old for him, but you're probably close to his age."

"I hope so."

"He's thirty-four."

Kate smiled. "I'm thirty-two." She looked over at Tom, who was paying the cashier for his tray of food. He then walked back over to their table and sat down.

Nancy asked, "Did you choose turkey on purpose, so you'd have the same food as Kate?"

Tom looked at Kate's plate and then over at his own. "Actually, I really wanted the turkey and mashed potatoes."

"You chose the same vegetable and dessert items too," Kate said.

Tom smiled. "Okay, I did choose the same items as you did, but I really like what you chose."

For the next minute, Tom and Kate silently ate their food while watching each other's movements. Kate ate a piece of turkey, and Tom did the same thing. Then Tom moved a forkful of mashed potatoes over to the carrots and swirled them together. Kate did the same thing on her plate. Tom's eyes widened, showing his surprise. He looked at Kate's face, which was smiling broadly. He then smiled in the same way that she was.

Nancy said, "I really need to get back to work."

Kate's eyes kept on watching Tom as she said, "Thanks for introducing us, Nancy."

"You two actually introduced yourselves."

Kate and Tom laughed while still staring at each other. After a few seconds, Kate said, "You're the one, Nancy, who brought us together. Thanks."

Tom added, "Thanks so much, Nancy."

"I'll call you tomorrow, Kate, and I'll see you, Tom, in the gym on Saturday."

"Okay," Kate and Tom both said at the same time.

Nancy stood up, waved at them, and walked over to one of the cafeteria's exit doors. She then turned back to look at Kate and Tom, pulled her cell phone out of her purse, and took a picture of them. They were still seated at the table and smiling at each other. They did not notice the flash from the picture being taken, followed by Nancy leaving the room.

Kate looked at her watch. "I need to make certain I'm back at work on time."

Tom laughed. "Don't we all, at least those of us who want to keep our jobs?"

"How much longer can you stay, Tom?"

He looked at his watch. "I should probably leave in about ten minutes."

Kate smiled. "That's the same as when I have to leave."

"Do you work somewhere in this building?"

"Yeah, I'm at the New World Bank. Where do you work?"

"Normally, I'm at the Providence Fire Department, but I had to come here today for a meeting about federal and state fire regulations." He looked down at the table like he was trying to hide something. After a few seconds, he looked back up at Kate. "As you can imagine, some of these regulations are important after what happened in the building next door."

"I know you can't tell me everything, but thanks for trying to be as honest as possible."

Kate and Tom both ate the last piece of turkey on their plates at the same time. Tom then asked, "Do you like working in this building?"

"No, I hate the elevators."

"A lot of people hate elevators, but going up and down in an elevator is a lot safer than people think."

"Is it really?"

"Yeah, there's even a National Association of Elevator Safety."

"I've seen inspection forms inside of elevators, so I guess inspectors must look at them fairly often."

"Yeah, elevators are inspected a lot, so they're safe to use. On the other hand, people often get injured while walking up and down the stairs."

"Even if people fall down the stairs, the stairs are usually still better for them."

"Why do you think that?"

"Running up and down the stairs is a good way to get some exercise. It's better to get a bruised knee once every few years while also getting a healthier cardiovascular system."

"You're right about that." Tom hesitated and then asked, "Do you use the stairs in this building? I thought the bank where you work is fairly high up."

"I'm on the twenty-first floor, so I've been using the elevators. However, I might try going down the stairs tonight."

"Using the stairs is a nice way to get some exercise, but just be careful."

"Thanks, I will be. If I get too tired, I'll just walk over to the elevators. I can then finish my trip to the ground level in an elevator."

"If you ever get stuck in one of the elevators, there are a lot of safety devices."

"I've noticed an alarm button on the control panels."

"The elevators also have speakers. Whether an elevator's broken or not, you can still talk to people."

"I'd go crazy if I were stuck in an elevator." Kate hesitated and then added, "I'd probably call my parents on my cell phone before dialing 9-1-1 or hitting an elevator's alarm button."

"In emergencies, people most often do what they're used to doing, so many people actually do contact their friends and relatives before they call 9-1-1."

Kate sighed. "What happens if people are really stuck in an elevator? Can you rescue them without having to cut through the metal walls?"

"Yeah, with the correct tools, the doors can be opened from the outside. Also, an elevator's roof often has some easily opened sections. Usually, there's a service hatch, so the lights can be changed or fixed. Sometimes, just a screwdriver is needed to open up the part of the roof where the light fixture is."

"That's interesting." Kate looked over at the library book on the right side of her plate. "Roger Williams would have hated being trapped inside an elevator."

"I think you're right. He ran away from England. Then he ran away from his home into a New England blizzard because he knew some officers were coming to send him back to England and prison."

"You know a lot about Roger Williams. Do you like history?"

"Yes, I do. I'm a descendant of William Bradford and Isaac Robinson."

"William Bradford came over to New England on the *Mayflower*, right?"

"Yeah, he did."

"I'm a descendant of Roger Williams, who came over to the new world on the *Lyon*."

Tom smiled. "That's so interesting. Isaac Robinson and Roger Williams both came over on the *Lyon*."

"So they came over on the same boat, but did they travel together at the same time on the same trip?"

"I don't think so. They probably came over on the *Lyon* at different times, but they arrived within a year of each other."

"They were close to each other and must have known each other." Kate smiled at Tom.

"I'm sure they did. Isaac Robinson and Roger Williams were both disliked by a lot of people in their century because they helped the Quakers."

"Religious debate back then happened so much."

"Roger Williams was a minister who wanted people to have religious liberty."

"You're right." Kate looked over at the book that the librarian had left for her. When she reached for it, Tom said, "There are some papers sticking out of the top."

Kate took one of the papers out of the book, looked at it, and then said, "Nancy listed some other Roger Williams books for me. There are also some quotes here. One of them is from a book by James Byrd: *The Challenges of Roger Williams: Religious Liberty, Violent Persecution, and the Bible.* James Byrd said that Roger Williams 'made the first sustained defense of religious liberty in American history. Over a century before Jefferson and Madison proclaimed that religious liberty was essential to the new nation, Roger Williams had waged his own polemical war for the cause.'[27]"

"What does 'polemical' mean?"

"I think it means controversial or argumentative."

"That makes sense. Roger Williams argued with a lot of ministers and politicians in his time. He thought true worship meant to be free to worship God by following one's own conscience. Especially if politicians tried to tell him how to worship God, he was really against it."

"He didn't like being told how to worship by the king of England or the governor of Massachusetts. He needed the freedom to worship God within his own heart and soul, rather than inside the metal walls of someone else's prison." Kate looked over at the library book by Edwin Gaustad. Another piece of paper was sticking out of the top of the book. She opened to the page where the paper was and said, "Here's an interesting quote in Gaustad's book: 'The sanctuary of the soul should never be invaded by sheriffs or jailers, by judges or soldiers. That sanctuary was, is, and will ever be God's own sacred place, reserved to him alone.'[28]"

Tom looked down at the book that Kate had moved in front of him. "Those sentences about the sanctuary of the soul are interesting. They show the importance of what is sacred."

Kate asked, "Do you go to church often?"

"Yes, I go every Sunday. Do you also go to church?"

"I go almost every week." Kate smiled as Tom reached over and held onto her hand. She then noticed the time on his watch and said, "I really have to get back to work."

Tom sighed before saying, "I have to go too."

Kate reached into her purse, tore out a deposit ticket from her checkbook, and said, "My phone number is on here."

Tom placed the deposit ticket into his billfold. He then took out a piece of paper, wrote his phone number on it, and gave it to Kate. They both returned their trays, and Kate bought three pizzas to bring back to her office. They then walked out to the elevators together. Almost immediately, one of the elevator's doors opened up. Tom held onto the pizza boxes while Kate pressed the elevator button for the twenty-first floor. She asked, "What floor do you need?"

"I'll first go up to your floor with you, and then I'll go back down to the lobby on the first floor."

As they rode upward, they stood close to each other and talked about their churches. When the door opened for the twenty-first floor, Kate took a step toward the elevator's doors. She then turned around to face Tom. They looked at each other silently for a few seconds before waving good-bye. Tom gave Kate the pizzas, and she stepped out into the hallway. She turned around again to watch Tom. He pressed the button to keep the elevator's doors open; he and Kate stared at each other.

There were three other passengers on the elevator. One of them smiled sweetly at Kate and Tom. The second passenger looked over at the control panel and moved his hand toward the close button while Tom was still pressing the open button. The sweetly smiling lady moved her right hand in front of the second passenger's hand; he was now unable to press the close button.

The second passenger said sarcastically, "Why don't we just all stand here for the whole day? It's not like anyone has to go back to work."

The sweetly smiling lady said, "I think we all have an extra few seconds."

Tom looked over at the three other passengers before saying, "I'm sorry. I didn't notice anyone else on the elevator with us." He then waved at Kate and pressed the close button on the control panel.

Kate leaned forward, but she was unable to stop the elevator doors from closing. When she could no longer see Tom's face, she sighed, turned around, and walked slowly over to the front door of the bank's office.

Carol took the pizzas from Kate and asked her about lunch. Kate said, "I had so much fun."

"Did you see the librarian?"

"Yeah, I did. Nancy and I began eating lunch together. Then I also met Tom, who is one of Nancy's friends." Kate's eyes lit up.

"Is Tom a boyfriend or just a friend?"

"I'm hoping we'll become more than friends. In fact, when I was in the elevator with him, I really wanted a lot of people to be in there with us."

"Really? Most people would have liked to be alone."

"We just met, so we couldn't do anything if we were alone. However, if a lot of people had been with us, we would have been standing super close to each other."

Carol laughed. "How many people were in the elevator with you and Tom?"

"I didn't notice. I think there were two or three, but there could have been four or five."

A customer came into the bank, and Carol walked to her teller station. Kate hesitated between going to her desk and staying in the lobby. Then more customers walked through the front door. Kate moved to her teller station and began helping multiple people with their transactions.

The bank stayed busy until closing time. About fifteen minutes after four o'clock, Kate said good-bye to several of her colleagues; she and Sue then left the bank's office to go home. They walked out to the elevators. Kate said, "After lunch today, I liked my elevator ride with Tom."

"That's so nice."

"However, my ride this morning was different. It was a little scary."

"Really? What happened?"

"The elevator was making noises."

"They sometimes do that."

"Also, too many people were in the elevator."

"How many were there?"

Kate paused for a few seconds and then answered, "I think there were eleven, including myself."

"If it's any consolation, I've been on an elevator with fourteen people."

"On one of these elevators?"

"Yeah."

"Now I really want to take the stairs." Kate and Sue both laughed as Kate moved away from the elevators and toward the red exit sign that was hung over a doorway leading to the stairs.

"I'll see you tomorrow," Sue said.

"Okay. I'm really fast walking down the stairs though, so I might see you in a few minutes. I'll look for you in the big hallway on the first floor of this building."

"I'll send you a text when I get to the first floor. We can then see how much faster the elevator is than the stairs."

"No, the stairs will be faster at this time of day. There are too many people leaving at the same time. The elevators will all have to stop at a lot of floors."

The elevator door opened up, and Sue waved at Kate as she stepped through the doors. "I'll text you when I get to the bottom floor."

Kate waved and then moved quickly through the doorway to the stairs. On each stair, one of her feet stepped so quickly that she appeared to be flying down the stairwell. When she was almost halfway to the ground floor, a loud exploding sound made her stop and grab onto the railing. The explosion expanded its sounds into even louder crashing noises. One of the sounds was above Kate's head. She looked upward; pieces of glass and metal rods were falling toward her. The rods had the same color as the hand railing that she was tightly grasping in her right hand. She began to run down the stairs again, but the pieces of metal were moving too quickly. A six-inch segment from a metal pipe landed on a stair as her foot stepped down onto it. She tripped, fell down several stairs onto a landing, and then rolled sideways.

After a few seconds, she tried to stretch out her right arm, but she was unable to move it because she was lying against the wall on the staircase's landing area. She looked to her left. Her coat was nowhere to be seen, but her purse was lying next to her. A book about Roger Williams had fallen out of her purse and was propped upward by a piece of the stairway's hand railing. Some paper with Nancy's handwriting on it was sticking out of the book's right side. Her writing was a quote from a letter written by Roger Williams on December 18, 1675: "If We cannot Save our Patients, nor relations nor Indians nor English Oh let us make sure to Save the Bird in our bozome."[29]

Below the quote was Nancy's reaction to it: "Roger Williams was able to help a lot of people, but he was not Jesus. He knew that he couldn't save other people like Jesus could. However, he wanted to save the bird in his bosom, so he wanted to do what was right for his soul."

While Kate was still staring at the piece of paper, a piece of metal hit the light on the wall above her. Bits of shattered glass rained downward. She twisted her head until she was facing the floor; her arms automatically moved up around the back of her head. Small pieces of glass hit her hands, shoulders, and back. Then a big heavy object hit the back of her head. The stairwell became dark as Kate lost consciousness.

A "BLOUDY" NIGHTMARE

While still unconscious, Kate started to dream. She found herself to be standing in her bedroom, right in front of an open closet door. A stack of towels was folded up on one of the shelves. While watching the towels, Kate's eyes moved horizontally and vertically multiple times. She then said, "You're not folded up too well."

She removed the top towel and began to unfold it. A blue bird suddenly flew out from an inner fold of the towel. It fluttered in the air for a few seconds before attacking Kate's right hand with its beak. Her hand began to bleed. Kate moved the towel onto the top of her hand and wiped off some drops of blood. Bloody red marks now appeared on the towel and formed themselves into the words "The Bloudy Tenent of Persecution."

Kate said to the towel, "You're the name of a book written by Roger Williams in 1644. He was trying to show that persecuting people because of their religion was very wrong and very bloody."

When Kate wiped off more blood from her hand onto the towel, the blood formed itself into more words, which were an excerpt from the book: "God requireth not a uniformity of religion to be enacted and enforced in any civil state; which enforced uniformity (sooner or later) is the greatest occasion of civil war, ravishing of conscience, persecution of Christ Jesus in his servants, and of the hypocrisy and destruction of millions of souls."[30]

"Roger Williams is so correct. Forcing people to be uniform in their beliefs is the biggest reason for civil war. I hate civil wars as much as I hate world wars, money wars, and any kind of wars. They're all so violent."

"Then why did you try to make my towel exactly like all the other towels?" the bird asked.

"I was just trying to organize things. If anything's out of place, I get nervous."

The bird attacked the towel, shredding the cotton fiber in several places; the shredded sections looked like bits of brown straw sticking out of the towel's main section. With a loud squawk, the bird bit through a hole in the towel and into Kate's bloody hand before flying away into the center of the bedroom and out into the hallway.

Kate's face showed her anger. She squeezed the towel more tightly onto her bleeding hand. She then started to walk toward the open door through which the bird had just flown. A blast of cold air hit her face, but she kept on walking forward toward the coldness. With every step that she took, her feet began to strike more heavily onto the floor. She soon was stomping so strongly that the floor began to shake. When she was almost at the door leading out into the frozen hallway, her toes were numb.

Kate stopped moving and asked herself, "Did I hurt my toes by my stomping, or was it the cold air that did it?" She bent over and wrapped the towel around her feet. As she stood up, she glanced at the scratches on her hand. The bleeding had stopped. She next tried to look out into the hallway. It was too dark for her to see anything. "Are you out there, bird?" she asked.

A chirpy voice replied, "Yes, I'm still close by." The bird was now partially visible in the doorway, but it no longer looked like a healthy bird. It was gray with streaks of red that looked like blood upon its feathers. "I'm so sorry for leaving in such an evil way. I didn't mean to hurt you, and I went through the wrong door. Can you forgive me?"

A voice from the ceiling said, "If we confess our sins, he who is faithful and just will forgive us our sins and cleanse us from all unrighteousness" (1 John 1:9, RSV).

Kate looked up toward the direction of the voice. Her eyes stopped moving when they saw a bright light in the center of the ceiling. She said, "Please forgive me too, Lord. When I was yelling and stomping around, I was doing things against the bird in my bosom. I was trying to hurt my very soul. I'm so very sorry for doing that."

The voice said, "He is so rich in kindness and grace that he purchased our freedom with the blood of his Son and forgave our sins" (Eph. 1:7, RSV).

Kate knelt down on her knees, bowed her head, and said, "I'm also so thankful that our Lord has given me freedom from my sins."

The bird chirped, "I'm thankful too for having freedom from sinfulness. Will you forgive me too, Kate?"

"Of course I will." Kate stood up and smiled at the bird.

"It's too dark and cold out here. Can I please come back into the warm room again?"

"Of course you can," Kate said.

When the bird flew into the room, its feathers were again pretty and blue. The ugly bloody streaks were gone. It asked, "Can I have my warm spot back in that towel?"

Kate took the towel off her feet and stretched it out wide. When the bird flew back into the towel, she softly twirled the cotton edges around it until the towel took on the form of a nest. As Kate slowly carried the nested bird over to the closet and set it down softly on its shelf, the bird began to sing thanks to God. Kate heard some words from the beginning of Psalm 136: "Oh give thanks to the Lord, for he is good, for his steadfast love endures forever" (Psalm 136:1, RSV). Relaxing to the sound of the bird's song, Kate fell into a deeper sleep within her unconscious state.

After almost an hour, she became conscious. She tried to sit up, rubbed her throbbing head with her bloody hand, and then put her hand back down again. Uncertain if she was awake or asleep, she tried to open her eyes, but she could only see darkness. "Where am I?" she asked.

A voice said, "You're in the middle of a war."

Kate looked at the man who had just spoken. He was standing in front of her, wearing armor, and carrying a spear, a gun, a bow, and an arrow. His left hand was resting on the neck of a horse that was also dressed in armor.

Kate said, "I remember now. There was an explosion."

"You were in the wrong place at the wrong time."

"Am I still in the wrong place at the wrong time?" Kate sat up and looked around. She was sitting in the doorway of an old wooden house.

The man in front of her was standing outside in at least a foot of snow. He said, "You're in a house that belonged to Roger Williams."

"Oh, that's really neat." Kate turned around and looked at the wooden furniture, fireplace, metal buckets, bed, and books. One of the books was a 1611 King James Version of the Bible.

"I thought the Puritans used the Geneva Bible."

"Some of the Puritans, like the ones leaving from Amsterdam in 1620 on the *Mayflower,* did use the Geneva Bible. However, it was banned in England in 1616, so the Pilgrims leaving from England in later years often used the King James Version."

"I didn't know that."

"Yeah, you did know that. It's in your own mind, just like I am."

"You don't look like you're in my mind."

"Even so, I'm there. You're not feeling too well right now, so I'm the stronger part of your mind."

"Are you sure Roger Williams really used the King James Bible?"

"Yes, he did. You actually know about a recently published book: *Decoding Roger Williams.* This book says that Roger

Williams quoted Scripture that was 'generally consistent with the 1611 King James Version.'[31]"

"Can Roger Williams really be decoded?"

"Yes, his theories, handwriting, and use of shorthand have all been decoded by many historians."

"Since you're telling me all this, I'm starting to remember some things. I now know what happened to me. I was walking down the stairs when something broke or exploded." Kate paused, touched her head, and then asked, "Do you know if I was hurt?"

"Absolutely!"

"Are you saying I was hurt?"

"Yes, you were really hurt."

"Am I awake or asleep?"

"You're unconscious."

Kate rubbed her head again. "So what war is this?"

"Roger Williams is fighting for separation of church and state."

"I thought he debated his ideas with people, rather than being at war with them."

The man moved his shield and then said, "A debate is a kind of a war—people are fighting with words. Then their debates sometimes turn into more violent wars with real weapons."

"I think Roger Williams did more than just talk."

"He did a lot of writing. Back then, people often debated publicly by writing books, pamphlets, and letters. For example, Roger Williams and John Cotton kept on debating each other's ideas by writing responses to each other's works. The written responses would be held in a public forum because their written responses were published. An article you've already read said that Williams and Cotton 'would have a longstanding intellectual feud...in 1644, Williams would publish his most famous work, *The Bloudy Tenent of Persecution*, as an attack on Cotton's conservative beliefs.'[32]"

"We debate publicly in our society too. In addition to writing and talking, we have TV and the Internet. Blogs sometimes have interesting public debates." Kate paused and then added, "I'm trying to remember more about what Roger Williams wrote. I know he wrote some books, but did he also write letters?"

"Yes, he wrote some really great letters. One of them was his 1655 'Liberty of Conscience' letter. Roger Williams compared the people in a commonwealth to a group of people on a ship. He said, 'There goes many a ship to sea, with many hundred souls in one ship... is a true picture of a commonwealth, or a human combination or society.'[33]"

"That comparison of people on a single ship to the people in one society is interesting. He's saying that a ship is like a colony or a city."

"He also used the word 'many.' While comparing a ship and a society, he's also saying there are many different settings with a lot of people in each setting."

"Even workplaces have their own unique settings. My new office is different from my old one, and the reason is each office has a different group of people who are working together in different locations."

"The different settings are sort of like being in separate ships at sea." The man moved his shield over to his other arm. "Even my shield feels differently on my two arms."

"Yeah, sometimes a single entity will have very different parts to it. The elevator culture in my workplace has been strange. Depending on the number and personalities of the people, different trips on a single elevator are often very different."

"Back in 1620, when the Pilgrims came over on the *Mayflower*, there were three different groups of people: the crew members, the saints (who were Puritan passengers), and the strangers (who were British passengers)."

Kate laughed. "The different groups of people must have had some debates on that voyage."

"They did, which is partially why the 'Mayflower Compact' was created and signed.

"Traveling away from England did not mean that everyone was free."

"Back in the seventeenth century, groups of people on some boats used to have more freedom of worship than when they were on shore. Roger Williams, in his 1655 'Liberty of Conscience' letter, explains how people on boats back then were able to pray in their own way: '[N]one of the Papists, Protestants, Jews, or Turks be forced to come to the ship's prayers or worship, nor compelled from their own particular prayers or worship, if they practice any.'[34]"

"That's interesting. People who were confined to small areas on boats were free to pray, but people in larger geographic areas on shore were not free to pray," Kate said.

"Roger Williams did create Providence as a geographic area where people had the freedom to worship God in their own way. One article about Roger Williams said that his 'contribution was not simply that he espoused tolerance of racial and religious difference but that he created a geographical space where those principles could be put into action.'[35]"

"Roger Williams did not just talk about his ideas. He established a physical area where his abstract ideas became a physical reality." Kate smiled.

"In Providence Plantations, people were free to be different. They could not be legally persecuted for being different in their religious beliefs and practices."

"Persecution happens a lot, even today in the twenty-first century."

"People in your time should know better."

"They don't."

"Back in the seventeenth century, Roger Williams not only wanted people to have the freedom of worshipping God according to their own souls, but he also wanted churches to have worship services in which people were there by choice, not by force."

Kate smiled. "Roger Williams was trying to change things with his words. Some other people back then were trying to change things by hurting other people."

"That's essentially what 'persecution' is—it's hurting others. In one of his writings, *Bloudy Tenent of Persecution*, Roger Williams explains why it was wrong to persecute people for their religious beliefs. In the first paragraph of the preface to this book, the first reason that he mentions is 'the blood of so many hundred thousand souls of Protestants and Papists, spilt in the wars of present and former ages, for their respective consciences, is not required nor accepted by Jesus Christ the Prince of Peace.'[36]"

"Roger Williams knew that Jesus didn't like religious wars. The fighting between the Church of England and the Catholics was really bad. Too many people were killed."

Gunshots and other loud noises made Kate and the man in armor turn to look out the window. Two men with shields and spears were riding horses on the dirt road and moving toward the Roger Williams house. They stopped in front of the door, pulled out a variety of weapons, and then rode off quickly into the approaching darkness of a night sky. Loud screams were heard in the distance as Kate tried to figure out if she was awake or asleep.

YELLING ELEVATOR

———•———

K ate heard the sound of a distant voice scream "help!" She sat up and tried a reality check to see if she was still dreaming or was now awake. She looked at her watch. It was just after six o'clock at night. She turned away and then looked back at her watch again. The time was the same. "I'm awake," she said out loud.

The same voice screamed "help" again. Kate turned her face toward the sound of the voice. However, she was unable to see anything at all in the complete darkness of the stairwell. Kate slid her right hand along the floor; her thumb hit a piece of metal tubing. She tried to push it aside, but other objects were in the way. She then shook some sharp pieces of glass and metal off her left foot. Slowly, she stood up and turned around in a circle, trying to see some light. Only darkness was present.

Kate rubbed her head in the place where she had been hit before losing consciousness. A bump was there now. Sitting down again on the floor, she carefully felt around until her right hand landed on her purse. She pulled it carefully into her lap and then opened it up. On her keychain was a small LED (light-emitting diode) flashlight, which actually worked when she turned it on. Kate smiled, but only until her eyes moved away from her purse. As soon as she saw the damage surrounding her, the smile on her face disappeared. The stairway below her landing was covered in debris. Parts of the red metal railway were mixed in with broken stairs, pieces of glass, tangled electrical wires, and large chunks of cement. She took a few steps forward and tried to shine her flashlight through some of the debris on the stairs below her feet, but she couldn't see anything. The pile of debris was too high, and her flashlight was too small. There was no way she could go down those stairs.

Kate shined her light at the stairs above her. There were fewer pieces of debris, but the railing and many of the stairs were missing. She said out loud, "I don't see my coat anywhere, but at least it's not too cold in here."

The distant voice yelled, "Help!"

Kate turned toward the sound of the voice. Her flashlight now was shining on a door leading into the building's interior. One of the door's hinges appeared damaged. The top of the door was slightly open and slanted into the stairwell. The number "twelve" was just barely visible near the top of the door.

Kate moved closer to the door before asking loudly, "What kind of help do you need?" She paused for a few seconds, but the distant voice was silent. Kate then yelled out, "Is it safe to open this door?"

The door itself seemed to be answering her by dropping some dust from its top section down onto the floor. Kate shined her light at the dust near her feet and then sneezed.

The distant voice yelled, "Help!"

Kate moved the light into her left hand and moved her right hand slowly forward until it was resting on the door's handle. After pausing for a few seconds, she pulled softly at the handle. When the door did not move, she twisted the handle and pulled harder. It opened several inches. Kate moved closer to the opening and shined her light through the empty space. Because the only light in the area was from Kate's small flashlight, only the first ten feet of a corridor could be partially seen. The floor in this section of the corridor was covered in tiles from the ceiling, pieces of furniture, office supplies, glass, a coat, a large black purse, and a red hat.

Carefully, Kate walked down the left side of the corridor, which had the fewest pieces of broken and dusty objects. Rather than walking on the floor, she was stepping on top of broken pieces of plywood, glass from light fixtures, ceiling tiles, pipes, white particles, electrical wires, dust, a computer keyboard, papers, and pieces of two doors. After passing an elevator, a restroom, and a partially demolished accountant's office, Kate had to stop. A large five-foot tall file cabinet was in front of her, and the rest of the corridor now had so much debris that she could no longer move forward, unless she wanted to step on top of at least three feet of broken items.

Kate went back to the accountant's office. In front of the door was a large pile of debris, including a lot of glass pieces. Removing the items would probably take at least half an hour. Kate shined her flashlight along the wall until the light fell onto a section of the wall that was pushed outward into the corridor; she walked over to this section and found a small gap in the plywood. She shone her flashlight through the gap and into the interior of the office. The left side of the room was only a few feet away. Against the wall was an unbroken table holding multiple items: a box of candy, a cake, some wrapped presents, and several lunch bags. Kate's eyes stared at the food items for several seconds before moving her flashlight quickly around to other sections of the room. Some pieces of broken furniture, glass, and other items were on the floor.

Pulling her flashlight away from the wall's gap, Kate walked back down the corridor until she came to the restroom. The door opened easily. Once inside, she noticed pieces of ceiling tiles in the sinks, as well as broken chunks of pipes and bits of fluorescent lights scattered across the floor. She turned her flashlight toward the ceiling. Two partial water pipes were visible, but no water was flowing out of them. Kate walked over to one of the sinks. She pressed against a faucet; no water came out. Sighing, she left the restroom and walked over to the elevator. She pressed both the "up" and the "down" buttons, but nothing happened. No lights turned on near the buttons, and no noises came from the elevator.

The distant voice yelled "help" again. The voice still sounded far away, but it was clearer and seemed to be coming from inside the elevator shaft.

Kate yelled, "Where are you?"

The distant voice replied, "In the elevator." The voice sounded from below where Kate was standing.

Shining her flashlight onto the elevator doors, Kate started to laugh. The doors were partially open, and she hadn't even noticed the opening until now. She took a step forward and peered down into the elevator shaft. The beam from her flashlight only showed a small part of the shaft's interior, but she could see the top of an elevator about ten feet down. She yelled, "What floor are you on?"

"I don't know for sure, but I think I'm on floor nine or ten."

"Are you okay?" Kate asked.

"I'm not hurt, but I'm stuck in a broken elevator." The voice paused and then asked, "Are you a first responder?"

Kate laughed. "I wish I was a police officer or fireman. I'm stuck here too."

"Are you also in an elevator?"

"No, I'm in a corridor, but I still can't find a way out."

"All you have to do is to look for a window."

"That's a great idea! I could go back to the accountant's office and see if there's a window to break. Then I can keep throwing stuff out the window until I'm noticed and rescued."

"If you're rescued, will you tell them about me?"

"Of course I will."

"Thanks."

"Why have you been screaming 'help'?"

"I was hoping someone would hear me and help me to get out of here."

"If I could help, I would."

"Thanks."

"Is anyone else in the elevator with you?"

"No, I'm all by myself."

"That's sort of strange. Usually the elevators in this building are packed."

"I know." The lady paused and then added, "Right now, I think I'd prefer one or two more people in here with me."

"Do you have anything to do?"

"I have a few games on my phone, but I'm trying to save the battery for phone calls."

"Does your cell phone work?"

"I don't think it's broken. I can turn it on, but I can't make any phone calls or get Internet access. How's your phone?"

"I haven't tried it yet. I'll try using it right now." Kate opened her purse, took out her cell phone, and smiled to see its light working. She then tried to dial "9-1-1." Nothing happened. She next tried to call her parents. Again nothing happened. After sighing, she said, "My phone turns on, but I can't make any calls on it."

The yelling lady said, "I hate it when my cell phone doesn't work."

"Something happened. The electricity's also not working."

"Do you know what's happening?"

Kate frowned. "I think there was some kind of bomb or gas explosion."

"Is just this building messed up?"

"I don't know. Because our cell phones aren't working, there are probably problems in other places too."

Kate and the lady were both silent for a minute. Then Kate said, "I'm going back to that office in the corridor to see if there's a window somewhere."

"Before you leave, can you help me to get out of this elevator?"

"I don't think I can help, except by telling rescue people where you are."

"I can't wait that long."

"I don't have any tools. I'd need something to break the metal."

"I think the ceiling of my elevator is already partially broken. Can you see the light coming through from my laser light?"

"Yeah, I can a faint glimmer of light in the center of the roof. There might be a small crack in the top of your elevator."

"Maybe you can pry it open."

"Okay, I'll first go to that office and see if I can find some kind of tools. I'll also get some food."

"Is there really food in that office?"

"Yeah. I'll get us both some food."

"How will you get the food into my elevator?"

"There's a crack between the doors up here. If I can find some scissors or a screwdriver, I might be able to pry the doors open."

"Then you can try to squeeze some food through the crack in my elevator's roof."

"I'd have to somehow climb down the elevator shaft to get to your elevator, but I can probably figure out some way of doing that."

"There might be a ladder on the wall of the elevator shaft."

"Well, if I can open up the doors and get into the elevator shaft, then I'll be able to look around for a ladder, a rope, or some other way to climb down." Kate paused and then added, "I'd better get going."

"Are you really planning on coming back and bringing me some food, instead of just trying to escape through a window?"

"Yes, I promise I'll be back here in less than an hour."

"Why will it take you that long?"

"I have to move some debris before I can get into the accountant's office."

"Okay. Thanks for saying you'll help me, whether you actually do or not." The elevator lady's voice sounded sarcastic.

"I'm not lying to you," Kate said. "It really will take me awhile to bring food back here."

"I really believe you." The lady's voice still sounded sarcastic.

Kate sighed before saying "good-bye." Then she walked back to the accountant's office and began moving the debris away from the door. In order to move items with both of her hands, she had to hold onto the flashlight with her mouth. Every few minutes, her neck muscles became tired from the weight of the flashlight, so she kept on having to remove the light from her mouth and stretch out her neck muscles. After about thirty minutes, she had moved enough of the debris so that she could open the door. Once inside, she kept the flashlight in her right hand while moving to the opposite side of the room. Moving the flashlight's beam around the room, she could find no windows. Sighing, she checked out all the other walls and walked into several different rooms, but still she found no windows.

Walking over to a desk that was still standing, Kate looked inside its drawers; besides lots of files and papers, she found a screwdriver, scissors, some cereal bars, and a backpack with some workout clothing in it. After dumping the clothing out of the backpack, she put the screwdriver and cereal bars into one of its sections. Then she walked over to the table next to the other wall. "Birthday Bill" was written on the cake. "Does this mean I'll be billed for taking this cake?" Kate asked out loud. She looked again at the cake and realized that her flashlight's beam had only fallen on the bottom part of the cake's decorations. Now her flashlight was showing her all the words: "Happy Birthday Bill." She pulled at the corner of the cake. A two-inch square piece fell into her hand. She first licked some frosting off her thumb and then ate the piece of chocolate cake. Grabbing a tissue from a box on one of the desks, Kate rubbed it on her sticky hand. As she dropped the tissue into a pile of trash in the middle of the room, she noticed several desks that were partially broken. She checked out their drawers and found a few more food items, some bottled water, and a small bottle of cranberry juice. She put these items into the backpack. Then she tripped over an extension cord. After standing back up again, she shined her light on the thick orange cord. She said out loud, "You're almost as good as a rope." She disconnected the cord and looked around for some more cords. She found two more of the thick cords and tried to place everything into the backpack. With her purse and food items inside, only two cords would fit into the backpack, so she had to wrap one of the cords around her waist. She went over to the only remaining desk that she had not yet examined. Inside one of the drawers, she found a cap, some duct tape, and a flashlight with extra batteries. After using the tape to attach the new flashlight to the cap, she put the tape, batteries, and her tiny flashlight into her backpack. She then placed the lighted cap on top of her head.

As she started to walk out of the office, her flashlight's beam fell onto a "Sales Reporting" form. Kate paused, picked up the form, and started to write a note: "Because of the emergency, I'm taking some items, but I'm leaving you some money for them." She then looked in her billfold, but before she had a chance to withdraw any money, a loud noise of breaking glass made her jump. She pointed her flashlight toward the noisy area. A ceiling tile fell down onto an already-broken picture frame. Her right hand began to shake. "Why is stuff still falling down?" she asked out loud. Another tile fell from the ceiling. This one landed only inches away from where she was standing. She dropped the "Sales Reporting" form and took a step backward.

Then the elevator lady with the distant voice yelled, "Help!"

Kate quickly left the accountant's office and walked back to the elevator, where she yelled out, "Are you okay?"

"Yeah, I am. I just heard some noises. I think something above my elevator fell down."

"What did it sound like?"

"I don't know."

"Was it soft or loud?"

"I don't know!" The lady screamed for a few seconds and then started to cry.

Tears began to form in Kate's eyes. She tried to wipe the moisture away, but her eyes were still tearful. After a minute, she said, "I found some food."

The lady coughed a few times and then asked, "Really?"

"I also found a screwdriver."

"Oh, you're so wonderful! I can't believe you came back to try and help me."

"I wanted to bring you some food."

"Did you find any way out of the building?"

"No, most of the corridors were blocked off. I could only get into one office, which didn't even have a single window." Kate sighed. "I guess I'll just have to keep on looking."

"Can you get into the elevator shaft? If you can climb down to a different floor, you might be able to find a window."

"I was planning on trying that, but first, I should try to get to your elevator."

"Is there anything I can do to help?"

"Yeah, can you shine your flashlight for a few seconds? I might be able to see the light from up here."

"The only light I have is that one tiny laser light."

"Can you try to shine it again through the torn ceiling section of your elevator?"

"Okay." After about thirty seconds, the yelling elevator lady said, "Can you see it?"

Kate said, "No, but please be ready to turn it on again in a minute."

"Okay."

Kate pulled the screwdriver out of the backpack, put its metal blade into the crack between the elevator's doors, and pushed the top of the screwdriver toward the right. The doors opened some more; there was now a six-inch opening between the doors. Kate leaned against the left elevator door, put her right foot between the doors, and kicked at the right-side door with her foot. The doors slowly opened more and more until there was a three-foot opening between them.

Kate stuck her head, shoulders, and right arm between the doors. She shined her flashlight downward and asked, "Can you see the light from my flashlight?"

The elevator lady said, "No, I don't think so." After a pause, she added, "Here, I'm shining my laser light into the crack in the ceiling. Can you see it?"

"Yes, I can!"

The lady in the elevator clapped loudly before yelling, "Thanks so much! Maybe now, I'll get some food and water."

"If I can figure out some way to climb down to your elevator, I might be able to somehow get some food into your elevator."

"What kinds of food do you have?"

"I have bottled water, cereal bars, and some other things," Kate said as she moved her head and shined her flashlight around the four walls of the elevator shaft. Immediately to her right was a rusty metal ladder that was attached to the shaft's wall. She turned sideways, grabbed onto one of the ladder's rungs, and pulled at it. The ladder seemed sturdy, so she moved her right foot onto one of the rungs, hesitated, and then placed her other foot onto the same rung. The ladder still seemed strong. Gripping the rungs tightly, Kate began to climb down. After every five or six steps, she paused and looked at the rungs on the ladder below her. They were all rusty, but none of them were missing or broken.

The elevator lady asked, "Is there any way you can climb down to my elevator?"

"Right now, I'm climbing down to your elevator."

"Your voice sounds much closer now than it did before."

"Your voice too sounds much closer."

Finally, Kate's feet landed on a ledge right next to the ceiling of the elevator. She knocked on the elevator's metal roof and asked, "Are you in here?"

"Yes, I am. You found me!"

"I found your elevator, but I haven't really found you, at least not yet."

The elevator lady laughed. Kate then said, "I'm going to step onto the roof of your elevator. Please tell me if the elevator shakes, blinks its lights, or does anything else strange."

"Its lights are broken, so it won't be blinking or lighting up."

"Okay," Kate said as she slowly moved her right foot onto the elevator's ceiling; then she shifted her weight over to her right side before having her left foot also step onto the ceiling. She finally asked, "Can you shine your laser light through the hole in the ceiling again? I think the hole's near the center of the roof, but I'm uncertain about exactly where it is."

The yelling lady shined the laser light into a crack in the ceiling again. Kate walked across the top of the elevator to the center of the roof. She was now standing over the area where the laser light was shining. Kate pointed her own flashlight down toward the roof. She could see a wide crack. "I think the elevator's light broke, which made this crack in the roof."

"Can you make the crack bigger, so I can get out of here?"

"I'll try." Kate knelt down on her hands and knees. She pulled the screwdriver out of her backpack and used it to hit the elevator's metal near its crack. "I don't think this is working."

"Please don't give up! You have to rescue me!"

Kate tried to pry up a part of the elevator's roof by inserting the screwdriver into the crack and then pressing against its plastic handle. Nothing happened. "The metal up here is so strong that the screwdriver can't do anything to it."

In a loud voice, the yelling lady started screaming "Help!" multiple times.

Kate said, "I'm only one person. I can't do everything."

"Maybe someone else will hear me and be able to help. You obviously aren't doing too well."

"I'd be really upset at you for saying something so mean, but I know you're stressed out."

"I don't even remember what I just said, but I didn't mean to hurt you. I'm sorry."

Kate sighed and then asked, "How would you like some food? This crack in the ceiling is large enough for me to give you some of the food that I found."

The lady was silent for a few seconds before saying, "I'd love some. Thanks."

Kate forced one of the cereal bars through the wide crack in the roof. As soon as the bar hit the floor, the elevator lady picked it up, took off its paper wrapping, and began to eat it. Kate also began to eat, but she ate several pieces of candy.

"Here's some chocolate too," Kate said as she dropped two pieces of chocolate candy through the crack. They hit the floor. Even though there were no paper wrappings for the candy, the elevator lady still picked them up off the floor and ate them. She then asked, "Do you have anything to drink?"

Kate hesitated and then said, "Yeah, but I only have one bottle of water."

"Is there some way we can share it?"

"I don't know." Kate touched the orange cord around her waist. "If I tie the bottle to this cord, the bottle with the cord will be too big to fit through the crack in your elevator's roof. I think the bottle all by itself, though, may fit through the hole. However, when you're done drinking half of the water, will you be able to push the bottle upward through the hole in the ceiling? Are you tall enough to do that?"

"I don't have to be. This elevator has a little bench."

Kate said, "Okay." She then pushed the bottle of water through the crack in the roof.

The yelling elevator lady caught the water bottle before it hit the floor. She said, "Thanks so much."

"You're welcome. I'm just glad to have more freedom than you do right now."

The elevator lady didn't say anything. Kate could hear the sound of the cap being taken off the bottle of water. A minute later, the elevator lady said, "You're such a nice person, but you're really too trusting of strangers."

"You're not a complete stranger. We work together in the same building."

"Actually, we don't work together. I was just meeting someone who works here. And I don't even like him that much."

"Oh, so you're dating someone in this building."

"Not really. I just said yes to the dinner date because I was bored and had nothing better to do."

Kate was silent for a few seconds and then asked, "Can you send the bottled water back up to me?"

"No."

"What do you mean?"

"I mean what I said: No. I lied about there being a bench down here, and I'm not tall enough to put the bottle up through the crack in the ceiling."

Kate screamed, "This isn't fair! I was trying to help you!"

"You can go back to that office and find more water."

"I already checked all the desks in that office. There's no more water."

"You have a lot more freedom than I do."

"What good is freedom if I die of thirst?"

"You can go find another office with some water in it."

Kate began to hit the top of the elevator with the screwdriver.

The elevator lady yelled, "I can live more with that noise than I can without water."

Kate yelled back, "Because I was scared you were hurt, I didn't even bother to leave any money for the items I took. You made me into a thief!"

"So I stole water from a thief who stole water?" The elevator lady laughed and then remained silent. Kate's screwdriver began to make even louder noises on the elevator's metal roof.

The yelling elevator lady remained quiet.

Kate finally said, "Okay. I'm leaving to find a window, and I won't give you any more of this food."

The elevator lady still said nothing. Kate hit the roof a final time and then moved her head upward, shining her flashlight up the elevator shaft's ladder. She frowned while trying to look up into the shaft. She could not even see the doors that she had pried open.

ACCOUNTING ELEVATOR

Kate moved her head, shining her flashlight around the walls of the elevator shaft. She climbed upward on a ladder until she found a large metal opening to her left. It was either a ventilation vent or some kind of connecting passageway. The opening was at least six feet tall, so she was able to walk directly through the metal opening into a metal corridor. She was moving slowly toward the interior of the building, but she kept on walking through the passageway.

After advancing for less than a minute, Kate found another elevator shaft. She moved her head, shining her flashlight up and down the shaft, but the beam of light wasn't strong enough for her to see an elevator anywhere. A metal shelf was circling around the interior of the elevator shaft. Kate carefully stepped out onto the shelf and then walked along the shelf on the inside of the shaft while leaning backward against the shaft's metal wall. When she arrived at the opposite wall of the elevator shaft, she stopped moving. Her left hand was touching a thick electric wire. Kate moved her head up and down, shining her flashlight along the length of the wire. Near her feet, the wire was split up into three different sections. When Kate looked at the one horizontal section of the wire, she noticed that it led into an opening in the elevator shaft. She slowly walked beyond the wire and across the metal shelf until she arrived at the opening. Inside was a different vent. It was curving slightly. It appeared to be going back toward the outer section of the building. Kate went into this vent and continued walking. After moving about twenty feet into the passageway, she paused and looked at the ground. There seemed to be a lot of plywood pieces and other debris in front of her. She continued walking through the debris for another ten feet until she was at the end of the passageway. Another elevator shaft was in front of her. Loudly, she said, "There are far too many elevator shafts in this building for the current number of elevators."

A voice above her said, "You're right. The old shafts have no working elevators in them."

The voice so surprised Kate that she jumped. Her cap with the attached flashlight flew off her head and landed on the metal walkway. Despite the loud noise that her flashlight made when it hit the walkway, it was still working. Kate picked up the cap with its attached light and put it back onto her head. Then she looked up to see an elevator's floor only a few feet above her head. She asked, "Is your elevator a new working one or an old broken one?"

"It's a new broken one."

Kate's laughter was drowned out by the louder laughs of multiple people who were inside the elevator. All of the laughter was jittery, rather than happy. After the nervous laughs stopped, someone hiccupped. Then soft crying noises were heard.

"Are you okay?" Kate asked.

The crying stopped. After a few seconds, a voice asked, "Are you a first responder?"

Kate laughed nervously again. "I've already been asked that question."

"What was your answer?"

"It was no. I'm not a first responder, and I'm stuck in this building, just like the other person who was stuck in an elevator."

"I don't think you're just like the people who are stuck in tiny elevators."

"I can't escape. I can't go home."

"At least you can walk around in a bigger area than we can."

"So you're stuck inside of your elevator?"

"Yeah, four of us are stuck here."

"That's too bad."

"We know."

"Okay, I have more freedom than you do, but I'm still stuck in this building." Kate paused and then added, "Debris and broken things are all over the place. I can't find a window or a door to get out of this building."

"Why are you outside of an elevator, rather than inside of one?"

"When I was leaving work, I took the stairs."

"Why?"

"I get nervous inside elevators, especially when they're crowded."

"After what happened today, I doubt if any of us will ever take an elevator again."

One of the other voices from inside the elevator said, "You're so right about that."

"What do you think happened?" the first elevator voice asked.

Kate replied, "I don't know for sure, but I'm guessing from the damage I've been seeing that it was more than one bomb."

"The four of us inside this elevator decided that it was a nuclear bomb."

"Why do you think it was that kind of a bomb?"

"It was really loud. Also, if it were a regular bomb, it was probably placed right inside this elevator's shaft. That wouldn't make much sense. Don't you think a bomb would be better placed at the door of a vault or some other place where the bombers could find some money?"

Kate replied, "It does seem a little strange that a bomb would be so close to an elevator, but maybe you just think it was closer than it actually was."

A different voice said, "I'm so glad that we left a few minutes earlier than we usually do. If we had left at the usual time, we probably would have been directly hit by the bomb. We'd no longer be here."

A third voice said, "I heard a lot of debris fall on top of our elevator, so the bomb was either in the elevator shaft or very close to it."

The first voice said, "About a half an hour after the explosion, I got an itchy rash, and John here got an upset stomach. It must have been a nuclear bomb."

"Who is John, and what's your name?"

The first voice said, "I'm Bill. I work in the MAX Numbers Accounting Office."

The third voice said, "I'm John, and the other people in this elevator are Beth and Ellen. We three work in a lawyer's office in this building." After a pause, John asked, "Who are you?"

"My name's Kate. I just started working in the New World Bank's main office."

Bill said, "Congratulations on the new job!"

"Thanks, but I'm actually working at my same old job. I was just transferred to the bank's Providence office."

Bill said, "I often meet with people at your bank. In time, we'll get to work together and will then know each other better."

Kate asked, "Since I'm a new person in this building, I don't know a lot about all the offices yet. Do you know where I can find an office with some windows in it? If I can find such a place, I can break a window, throw things outside, and hope that someone will notice and rescue me."

Bill asked, "Can you also tell people where our elevator is located?"

"Of course I'll do that. In fact, I'd really love to be able to do that."

"Finding an office with windows in it sounds like a good plan," John said. "Our lawyer office is on the twelfth floor. Even though it doesn't have any windows in it, the office next to ours does have some windows."

"Would it be right above us, by any chance?"

"Sort of," a female voice said. "You need to go this way about twenty feet."

"Which way is this way?"

John said, "It's this way." Someone knocked on the back wall of the elevator.

"Thanks," Kate said. "Before I try to move in that direction, is there anything I can help you with? Do you need some food?"

"Yeah, we do," John said. "Do you have anything?"

"Yeah, I have a few items."

"What kinds of food do you have?"

"A cake, some cereal bars, and some candies."

A female voice said, "A cake sounds really great."

John asked, "You're below us, right?"

"Yeah, I am. Is your elevator's door open at all?"

"No, it's completely closed." John paused and added, "Beth is good with mechanical things. What do you think, Beth?"

"If Kate can climb up onto the elevator's roof, she might be able to open up a hole in the roof. For example, where the light fixture is, there's probably some way to open it up and change the bulb. Once there's a hole or an open roof, then she can find some way to drop things down to us."

John said, "An open roof would be better. Then we'd be able to get out of here."

Kate said, "Okay, I'll see what I can do. There's a kind of a ladder here." She began to climb upward on skinny metal steps. Most of the steps had pieces of metal, wood, and glass on them. Kate used one of her feet to push the debris off each stair before she stepped onto it. After about five minutes, she was slightly above the elevator's roof. She stepped down onto the roof and kicked off some of the debris that was covering its rusty metal. She then took out her screwdriver and tilted her head so that her flashlight shone on the metal roof. Finally, she began to disconnect the elevator's light fixture. Before she removed the last screw from the fixture, she said, "Please stand away from the light. It might fall down."

John said, "We're all set. We've already been standing in the four corners in case pieces of the light fall."

The light fixture suddenly fell down into the center of the elevator. Pieces of glass made clinking noises as they bounced off the floor. Kate moved her head and looked down through the small hole in the top of the elevator. She saw one of the men pulling a piece of glass off the top of his shoe. She asked, "Are you okay down there?"

Kate knew the man with the glass on his shoe was John when his familiar voice said, "I think I'm okay." He looked around at the three other people in the elevator. They all shook their heads, indicating they were also okay.

Kate said, "I'm so sorry about the light. Should I try to fix it?"

John said, "Normally, I'd hate to have a broken light in here, but it's not working anyway. Do you know, Kate, if other parts of the building have any electricity in them?"

"I've only been to a few places. There's no electricity and no water anywhere. Also, my cell phone isn't working. Are your cell phones working, by any chance?"

"We can turn them on and use them for lights and music, but we have no access to the Internet or phone services."

Kate opened her backpack and removed a cake in a plastic container. She opened up the container, cut the cake into strips, and then folded the container around one of the three-inch wide strips of the cake. She then wrapped the end of an extension cord around the cake strip and lowered it into the elevator.

The other man in the elevator, Bill, asked, "Can you shine your flashlight this way? Then we'll be able to detach the food from the cord without breaking anything."

John suggested, "I can use my cell phone to help with some more light."

Kate said, "You should save your cell phone's battery, John. I'm using the flashlight anyway, so I can just shine it into different places." Kate shined her light onto the cake, which was now in Bill's hands. There was a wedding ring on his ring finger.

Bill laughed and then said, "I don't believe this. The cake actually has 'Bill' written on it. I wonder if you're giving me my own birthday cake, Kate."

"Could this really be a cake for you, Bill?"

"Yeah," Bill replied and then looked up at Kate. "My birthday's tomorrow."

"Happy early birthday, Bill!" Kate smiled. "If you send me back that container, I can send down more of the cake to you."

Bill sent the container back up to Kate several times. After she had sent down all parts of the cake, he put them together on top of a large piece of paper. Once the cake was completely put back together again, Bill asked, "Where'd you get this cake from?"

"An accountant's office."

"Was it MAX Numbers?"

"I don't know. My flashlight isn't that good, and I didn't notice."

"Because my birthday's tomorrow, someone probably brought this cake into the office right after I left work at four thirty."

"Were the food items yours, Kate, or did you also get them from the accounting office?" Ellen asked.

Kate looked guilty as she said, "The food was in the accounting office." After a brief pause, she added, "I tried to write a note and leave some money, but ceiling tiles were falling, and an elevator lady was screaming for help."

Ellen said, "Well, even if you have a good excuse for what you did, it's still theft."

Bill shook his head in agreement. "Some people would call that looting."

Kate sighed. "You're right; I did steal the food." After thinking for a moment, she added in a loud voice: "I'm also the one who carried it to different elevator shafts. I should get paid for transporting essential goods to feed people." Kate tightly gripped her flashlight as she shined it onto the four faces of the elevator people. They were looking at each other, but they all turned their faces upward at the same time to blink their eyes at Kate.

Bill asked loudly, "Did you only steal food items? That flashlight looks familiar to me."

Kate's face showed her anger as she yelled, "I only borrowed some items to help other people! I didn't steal any money or any expensive things!"

Ellen asked, "Why should we believe you? You're a stranger running around in a bombed-out building!"

Bill glared at Kate while saying, "We're possibly dying while stuck in this elevator, and you're running around free to do whatever you want to!"

Kate opened her mouth, but no words came out. She looked down at the four people in the elevator. Their faces showed their anger. "If I really had stolen items, would I be here trying to help you, or would I be stealing more things from other places?"

Ellen's eyes widened. She then smiled. "You're right, Kate. If you were really a thief, you would not be here arguing with us."

Bill looked around at the other three elevator people's faces before saying, "I'm sorry to be yelling at you, Kate. We're all just upset right now, so we need to scream at someone to make ourselves feel better."

John said, "I know what also happens when people are upset. They often do what they're used to doing, and this will make them feel better."

Ellen shook her head in agreement. "When my aunt was killed in a car accident, I went to work the next day. I actually felt better just being able to do something that I normally did."

Kate suggested, "Let's all focus on how I should repay you guys for the items that I took from your office."

Ellen said, "We need to decide on some specific payment amount."

John added, "Beth and Ellen both know a lot about Rhode Island's laws pertaining to economic matters. They can figure out what's most appropriate."

Ellen said, "John is the criminal lawyer. He can figure out what to do about the theft." She looked at John and added, "Is she a thief or a looter?"

"She's possibly both of those. She's maybe guilty of stealing and looting."

Kate said in a soft voice, "I'm innocent until I'm proven guilty."

John laughed. "Do you know how often I've heard that sentence?"

"I think we all agree that I have a good excuse for what I've done."

John laughed again. "I know what you're going to say. You're going to blame the bombs for your crime."

Kate smiled. "Actually, I was trying to save someone who was screaming for help."

John asked, "Were you able to save him or her?"

"She was healthy enough when I left her. Hopefully, she's still okay."

Ellen asked, "What other items did you take from the office? Are you also using MAX's extension cords as your ropes?"

"Yes, I am, but they were mixed in with all kinds of debris. Doesn't that make them trash?"

Ellen shook her head. "No, the cords weren't trash if they were inside an office. If they were in a trash container on the side of a road, then they could be claimed to be trash."

"But the office was all trashed by a bomb. There was even some trash, possibly from a wastepaper basket, on top of one of the cords."

"The trash still wasn't in a legal trash container."

"If the bomb was a nuclear bomb, like you four people think, then the extension cords could be radioactive." Kate paused and then added, "I also tripped on one of the extension cords. My ankle's been bothering me off and on since then."

Ellen asked, "Are you okay now?"

Kate rubbed her ankle. "It's okay right now, but it was aching about ten minutes ago."

Ellen whispered to the other three elevator people. After a minute, she said to Kate, "If we sign a statement that says we'll not file a suit prosecuting you for theft, then you'll also have to sign off on not filing for possible personal injuries due to your fall or the use of radioactive extension cords."

"Okay, I can sign some papers." Kate laughed before adding, "I've been signing a lot of papers at work this week."

Bill said, "There's also the cost of the cake, any other food items you've stolen, and the extension cords."

Kate asked, "How about payment for my services of delivering food items to you?"

Ellen said, "Let's do it this way. You can list the items you stole on a piece of paper. Bill and I will figure out the cost of the items, including the sales tax."

"Why do I have to pay sales tax?" Kate rubbed her head and then added, "I'm not buying anything from a store. I'm buying stuff from people to sell to other people."

Ellen asked Beth, "What do you think, Beth? Is this a casual sale or is it more formal?"

"We could try to claim it's a casual sale. However, if Kate will be earning money by buying stuff from us and then selling the items to multiple other people..." Beth looked at Ellen and shook her head in a negative way.

Kate said, "I won't be earning money. It's more likely that I'll be losing money."

Bill said, "I think John, Beth, and Ellen are just trying to follow state laws. As lawyers, they also know what the laws say should be done in situations like this one."

Kate sighed before saying, "You're right, Bill. I also really do want to pay any sales taxes correctly."

Ellen said, "What's happening now actually is different from a normal situation."

Beth shook her head in agreement. "Can we list the items being sold as medical supplies? Without any food at all, people will be dying."

Ellen looked around at everyone's faces and then suggested, "We could set aside some money for possible sales tax and then refund it to Kate if we don't have to pay any taxes for the items being sold. Considering our present situation, I'm guessing we'll be able to get a tax exemption."

Kate said, "A lot of people, including myself, hate to pay taxes. But I know the tax money is needed."

Beth shook her head in agreement. "Everyone hates paying taxes, but then everyone also wants all kinds of services, like schools, police, and fire departments."

Bill smiled. "People claim the sales tax in Rhode Island is really high, but there are no local sales taxes."

Beth said, "You're right. Also, not everything in this state is taxed. Food and medical supplies often aren't taxed. Also, clothing costing less than two hundred fifty dollars is not taxed."

Bill added, "I really love how one of the Rhode Island sales tax laws supports writers, composers, and artists. These people can sell their own creative works without paying any sales and use tax."

Beth shook her head in agreement. "Supporting people who are trying to communicate literary and artistic ideas is so neat. The law says 'an original and creative work...shall be exempt from the sale and use tax when sold by a writer, composer or artist who created such work.'[37]"

Bill said, "The tax people in this state are usually very helpful. I think the food and extension cords might be considered emergency medical supplies, which are intended to keep people alive."

Beth said, "John and I will word everything on his laptop."

"You have a laptop?" Kate asked.

John reached into his briefcase, pulled out his laptop, and raised it upward, showing it to Kate.

She asked, "Is it working?"

"It's only partially working. I turned it on right after the elevator was stuck. There was no Internet access, so I turned it off again. We've been using it occasionally when we need some extra light in here. It's better than our cell phones at lighting up this elevator." John turned on his laptop, and the bottom half of the elevator's interior was filled with dusty light.

"We'll write the document on my laptop and then read it out loud. If you don't like anything, Kate, we can rephrase it."

"Will you be able to print the document?"

"No, but once it's worded correctly, I'll just write it out with my pen on some paper. Then we can all sign off on it."

After the document was phrased in a way that made everyone happy, John pulled out a legal pad of yellow paper from his briefcase. The first few pages already had writing on them. He tore off a blank piece of yellow paper and wrote a handwritten copy of the document on it. The paper was then passed around and pulled up and down on the extension cord until everyone had signed it. They all also looked at each other's signatures. Kate was now able to legally keep the backpack, extension cords, and some food items.

Bill said, "We still have to fill in some forms to show such things as sales tax and payment for your transportation services."

Kate laughed and then looked at his face. "Do you have the forms with you?"

"No, I don't. They're in the office. Can you go and get them?"

"Can't we do the forms after we're rescued?"

Bill looked at Beth and Ellen before saying, "I guess we really should wait until then. This is sort of an emergency situation."

Beth added, "We've already come up with a few new rules for our own conduct."

Kate asked, "Really? What new rules did you create?"

Beth looked around the floor of the elevator. Her eyes rested on a brown sweater that was covering a boxlike item against one of the walls of the elevator. She replied, "The rules have to do with things like personal space, like where we can stand, sit, and sleep. We've also discussed sleeping times and using that container over there."

"What's that container used for?"

"I'll let you use your imagination."

Everyone, including Kate, laughed. Bill then said, "Yeah, this is really an emergency situation." After pausing a few seconds, he added, "We can wait, Kate, on doing the tax and compensation forms."

"Thanks, Bill. I need to try and get out of this building. In fact, after we all get out of here, I'll stop by your office."

"I don't think we'll be in our usual offices for a while. However, after we're rescued, I can contact you. What's your phone number and e-mail address?"

While Kate was telling him the information, Bill was writing everything on the back of one of his business cards. He then put the card into his billfold. John also recorded the information, but he typed it into a file on his laptop. Bill, Beth, and Ellen added their information into John's file. After he saved the file, he turned off his laptop.

Kate said, "When I get out of this building, I'll tell the police about you and other people being in some of the elevators."

Bill said, "You should make a list with everyone's name on it."

"Why should I do that?"

"If you get out of this building before anyone else does, I think most people would want you to give their names to the police. Then the officers could notify everyone's loved ones about who was alive."

"That's a good idea."

Beth said, "If you need a piece of paper, I'm sure John can give you one."

Kate asked, "How much money do you want for a piece of paper?"

John laughed. "I'll donate it for free. This way, we can help other people, as well as ourselves."

Kate sent the extension cord's end back down into the interior of the elevator. After she retrieved a piece of the yellow notary paper, Kate wrote down the names of the elevator's occupants, as well as the phrase: "Yelling elevator lady who stole my water." She then put the paper in her purse and the cord around her waist before saying good-bye.

Slowly, Kate moved down from the top of the elevator to the narrow metal shelf. She then crawled into the elevator shaft and began to move down a rusty ladder. Particles of dirt, glass, and other items made the ladder's rungs slippery, so she held tightly onto the edge of each step as she moved downward.

After going down two floors, Kate heard a couple of people talking. Their voices were off to her left. She stopped moving and tried to listen, but the voices were too far away. A minute later, the people stopped talking. Turning her head and shining her flashlight to the left, Kate saw a narrow metal walkway. She stepped over some broken pipes onto the walkway and toward the interior of the building.

Suddenly, a loud noise of metal hitting wood came from where the voices had been talking. Kate stopped walking and looked toward the noises. Two men, an axe, a backpack, and a small lantern were standing ahead of her on the walkway. She turned off her flashlight and tried to breathe slowly and quietly.

A man's voice said, "This is taking forever, Larry."

A second male voice, one that sounded familiar to Kate, said, "You're right, Henry. Breaking through these walls is taking too much time. It's also really tiring." Larry swung the axe into a wall. Pieces of plaster and wood flew out, fell down through the metal walkway, and made only a few soft noises as they landed many levels below.

Henry said, "Let me have that axe, Larry. It's my turn."

"Hitting walls multiple times with this stupid axe is tiring, but it's also a good way for me to get some exercise." He hit the wall another time before stretching his arms and giving the axe to Henry.

"Thanks. I think we're both getting enough exercise for today."

"We won't have enough time to go to our gym today anyway."

"I was hoping we'd find the hidden jewelry more quickly."

"We won't have enough time to check out every wall in this building."

"You said we'd probably find it in the first few walls."

"We'll have to just keep trying, at least until people figure out how to get into this building without endangering any lives."

"Your idea of blowing up multiple areas at the same time was a great one."

"Thanks. The building looks in much worse shape than it actually is. Plus, with people stuck in elevators, the police have to be careful about how and where they get into the building." Larry laughed before adding, "Besides, the police know there are still a few bombs that haven't exploded yet."

"Really? You didn't tell me about any extra bombs."

"I didn't want you to get worried. The bombs will only go off if someone enters or leaves the building where a bomb is located."

Henry was quiet for a moment. He then cleared his throat and said, "I haven't seen any dead bodies. Do you know if anyone died?"

"I don't know. There have probably been at least a few injuries."

"With so many people stuck in elevators, crazy fights will be happening." Henry laughed and then added, "As time goes by, there will be more and more injuries, if not deaths."

"Because of the placement and timing of the bombs, I can tell you about a possible war that could be happening inside of one of the elevators."

"Really?"

"Yeah. There are three people who all work in the same lawyer's office. When they leave work, they usually take the same elevator because they leave at the same time. One is John, a liberal democrat and a criminal lawyer who has completely messed up. One of my friends, who only stole fifty dollars, wound up having to go to jail because of John."

"Was this friend of yours the thief who killed someone at a fast-food restaurant?"

"Jim didn't kill someone on purpose. He was attacked by the person at the cash register. To save himself, Jim had to shoot the cashier."

"The cashier was attacking Jim to save just fifty dollars?"

"Yeah. That cashier was so stupid." Larry lifted the big axe and struck so hard at the wall that a wooden beam tilted outward toward him. He quickly moved to his right as the beam broke off. It then hit the walkway and bounced off into the dark emptiness below.

Henry stared at Larry for a moment before asking, "Who else is in that lawyer's office with the liberal lawyer?"

"Beth works there too. She's an ultraconservative republican who does a lot of things related to money matters."

"Really?"

"Yeah. She's really pretty too."

"She sounds interesting."

"I know, but she's married."

"Rats!"

"Another female lawyer, Ellen, also gets on the elevator with John and Beth."

"Do any of them have guns?"

"Beth probably does."

"Okay, tell me the truth. Did you place one of the bombs to try and kill John?"

"Well, it just so happens that I knew which elevator he would be taking—the one that's closest to his office."

"Is he usually boarding that elevator every day at four thirty-four—the time when the bombs were set to go off?"

Larry said in a sarcastic tone, "Coincidences happen so often in our lives. In fact, if John left at the exact same time when he has been leaving in the past, he's probably not alive anymore."

"What if he survived?"

"Then he'll be fighting with the other people in his elevator."
Larry laughed before adding, "If we have time, we can go and
check out his elevator."

"We could also just leave the building and find out if he's one
of the survivors or not."

"I like that idea better. If we find out that he's still alive, I'll
figure out what to do then." Larry raised the axe and hit the wall
strongly a few more times. "This wall doesn't look like the one
we're trying to find."

"Should we move on to the floor below us?"

"Yeah, that makes sense."

Kate held her breath as she waited to see if they came toward
her or went off into a different direction. After a minute, she
heard their voices again, but this time, they were further away.
They began to talk again, but she could no longer understand
what they were saying. Exhaling and sighing at the same time,
Kate turned on her flashlight, looked down at the thin metal
walkway, and started walking backward to the elevator shaft.
When she reached the shaft, she heard some voices coming
from a lower level. She sighed and began to climb upward on the
elevator shaft's narrow metal ladder.

1663 Rhode Island State Charter,
Courtesy of Rhode Island State Archives

First Section of the 1663 Rhode Island Charter,
Courtesy of Rhode Island State Archives

LIBERTY ELEVATOR

When Kate reached the next floor, she stepped off onto a small walkway and stopped for a minute to rest. She then heard some voices coming from her left. She shined her light across a walkway and saw another elevator. Something smelled funny. She paused for a moment to shine her light around the area, but she could not find anything besides the normal rusty metals, old walls, and some debris. After looking very closely at the walkway, she moved across to the new elevator and asked, "Is anyone in here?"

A familiar voice replied, "Yeah. Do I know you?"

"Possibly. My name is Kate Odyssey. I just started working in the New World Bank this week."

"We do know each other. I'm Nancy Bradford—the one who works in the library. I loved our lunch today. My chicken was so great!"

"I loved my turkey, and our talk about Roger Williams was so neat!"

"Do you see anything unusual out there?"

"Besides a fallen-down building and lots of debris, everything seems normal," Kate said sarcastically. After pausing for a few seconds, she added, "Your elevator does smell a little strange."

"Is it the elevator that smells strange or is it the surrounding area?"

"I think it's the elevator."

"We thought some kind of biochemical hazard was happening, which made that strange smell."

"I don't think any biochemical thing is happening."

"Why not?"

"There were some bombs. They blew up sections of the building."

"The criminals could have used bombs and biochemical weapons at the same time."

"Whatever happened, I wish we were back at lunch again. In addition to the chicken, I completely loved the chocolate fudge brownie that we split in half."

"Okay, my half of the brownie was also really good."

A male voice from inside the elevator asked, "When did you two have lunch?"

"Earlier today," Kate said.

"Between twelve and one, but our lunch together seemed like it was so long ago," Nancy said.

The male voice asked, "Did you save the other half of the brownies?"

Nancy laughed. "No, we bought only one brownie, and each of us ate a half of it."

Kate said, "I don't have any brownies with me, but I do have some chocolate candies, cereal bars, celery sticks, and almonds."

"Really?" the male voice asked.

"Yeah, I'm so thankful right now to just have any food at all." Kate paused and then asked, "What's your name?"

"Roger Clarke."

Kate opened up her backpack, took out her purse, started to write down his name in her listing, and then asked, "How do you spell your last name?"

"It doesn't really matter right now, does it?" he asked.

"It does. I've been writing down a list of names of people in different elevators. That way, if I can escape from this building, I can tell the police about who's alive and stuck in an elevator."

"Oh, that's a good idea." Roger spelled out his name.

Nancy also spelled out her name and then said, "Roger's a professor at one of the colleges in Rhode Island." After pausing, she added, "There are two other people in this elevator. Lydia Cranston works at a museum and lives in Cranston. Providence Williams works in the library with me." Lydia and Providence both spelled out their names.

After finishing the listing of names, Kate asked, "Do you live in Providence, Providence?"

"Actually, I do."

"Are you, by any chance, descended from Roger Williams?"

"Yes, I'm descended from one of his kids, Joseph Williams, who married Lydia Olney."

"That's so neat!" Lydia said. "I'm also a descendant of Joseph and Lydia!"

Kate said, "I'm a descendent of Roger Williams too. It's so neat to meet some of my extended family members."

Nancy asked, "Kate, do you have the book that you borrowed from my library?"

"Yeah, I do. It's in my backpack, and I've actually been reading it."

"That's great. I have a whole cart of over twenty books in here right now."

"Do you normally have that many books with you?"

"Sometimes I do. When the bombs went off, I was moving these books to one of the library's storage areas."

"Do you have enough flashlights and batteries to keep reading for a few days?"

"We might have enough light for another day or two. We've been taking turns with three different flashlights. One person will use a flashlight and read a part of a book out loud. Everyone in the elevator will listen. Then after a page or two, the flashlight is turned off, and we talk about what was just read."

"That's a good way to stay busy. I don't know how long only three flashlights will last though."

"We also have some other light sources, like our cell phones and an iPad."

"Are your cell phones working?"

"They can turn on and light up, but we can't call anyone. Is your cell phone working any better?"

"No, it's not."

"For right now, we're not using our cell phones for light. Instead, we're using the flashlights and iPad. That way, whenever things get better, we'll be able to use our cell phones to call people."

"It's really great that you have enough light and books to keep yourselves busy."

"I agree with you. In fact, I love being able to just read books in here. It's one of the few things I like about being stuck in this elevator."

Kate laughed. "You're the first person to say a single positive thing about being stuck in an elevator."

"Thanks." Nancy smiled before adding, "Can anyone think of any other positive things?"

Providence said, "I'm just so thankful that we're still alive."

Roger, the professor, said, "I'm getting firsthand experience with the creation of common law in a small community."

All the elevator people laughed. Kate asked, "How does common law work in an elevator?"

Roger replied, "We've been debating things and making our own rules, like when we should all go to sleep, when we should all wake up, and who should have which section of the elevator."

Lydia said, "That's the problem with being in such a small area. Everyone's trying to tell one another what to do. Our differences don't seem to matter. Those of us who are dating have to follow the same rules as people who are not dating."

Kate asked, "Who are you dating?"

"Providence."

Kate said, "It's wonderful that you two are stuck in the same elevator together."

"Yes, it's great that we're together, but there's one problem."

"What's that?"

"We're not alone in here. There are other people with us."

Laughter erupted from inside the elevator. Then Roger said, "We've actually been voting on rules for correct behaviors and ownership of this elevator's space."

Providence said, "We're still dating, Lydia. We just can't act like we're all by ourselves."

"Why can't we just kiss? We're only trying to express our love for each other. It's not like we want to do anything illegal, like getting naked or having sex in front of other people."

Kate's face showed her surprise as she asked, "Were you told that you can't kiss each other?"

Roger said loudly, "Yes, they were told to stop kissing each other. Two of us voted against that behavior."

"What's wrong with kissing in an elevator?" Kate asked.

Roger said, "They were doing it too much and making us nervous."

Lydia said, "Being in this elevator is like being in a prison."

Roger said, "I agree with you about this elevator being a prison. Actually, this elevator is an example of people being put into prison by mistake."

Lydia said, "We could be freer than we are, if you would just let us kiss. This elevator is a mistaken prison."

Nancy said, "Roger Williams used the word 'misprision' to refer to being mistakenly in a prison."

Kate asked, "Do you know more about his use of the word 'misprision'?"

"In one of his letters, Roger Williams once said something about misprision. I think this book on the book cart has the quote I'm thinking of." The noise of shuffling pages was followed by Nancy reading a quote from Roger Williams: "Sir, I dare not stir coals, but I saw them to be much disregarded by many, which their ignorance imputed to all, and thence came the misprision, and blessed be the Lord, things were not worse."[38]

"Which letter are you reading from?"

"It was written to Governor John Winthrop and dated August 20, 1637."

"You're reading from a letter that's contained in a book, right?"

"It's in the first volume of a book called *The Correspondence of Roger Williams*."

"Other letters by Roger Williams must be in that book too."

"Yes, there are some nice letters, as well as commentary about them."

"Can I borrow the book now, or do I have to be in the library to check it out?"

"I'd let you borrow it right now—if I could get out of this elevator."

"If I can open up a part of this elevator's roof, then I might be able to send down a cord and get the book."

"If that happens, you can just write down your name and library card number on some paper."

"Thanks so much."

"You're so very welcome." Nancy paused for a moment before adding, "I was moving that book on a cart with some other books to a storeroom when our building was blown up. I'm guessing some terrorists did it."

"Do you really think it was blown up by terrorists?" Roger asked. "I don't think there would be any logical reason to blow up our building, especially after a lot of the people had already left for the day."

Lydia said, "It could have been some kind of an accident, like a gas line blowing up."

"The damage seems more like something done by bombs," Kate said.

Roger asked, "Wouldn't gas line problems end up causing fires?"

"I don't know." Kate paused and then added, "I didn't see anything that was burned up. I also know that a couple of thieves are running around inside this building. If someone used a bomb, it was probably those thieves, rather than terrorists."

"Thieves often try to steal things during emergency situations." Roger sighed. "I once was in a car accident, and a thief stole my wife's purse."

"Why would thieves blow up a building this size? If they're trying to steal something, they could just steal it," Nancy said. "Thieves broke a lock in one of the library's closets, but they didn't have time to steal anything."

"In a library, they'd probably only want to steal books."

"Archived books can be worth a lot of money."

"You're right. I didn't think about that."

"The security devices in the library's doors would have to be turned off for someone to steal the books." Nancy hesitated before adding, "The security devices are never turned off."

"Thieves are probably looking for something inside the walls," Kate said as she began to climb up to the top of the elevator.

"I know some parts of this building have new walls built on top of older walls."

"Blowing up the whole building, instead of just one part, doesn't seem to make much sense," Roger said.

"Well, criminals aren't always too smart." Kate shined her flashlight toward the elevator's lighting fixture.

Nancy said, "Oh, I can see a small light in the top of this elevator. Is the light yours?"

"Yeah, it is. If you're okay with this, I'm going to try to disconnect the lighting fixture; then I can send some food down to you."

"That sounds really great! If you have some rope or a string, I can also send the library book up to you."

"I have some extension cords. I've been using them as ropes."

"I'll turn on my flashlight and shine it upward so that you can better see what you're doing up there."

"Thanks, Nancy. The extra light will help a lot. Please just step away from the middle section of the elevator. I don't want anything to fall on people and hurt them." Kate quickly disconnected the light fixture. She then pulled the extension cord off her waist and withdrew one of her checking account deposit tickets from her purse. After she wrote her name, library card number, and book information on the back of the deposit ticket, she attached it to the extension cord with an elastic band and pushed it downward into the elevator. While she pointed her flashlight at the lowest section of the extension cord, Nancy took off the deposit ticket and tied the cord around the Roger Williams book. Kate pulled the book upward and maneuvered it through the hole in the roof. She then dropped four cereal bars and some candies through the hole in the roof.

Each of the elevator people picked up a cereal bar and some candies. They all said "thanks" and smiled up at Kate.

Before Nancy opened up her cereal bar, she coughed and then said, "I'm really thirsty, and my throat is very dry. I'm thankful that you gave us some food, but do you also have anything to drink? Even if it's something small, I can share it with the other people here." She looked around at the three other elevator people; they all smiled, showing their agreement.

"I have a bottle of water." Kate attached the bottle onto the extension cord on her waist and then lowered it through the hole in the elevator's roof. "Can you untie the bottle from the co-rope okay?"

"What's a co-rope?"

"I meant the extension-cord rope."

Nancy took the bottle off the rope before saying, "I untied it okay, but before we drink this and eat the cereal bars and the candies, I should ask you how much we should pay for them."

"Ten dollars should be okay."

One of the elevator people, Roger, said, "Cuppaimish ten dollars."

Nancy laughed. "I don't think Kate knows what that word means."

"No, I don't. What language is it?"

151

Roger explained, "It was a seventeenth-century word that Roger Williams claimed was 'newly made from the English word pay.'[39] He listed this new word in his 'Of their Trading' chapter in his book *A Key into the Language of America.*"

"Are you telling me that word was a new one used by the natives while trading with Roger Williams?"

"Yeah, it was. Friendship often means that people learn each other's words. For example, when Roger Williams was met by the natives at Slate Rock, one of them greeted him 'with the phrase "What cheer, netop?"—essentially, "What's up, bud?" in a mixture of old English and Narragansett.'[40]"

"What's Slate Rock?"

"In 1636, when Roger Williams had to move from Rumford to the other side of the Seekonk River, Slate Rock is supposedly where he first stepped from his canoe onto the west side of the river. It's in Slate Rock Park in Providence, Rhode Island."

"I've driven past that park before. I think my mom called it 'what cheer square.'"

"Slate Rock is Rhode Island's version of Plymouth Rock in Massachusetts. As you probably already know, Plymouth Rock is where the Pilgrims possibly first stepped ashore."

"Sometimes people combine words together from different languages, but sometimes they make up completely new words." Kate paused for a second and then added, "My word 'co-rope' is one that I've just started to use today."

"You're talking about that extension cord you're using to lower the food to us, right?"

"Yeah, I'm not thinking of it anymore as an extension cord, but rather as something that connects people who need food and other items." Kate paused and then added, "I like 'co-rope' better than 'extension-cord rope.'"

Nancy laughed. "I like that word too. If we all start to use it, within a few years, it could wind up in one of the dictionaries as a real word."

Kate looked into her backpack and brought out a bottle of cranberry juice. "Since it'll probably be awhile before people are rescued, you might need something else to drink. Would you like some cranberry juice?"

Nancy said, "I don't know about anyone else, but I love cranberry juice!" The other elevator people smiled at Kate while they shook their heads up and down.

Kate attached the juice onto her extension cord and began to lower it into the elevator. When the juice had only gone down about two feet, its cover fell off. About half the juice spilled out of the bottle; some of the juice landed on the elevator's floor, and some splashed onto the books set up on the library cart.

Nancy yelled out, "Oh, no! A couple of these books aren't even in print anymore."

"I'm really sorry," Kate said as she looked in her backpack and took out some facial tissues. She threw the tissues down through the hole in the elevator's roof.

Providence grabbed the tissues and gave them to Nancy. She tried to rub some of the juice off the books, but she was only partially successful.

Lydia took out some hand cleaner from her purse and said to Nancy, "Can this hand cleaner be used on the books?"

Nancy looked at the cleaner and said, "I can't use it on the books, but I'd love to use it on my hands. They're all sticky."

Lydia gave her the hand cleaner. After Nancy was done cleaning her hands, she looked up at Kate, who apologized again.

Nancy said, "It's not really your fault. You were just trying to help."

"I should have made certain that the top was on tight enough. I could have also tried to attach it better to the extension cord."

Nancy looked at the bottle of cranberry juice. It was now standing upright on the floor with about half its juice still inside. "What's more important is that we now have another half a bottle of liquid to keep us alive a little bit longer."

153

Kate said, "Under the circumstances, I can't collect any money from you for the food that I sent down to you earlier. If anything, I need to pay you some money for the damaged books."

Nancy said, "Thanks. Let's do it this way: we won't pay you for the food and drinks, and we won't charge you for the books. That way, we're both contributing something for the damage."

"You're so nice, Nancy. I'll tell you what. I'll write you out a check for a library donation. That way, I'll get the tax benefit, and you'll get some of the money for the books."

Nancy looked up at Kate and smiled. "I should be able to write off the books as being damaged directly or indirectly by this disaster. That way, if you want to make a donation, you'll be able to legally write out a small check."

"Thanks, Nancy. You're already one of my best friends, and we only just met earlier today."

"You're one of my best friends too, Kate." Nancy looked at her cereal bar and candy before adding, "While we're eating together again right now, I can tell you more about Roger Williams."

"I'd love to hear more about my ancestor! Especially when we're stuck here with no freedom, thinking about Roger Williams will be so nice."

"Just like we're relying on you today, Kate, back in the seventeenth century, the New England colonies had to rely a lot on other people. The natives helped them out a lot, as did some of the people in England. They were always needing supplies and financial help from England. Even such things as paper came from England."

Providence agreed. "Roger Williams didn't always have enough paper. Near the end of his life, he wrote an essay in the margins of a book."

"Did he really?" Kate asked.

"Yes, he did. His essay was titled, 'A Brief Reply to a Small Book Written by John Eliot.'"

Kate laughed. "Since he was writing in the margins, it definitely had to be a brief reply."

Providence thought for a moment and then added, "The symbolic aspects of this essay are very interesting."

"How so?"

"Williams used the words 'brief' and 'small' in his essay's title while responding to a book by Eliot. Eliot's book also had the words 'brief' and 'small' in its title: *A Brief Answer to a Small Book Written by John Norcot Against Infant-Baptisme.*"

"Did John Norcot's book also have the words 'brief and 'small' in its title?"

"No, Norcot's book, which was published in 1672, was called *Baptism Discovered Plainly and Faithfully, According to the Word of God.*"

"So only John Eliot and Roger Williams used 'small' words in their titles."

"Roger Williams went further than that. He used shorthand while writing his brief reply to a small book."

Kate laughed. "Did he really use short words in his short essay?"

"Yeah, he did. Roger Williams was experienced in using shorthand. When he was young, he took notes in church."

"I heard about his use of shorthand to take notes."

"Roger Williams began working as a scribe for Sir Edward Coke, who paid for him to go to college."

"That was nice of him."

"Yeah, he became like a father to Roger Williams."

"Was there really a shorthand system back in the seventeenth century, or did Williams just make one up?" Kate asked.

Nancy said, "Yeah, shorthand systems have been around for ages. There was a Roman shorthand system called the Tironian Notes. It was used for over a thousand years."

"Is that the shorthand system used by Roger Williams?"

"No, Roger Williams 'adapted and customized' John Willis's 1602 stenographic system.[41]"

"So he used an actual shorthand system, like our modern Gregg system?"

"Yeah, he did. In fact, it took a while to figure out that the shorthand essay in the margins of that book was written by Roger Williams. Some people then decided to try to decode the essay." Nancy opened up her purse, took out a book, and waved it around so that everyone could see it. "You can see the code used by Roger Williams in the picture on the cover of this 2014 book: *Decoding Roger Williams: The Lost Essay of Rhode Island's Founding Father.*"

"So what does that book say about Roger Williams?"

"I haven't had a chance to read the whole book yet, but there's a lot about decoding seventeenth-century shorthand. Also, the author mentions what people today think about Roger Williams." Nancy opened up the book and read: "Roger Williams has long loomed large in the historiography of colonial America as well as in the popular imagination, sometimes viewed as the prescient promoter of full religious liberty in the early modern world with his 'lively experiment' of Rhode Island."[42]

"Why was Rhode Island called a lively experiment?"

Nancy looked at a stack of printed material in the library's cart. She pulled out a copy of the *Rhode Island Royal Charter of 1663* and read a short section out loud:

[I]t is much on their hearts (if they may be permitted) to hold forth a lively experiment, that a most flourishing civil state may stand and best be maintained, and that among our English subjects, with a full liberty in religious concernments and that true piety rightly grounded upon gospel principles, will give the best and greatest security to sovereignty, and will lay in the hearts of men the strongest obligations to true loyalty.[43]

Providence asked Nancy to read the excerpt for a second time. After listening closely, he said, "The experiment was that Rhode Island and Providence Plantations would be a civil state and would give its citizens freedom to follow their own religion."

Nancy said, "That's right. What I really think is interesting about the 1663 charter is that other freedoms, in addition to freedom of religion, are mentioned."

Providence asked, "Can you read us some section of the charter that mentions a different freedom?"

Nancy looked at the charter and said, "The freedom to go fishing is one example of the freedoms mentioned: 'they, and every or any of them, shall have full and free power and liberty to continue and use the trade of fishing upon the said coast.'[44]"

Professor Roger Clarke said, "Freedom was mentioned in other places, in addition to the 1663 charter. In an earlier legal document, the 1643 patent, Rhode Island was first allowed to have a political community with no religious requirements. Once Charles II became the king of England, the 1643 document became invalid. A legal document signed by the king was needed. After Charles II became the English king, he signed Rhode Island's 1663 charter. His picture is in the top left corner of the charter document."

Lydia said, "Because I work in a museum, I love to talk about historical documents. I know the 1663 charter is now in a steel vault."

"Have you ever seen the actual charter?" Roger asked.

"Yeah, I have. Right now, it's attached and held up by some threads. It used to be attached to some cardboard, but in 1996, its storage system was changed to the current one."

"Why does it have to be suspended by threads?" Roger asked.

"The charter was written on parchment from sheep or goat skin, so 'it needs to expand and contract, just like your own skin.'[45]"

Providence said, "Just like the charter, I think all of us need to expand and contract too. Being stuck in this steel elevator is just like being stuck inside of a steel vault right now."

Nancy laughed. "We don't just like the 1663 charter, we're also living just like the charter is right now."

Kate said, "We do have more freedom than the charter does."

Nancy looked up at Kate and said, "You have more freedom than the charter does, but those of us stuck inside this elevator are living more like the charter does."

"Even in an elevator, you have more freedom than a locked-up piece of parchment does. You're alive with a brain, so you can do things like reading books, talking to people, and imagining a day when you'll be rescued and freed from this place."

Everyone in the elevator silently looked at Kate for a moment. Then Providence said, "You're right. We do have some freedom here. One of my favorite quotes from my ancestor, Roger Williams, is the last statement in his 'Liberty of Conscience Letter.' In this letter, he was trying to help people locked up in a trip on a boat. The boats back then were really crowded. They were seventeenth-century versions of elevators. Roger Williams said, 'I remain studious of your common peace and liberty.'[46]"

Roger laughed. "I'm a professor in the legal field, and I know people should not be given freedom to do what they want. The result will be too many criminals."

"Roger Williams was talking about freedom of conscience, not the freedom to hurt other people. He was saying that people should have the freedom to worship God according to the desires of their souls, rather than having to follow the laws of politicians."

Nancy said, "Politicians have a really tough job: they're supposed to make everyone happy. They also have to create laws to try and keep everyone safe."

Roger shook his head in agreement before saying, "Back in the seventeenth century, the legal systems were different than they are now. Back then, politicians were expected to create religious laws. These laws would tell people how to worship God."

Nancy looked at a printed essay in the stack of books on the cart. She then said, "You're right about the laws in the seventeenth century. For example, this one source says that 'in England, the Clarendon Code (1661–1665) firmly reestablished the Church of England and punished dissenters, barring them from holding public office, attending the universities, preaching, teaching, or attending dissenting services, and requiring strict conformity to the *Book of Common Prayer.*'[47]"

Providence said, "We do have liberty of conscience in this elevator. We're free to love God." He smiled at Lydia and added, "We're also free to love each other."

Lydia smiled back and then said, "Even in this elevator, Providence and I have more freedom than the people in seventeenth-century England did."

Providence kissed Lydia quickly on the top of her head.

Roger yelled, "You agreed not to kiss each other."

Providence kissed Lydia again. This time, he kissed her forehead and then looked at Roger. "We have some liberty in this elevator. Plus, what are you going to do to us if we show our love to each other? Are you going to beat us up?"

"No, I'd never do that."

"Are you going to behead us or burn us at the stake?"

Roger said, "No, of course not. We're not living in the seventeenth century."

"Will you put us in prison?"

Roger opened his mouth, closed it, and then smiled. "Okay, I understand what you're saying. You should have the freedom to love each other."

"We not only should have that freedom, but we do have that freedom, even in this elevator."

Roger said, "You've won the debate. Plus, you're already in prison, just like the rest of us are." He looked upward toward the ceiling and added, "Kate's also in prison, but just a larger one than we are."

"So do we have your permission to kiss each other?"

"Yes, you two can kiss, as long as you don't do it so much that it bothers everyone else."

Nancy shook her head in agreement. She then explained to Kate, "Initially, Providence and Lydia were kissing almost constantly."

Roger said, "They were trying to do a lot more than just kiss."

Kate said, "You can't always have a flashlight on in your elevator. How did you know what they were doing?"

Roger glared at Providence and Lydia before saying, "They wanted to put the library cart in the middle of our elevator. Then they wanted all the flashlights to stay turned off."

Providence said, "We just wanted some privacy. That doesn't mean we were going to do anything wrong."

Roger yelled, "You were trying to have sex in an elevator with other people near you! That's not right!"

Providence looked at Lydia and sighed. "We weren't going to have sex, but even if we somehow did have sex, it's none of your business. Lydia and I are engaged, and we're getting married in two weeks."

"Having sex in public is against the law!"

Providence frowned at Roger and then smiled as he looked back at Lydia. She moved his right hand up to her lips and kissed it.

Wanting to give them some privacy, Kate looked away from the engaged couple and glanced over at Nancy, who was still watching the couple kiss. After another minute, Nancy moved the library cart into the center of the elevator and positioned herself on the opposite side of the cart. Roger made a face at Nancy and then joined her on the opposite side of the cart.

Kate said, "I should get going and try to find an exit to this building. I can then tell the police about the elevators with people inside them."

Nancy looked up at Kate. "I already know your work phone number, but we will probably be in different buildings with different work phone numbers for a while. We should trade cell phone numbers."

"That's a great idea. After we all hopefully escape from this building, we can tell each other that we're safe."

"We can also get together for lunch sometime."

Kate, Nancy, and the other elevator people traded their phone numbers. Kate then asked, "Do you need anything before I leave?"

Roger yelled, "Liberty!"

Kate asked, "How about some more candy?"

All four of the elevator people looked up at Kate and then smiled as she threw a handful of candy into their elevator. Everyone then waved good-bye.

While eating a piece of candy, Kate climbed back down to the walkway and moved away from the liberty elevator.

WATERY ELEVATOR

---✦---

Kate kept moving across the narrow walkway until she came to a ladder in an elevator shaft. She paused for a moment and shined her light upward. Nothing was visible, so she went past the ladder and continued to walk horizontally along the narrow walkway.

After another twenty-five steps, Kate slipped and fell on the walkway. Her backpack landed next to her feet, slid sideways, and partially opened up. Some items fell out. Before the backpack could fall off the walkway, Kate grabbed onto one of its flaps, lifted it up, and immediately noticed that one of its zippers was broken. She sat up and looked inside her backpack. No water bottles remained, but there were still some food items, her purse, the screwdriver, and some extra batteries.

While still seated on the walkway, Kate looked at its shiny metal surface. She moved her head so that the light on her hat was closer to the walkway. She then touched the metal surface. It was shiny because it was wet. She slowly stood up. The walkway was too slippery to walk across. A drop of moisture fell onto the walkway in front of her foot. The water droplet was light brown in color and seemed too thick to be drinkable water. Kate said out loud, "I'm not that thirsty. I don't think I'll ever be that thirsty."

She turned around and carefully walked back to the ladder in the elevator shaft. She began to climb up the ladder. After a couple of minutes, she found a new elevator and said, "Hi." No one from inside the elevator replied.

Kate went back to the ladder and climbed up to another level. She then stepped onto a walkway and moved across to a different section of the Pilgrim building. A few minutes later, the beam of her flashlight shined upon another elevator shaft. An elevator was several feet above the walkway. As she stepped closer to the elevator, she heard some people inside its silver metal form. They were talking to each other.

"There was more than one explosion, which means this could be another 9/11 disaster."

"Why would terrorists blow up our office building?"

"Terrorists would have chosen a better location—one with some kind of importance, like the White House."

"Maybe they chose this building because it's called the Pilgrim building."

"I don't think so. A lot of places use the word 'Pilgrim.'"

"You're right. There are Pilgrim names for streets, businesses, schools, and even a Pilgrim post office."

"Maybe someone was trying to steal money from the New World Bank."

"That place is only a central administrative office. I don't think the bank keeps any money there—just a lot of paperwork."

From her position outside of the elevator, Kate said, "I work in that bank. I know there's some money in the office, as well as bank tellers and customers."

One of the people inside the elevator asked, "Where is that voice coming from?"

Kate said, "I'm on the outside of your elevator."

"Oh, really?"

"Yeah."

"Can you help us to get out?"

"I haven't found a way out of the building yet."

"I actually meant to ask if you can just help us to get out of this elevator."

"I can try, but I probably won't be able to do very much."

"How did you get out of your elevator?"

"I was taking the stairs when the explosion happened."

"You just said, 'the explosion.' Do you really think there was only one explosion?"

"There could have been more than one. I was knocked out, so I don't know for sure."

"Are you okay?"

"Yeah, I am for right now. How about all you guys in the elevator? Is anyone hurt?"

"No, no one's been hurt. We're mostly just anxious. It's tough getting along with one another in such a small space."

"I've had nightmares about being stuck in an elevator. That's partially why I was taking the stairs, instead of an elevator, when the explosion or explosions happened."

"Who are you?"

"I'm Kate. I work at the bank you were talking about. What's your name?" Kate took her purse out of her backpack and then withdrew a pen and the list of names from inside her purse.

"Mike."

"Can I have your whole name? I'm writing down everyone's names in case I escape. Then I can give the police a list of the people who are alive."

"That's a good idea. Then my wife and kids will know I'm okay. My name's Mike Waterman."

Kate asked, "Are your cell phones working?"

"We can't make any calls on them. Is yours working at all?"

"Mine's broken too."

The other people in the elevator all told Kate their names, and she added them to her list. Then one of the elevator people asked her, "Are you smoking?"

"No, I quit smoking ten years ago."

"But I smell smoke."

"Yeah, I do too," Kate said. She turned her head toward the right. "The smoke is coming from that direction."

"Which direction are you talking about?"

"The direction I was planning on moving toward."

"What's making the smoke?"

"It could be someone who's smoking."

"I guess anything is possible in this broken-down building."

A different elevator passenger said, "There's too much smoke for someone who is smoking. It's got to be a fire."

Kate's eyebrows furrowed as she said, "I doubt if it's an electric or a gas fire."

"Why do you think that?"

"The electricity hasn't been working for about four hours. Electrical cords or circuit boxes wouldn't be causing a fire now. Also, I think a gas fire would have become a giant fire before now."

"Can you still check out the smoke for us? I'd hate to have a fire burn us alive while we're stuck in this elevator."

One of the other passengers laughed. "What other option will we have?"

"Let's not talk about that right now."

Another passenger said, "With fires, people usually aren't burned alive. They first die from the smoke. They can't breathe."

Kate said, "Even if I find a fire, I don't have any water to stop it from spreading. I don't even have any water to drink."

"We don't have enough water to put out a fire, but we do have a little bit for drinking."

"Is it bottled water?"

"No, it's dripping down from the ceiling." After pausing, the elevator person continued to explain, "We thought that maybe the bomb explosions blew up some of the water pipelines."

Kate said, "That could have happened. I've found a lot of broken pipes all over the place in this building."

"Did you see water anywhere?"

"I found some water on a walkway at a lower level than your elevator. I wasn't able to figure out where it was coming from, but it might have been the same water that's going through your elevator."

"That's possible. After the water in here comes down from the ceiling, it trickles down along the floor. Then it disappears into the crack where the back wall and the floor meet."

Kate asked, "What does the water in your elevator look like? Does it look like normal water, or is it dirty?"

"We haven't been able to look at it too well. We have a little bit of light if we turn on one of our cell phones, but there isn't enough light to see if the water is completely clear or not."

"How do you know that the water is safe?"

"We've been drinking it, and no one has gotten sick yet."

"I guess it should be okay then." Kate paused and then asked, "Can I have some of your elevator's water to drink? I'm really thirsty."

"We'd be glad to share it with you, but we can't get out of this elevator."

"I can disconnect the light from the roof of your elevator. Then, there'll be a little space where I can drop down the end of one of my extension cords."

"Do you have a container for some water?"

"No, I don't think so." Kate frowned as she looked at the items inside her backpack. She then smiled as she picked up the celery sticks, which were in a covered plastic container. "Actually, I do have a plastic container that should work."

Mike said, "If you take the light fixture off, will you be able to put it back on again?"

"Yeah, I think so."

"Okay."

As Kate was removing the light fixture, the people in the elevator began talking to each other.

Janet said, "Once the lady takes the light fixture off, she should leave it off."

Mike said, "No, she should put it back together again."

Janet said, "If the light fixture is off, we'll be able to get out faster when the first responders get here."

"What if the electricity starts working while we're still stuck in here?" Mike asked.

"Oh, I didn't think about that. I'd hate to be in this darkness for longer than necessary."

Joyce said, "Even if we do have to go without lights for a while longer, the light fixture should be kept off the ceiling. Then the first responders will hear us better if we start yelling out "help.""

Janet said, "I've changed my mind again. It's more important to be able to yell to first responders than to have lights."

Mike asked, "So you don't want any light in here when the electricity starts working again?"

"I doubt the electricity will start working anytime soon," Josh stated in a stern fashion.

Jim said, "I agree with you three, so now four of us want the light fixture to stay off."

Mike sighed before he said, "Our elevator will be more dangerous with a hole in the ceiling."

"In what way?"

"What if more items start falling down again? Especially since I'm in the middle of the elevator, falling things will hit me."

There was a pause, and then Jim said, "It's been a few hours since anything's fallen down. I doubt if any debris will start falling again."

Mike's voice sounded angry as he said, "When first responders start rescuing people, then all kinds of things might start falling down onto our elevator."

Kate was almost finished with her task of disconnecting the light fixture from the roof. She could now see through a crack and shined her light at the elevator people. All five of them looked up at her for a few seconds of silence before they continued their debate.

"I think you're starting to make sense, Mike. Having a small hole in the elevator's ceiling will be more dangerous for you, and possibly for us too." Janet looked at the faces of the other elevator people. They were shaking their heads back and forth, indicating their disagreement.

Josh said, "We live in a democracy. Three of us want the light fixture to be off."

Mike's voice still sounded angry as he said, "Look, the middle area is my territory. The light's over my area. How my space is set up is for me to determine, not for all of you to vote on."

Jim said loudly, "This is an elevator! It's a public space. It's not your home or something that you legally own."

"We're no longer in a public space. Remember?" Mike asked sarcastically. "You all paid me a hundred dollars each, so I would stay in the center and you four could have the four corners. The center area is mine!"

When Kate pushed her plastic container on the edge of an extension cord down from the roof, the five elevator people stopped talking and watched the container's slow downward progress into Mike's hands. He took the cover off the container, placed it beneath the dripping water, and then said to Kate, "If you want this container back, you'll need to agree to reconnect that light fixture."

Kate immediately said, "I promise to do that."

Mike rubbed his neck and then said, "This container smells like celery. Did it have some celery in it?"

"Yeah, it did."

"Do you have any more celery up there, or did you eat it all?"

"I still have some celery."

"Do you have any really good food, like pizza, cheeseburgers, fries, chocolate, and beer?"

"I do have some chocolate, but my only other food items are celery and cereal bars."

The five elevator people looked at each other with wide, surprised eyes. Then they all smiled at each other. Jim, Joyce, Josh, and Janet moved close to Mike and placed their hands onto the container that was nearly filled with water.

Mike looked up at Kate and said, "If you throw down some food for us, we'll let go of this container. Then you'll be able to pull it back up and have some water."

Kate's flashlight suddenly stopped working. She shook it back and forth, but it still didn't work.

Mike's voice yelled, "Why did you turn your light off? Are you leaving us here with no food?"

Kate said, "No, of course not. I'm guessing that the batteries just died." She pulled out her other tiny flashlight that was on her keychain. It was still working. She used the tiny light to replace the batteries in the bigger flashlight. When she turned on the larger light and it worked, Mike said, "I'm glad your flashlight's working now. If you want to throw down some food to us, we'll let you have this water."

"Yes, I still would love some water, and I'm so glad my flashlight's working again. As soon as I find them in my backpack, I'll throw down five cereal bars and some pieces of chocolate candies."

"I think you should throw all your food down to us."

"I need some food too."

"But you're only one person. There are five of us in this elevator."

Kate sighed. "I've been sharing my food with people in other elevators. Plus, you want me to go and check out that smoke, right?"

Mike looked at the other four elevator people. All of them seemed uncertain about what to do.

Mike said, "Okay. We'll send up the water, as long as you send down the food you mentioned."

Janet said, "You should also promise to look for some beer. I'm so sick of drinking water."

Kate laughed.

Janet asked, "What's so funny?"

"Do you know how many people in this building would be really happy to just have some plain old water to drink?"

"Okay, we should just be happy to not be thirsty, but I still want something good to drink."

Josh, Jim, and Joyce looked at each other. Then all three yelled "soda" at the same time.

"Okay, so you all want either soda or beer. Where will I find these drinks?"

"A lot of people store beer or wine in their desk drawers," Janet said.

Josh smiled up at Kate. "Most offices have refrigerators in them. Soda will probably be inside most refrigerators."

"Fruit juice and milk would also be nice, but I really want either soda or coffee. Even iced coffee would be great." The other four elevator people looked at Jim and shook their heads in agreement.

Kate asked, "If I find anything good to drink, you want me to bring it back to you, right?"

"Definitely," all the elevator voices said at the same time. Mike then added, "Watching the water drip down from this ceiling has been so bad. Sometimes, it has even had stuff in it."

"What kinds of things are in the water?"

"I don't know. It just sometimes has looked sort of bumpy, cloudy, and dirty."

Kate frowned. "Didn't you already tell me that the water didn't make you sick?"

"It hasn't made us sick, at least not yet, but we still really need something good to drink."

Kate tossed down five cereal bars. She then said, "After I pull the container up here and drink it, I'll send it down for some more water. Once I have the container full of water for a second time, I'll send down some candies."

Mike said, "Okay. That sounds like a plan."

Kate pulled up the container, drank the water, and sent it back down again. She waited patiently for the five elevator people to add more water into the container. When she pulled up the water-filled container again, she put it into her backpack. After sending down some chocolates, Kate put the extension cord back around her waist and began to reconnect the light fixture.

Josh asked, "Why are you reconnecting that light fixture? Three of us want the fixture to stay off."

Mike said, "While only two of us want the light fixture to be reconnected, the light is in my space. My view is the only one that matters."

The four other voices in the elevator started yelling about their views being just as important as Mike's.

Kate stopped reconnecting the light fixture, turned off her flashlight, and waited until everyone in the elevator looked up at her. She said, "I think you five should decide in a nice way among yourselves if I should reconnect the light or leave the hole in the ceiling."

Mike's voice was loud as he said, "The hole from the light is a part of my personal space! You have to listen to me, Kate, and not pay attention to these other people."

Kate said, "I think everyone in your elevator needs to discuss things in a more civil fashion."

Mike yelled, "You can't tell us what to do!"

"You might not want to listen to me, but what about listening to Roger Williams?"

"What do you mean? Roger Williams isn't alive anymore. He can't talk to us."

"His writings and beliefs, though, can say something to all of us."

Mike said, "Okay, go ahead and tell us some idea about Roger Williams. Maybe it'll be logical."

Five pairs of eyes watched as Kate turned her flashlight on again. She took the piece of paper out of the Roger Williams book in her backpack and said, "One author wrote in 2001 about Roger Williams's view of people communicating in a civil manner. James Calvin Davis thinks that Roger Williams believed 'citizens of a pluralistic society may not agree on a complex set of moral norms, but among the basic values every citizen ought to honor are the appropriateness of tolerance, common courtesy, friendship, and truthfulness as parameters for the very act of engaging in public conversation.'[48]"

Josh laughed. "There are five of us stuck in this elevator together. I can understand how we will often disagree with each other, but how can we really be tolerant of each other?"

Mike thought for a few seconds before saying, "Instead of actually being friends, we can try to make believe we're friends."

Kate put the paper in her backpack and then said, "That's a great idea, Mike. If you could all make believe you're friends, perhaps you can get along a little better with each other."

Mike said, "We might be able to figure out how to solve the debate about the light fixture in a more civilized fashion."

Josh asked, "So if we're all of a sudden very close friends, what should we do about the light fixture problem?"

Kate suggested, "If Mike thinks it's too dangerous for him to be in the center of the elevator with a hole in the ceiling, how about if one of Mike's friends trades places with him?"

Josh, Jim, Janet, and Joyce all looked at each other, but not one of them volunteered to be the person in the middle of the elevator.

Mike said, "How about if I just get out of the center of the elevator, and we somehow split up the safe sections? Then we could leave the light fixture off, and I'd be safer than I am now."

His four new elevator friends all smiled at him. They then rearranged their positions, so Mike could sit down with his back against one of the elevator's walls. The center of the elevator became the spot where everyone now placed their backpacks, purses, and coats.

Kate moved the light fixture away from the hole in the ceiling and said, "I'll try to find the source of that smoke."

Mike smiled. "You'll also look for some beer, right?"

"Yes, I'll look for beer, soda, juice, milk, and coffee. I also promise not to drink it all, but I'll bring some nice drinks back here to your elevator."

Everyone in the elevator laughed. Then Mike said, "There's supposed to be a fire hydrant on every floor. You might be able to find one on your way to the fire."

"Okay. I'll watch for one."

Kate moved to the left side of the elevator and then onto the narrow metal walkway. After walking about twenty feet forward, she paused. Her flashlight was shining into another elevator shaft. She moved up to the edge of the shaft and then shined her light's beam up and down into empty space. She couldn't see an elevator either above or below her current position, but the smoke seemed to be moving downward from an upper level.

FIERY ELEVATOR

Kate started to walk carefully up to the skinny metal ladder inside of the shaft. After every few feet, she paused in her upward motion and looked at her surroundings. There were no openings, elevators, or different walkways. The shaft was getting colder and colder, but no windows or other exits were visible. Finally, after moving up three levels, Kate saw the floor of an elevator above her. She kept climbing up the ladder and went past the elevator's side wall. When she was horizontal to the roof, she stopped climbing upward and jumped over to the rooftop. She then placed her cold hands into the pockets of her slacks.

A voice from inside the elevator yelled out, "Is someone on top of our elevator?"

Kate said, "Yeah, I'm up here on the roof. My name is Kate."

"Hi, Kate."

A different voice from inside the elevator said, "There's a little bit of light coming in from a corner of this elevator's ceiling. Do you have a flashlight up there?"

"Yeah, I do. I might be able to make a small hole in the top of your elevator. Then you can see the light better."

"How will you make a hole in the ceiling? Do you have a drill?"

"No, I only have a screwdriver, but I can disconnect your elevator's light fixture."

"How big would the hole be? We're already cold in here."

"If your elevator is like the other ones, the hole will only be slightly larger than a bottle of water."

174

The voices inside the elevator became softer as they talked among themselves. Only a few of the words were heard by Kate: "...cold...light...fire..."

After a few minutes of discussion, one of the elevator voices loudly said, "Another fire will give us some light, as well as heat."

A louder voice said, "A roof hole will help us—there will be less smoke from our next fire."

All the voices were silent for a few seconds. Then one of them said, "Okay, Kate. You can try to open up a hole in the roof. Just be careful not to break anything."

A second voice said, "I don't think it would be a good idea for us to get cut up by glass and metal, especially since we're stuck inside this elevator."

"I'll be careful." Kate sat down on the roof, disconnected the light, took out the fixture, and moved her hat forward so that the flashlight was pointing into the hole in the elevator's roof.

Three women were standing in a triangular shape in the middle of the elevator. They were all wearing hats and coats. Two of the women were wearing gloves, and the third woman had her hands in the pockets of her coat.

"Why is it so cold?" Kate asked.

The woman wearing a gray coat said, "I don't know. Isn't the whole building cold?"

"No, it isn't. Just this section is really bad."

"We thought the whole building would be cold because the electricity's out."

Kate said, "I don't know what's happening. There must be some kind of backup generator for some parts of the building."

"Maybe some open windows are somewhere near our elevator. Are you feeling any drafts, like from an open window or a door?"

Kate stood up for a minute and turned around slowly in a circle. She then sat back down near the hole in the elevator's roof and said, "No, I can't feel any drafts at all. I'm just freezing." She moved her hands forward toward the hole in the roof. "Your elevator, though, is a little warmer than it is out here."

"Would you like to join us, Kate?"

Kate laughed. "No, I don't think so." She then took a pen and her list of people's names out of her backpack. "Can I have your names?"

"Why do you want to know?" the woman with her hands in her pockets asked.

"I'm writing a list of the people I meet. This way, if I find a way out of the building, I can tell the police the names of the people who are still alive."

Mercy and Patience gave Kate their full names. The third woman though did not tell Kate her name. She instead asked, "So has anyone died?"

Kate replied, "I don't know."

"So you haven't seen any dead people yet?"

"No."

"So why do you need a list of names?"

Kate frowned as she said, "An accountant suggested that I do this."

"Really?" the unnamed woman asked in a sarcastic voice.

"You don't have to tell me your name. I'll just write 'a lady' in my list."

Patience said, "You can call her 'So,' which is the word that Freeborn uses in most of her sentences."

Kate wrote down "So."

The unnamed woman said, "So you can call me either 'Freeborn' or 'So,' but neither one is my real name."

"Okay." Kate crossed out the "So" name on her list and wrote down "Freeborn." She then said, "So I think I smell smoke. Is there a fire in your elevator?"

"You can call me Freeborn."

Kate said, "Oh, I'm sorry. I was just saying so; I didn't mean to say your name."

"So you're now officially going to call me Freeborn?"

"Yeah, I will, unless you want me to call you something else."

"Freeborn is fine."

"Okay. So anyway, Freeborn, is there a fire in your elevator?"

Freeborn said, "There was a fire in here, but right now, the fire is out."

Patience added some more explanation, "There's only a pile of ashes in the middle of the floor."

Mercy said, "When we get too cold, we're warming up our elevator by burning the pages from a book."

"Do you think that's a good idea?" Kate asked as she moved her cold hands even closer to the hole in the elevator's roof.

"So what's a good idea? We're cold, and we don't like the book."

"Whether it's a good book or a bad book, you shouldn't start a fire." Kate paused and then asked, "What's so bad about the book?"

"So it has some letters from John Cotton in it. He was one of the Puritans who kept on fighting with Roger Williams."

Kate squeezed her hands together. "Back in the seventeenth century, everyone was fighting."

"So you're so right about that."

Mercy said, "Even in our century, everyone's always fighting."

Kate shook her head in agreement before saying, "You're right. We can just look at how people today drive on the roads. Fast drivers want everyone else on the road to be as fast as they are."

Mercy smiled. "Slow drivers want everyone else to be slow."

Kate laughed. "Whenever I get behind a slow driver, I get upset."

Mercy's eyes widened as she looked at Kate's face. "You're one of those crazy fast drivers."

"No, I'm just normal. The slow drivers are the crazy ones."

"Speeding is against the law."

Kate sighed. "I think John Cotton was a too-slow driver back in his century."

"No," Mercy said. "He was a too-fast driver. He was pushing people into banishment."

"We can debate if Cotton was too slow or too fast, but I think most people know that Roger Williams was definitely too fast."

Freeborn shook her head in agreement. "So I think they were both so very fast. That's why they kept on bumping into each other while they were debating how things should be."

Kate said, "Cotton wasn't trying to hurt anyone. He was just trying to establish a new colony with people who were just like himself. He ran away from persecution in England, just like so many other Pilgrims did. He then wanted to have a colony where he could worship God in his own way with other people like himself."

"So you sound like you like John Cotton."

"I don't know if I like or dislike him. I'm just trying to explain what I think happened."

"So because Puritans were persecuted, you think that it was okay for them to persecute other people, like Roger Williams?"

"Roger Williams was telling people in the Massachusetts Bay Colony about things he thought they were doing wrong. He wasn't able to just be quiet."

"So why should people be quiet when they see something's wrong? Horrors like the Holocaust have happened because supposedly 'good' people have said and done nothing."

Everyone was quiet for a moment. Kate then said, "You're right, and I'm wrong. It wasn't a good idea to banish Roger Williams. Especially in a New England winter, banishment is really bad." Kate squeezed her hands tightly before adding, "However, there were worse things that happened back then. Nonconformists in England were often imprisoned or killed. Roger Williams went running off into the New England winter to avoid being captured, returned to England, imprisoned, and possibly killed."

The three women in the elevator moved closer together. Then Mercy said, "I can't imagine spending a whole winter out in the cold weather away from my home and family."

Patience rubbed her hands together as if they were over a fire. She then said, "At least the natives helped him."

Kate said, "After Roger Williams started Providence Plantations, he helped some other people, like Anne Hutchinson, who was also banished."

Freeborn asked, "So what did Anne do that was so wrong?"

Patience said, "She was a midwife, so she helped many of the Massachusetts Bay women. She then had meetings in her house when they discussed sermons and religious matters. She began to disagree with some of the area ministers, so they banished her in 1637. They then excommunicated her the following year."

"So what's the difference between banishment and excommunication?"

Patience explained, "Banishment is a legal punishment, and excommunication is a religious one. According to a scholarly article by Nan Goodman, banishment 'varied by degree, ranging from extremely punitive—which might mean exile from an entire country—to very lenient—which might mean forced exclusion from a parish or town square.' Excommunication 'typically prohibited the excommunicate from taking the sacraments or from mingling with the Christian community.'[49]"

Kate said, "After Anne Hutchinson was banished, Roger Williams helped her and her family to find a new home in Portsmouth."

"So it was so nice that Roger Williams helped her out."

Patience said, "Roger Williams also helped a lot of other people, like Jews and Quakers, to find homes."

Kate asked, "Do you know how many other people were banished?"

"Quite a few were banished. According to John Barry, when the Massachusetts Bay Colony was small, in 1630 and 1631, fourteen people were banished. This number of people was almost 2 percent of the colony's entire population.[50]"

Mercy said, "That's so sad, but I'm glad that Roger Williams was later able to help some of the banished people."

Kate thought for a few seconds before saying, "We do similar kinds of things today."

Mercy asked, "What do you mean? Are you talking about helping people or banishing them?"

"We often do help each other, but I was thinking about banishment."

Mercy shook her head in a negative way. "No, I don't think we banish people anymore—at least, not in this country."

Kate asked, "What does it mean if someone's laid off or fired from a job? Isn't that banishment from a workplace?"

"No, I don't think so. People who are fired can still go back to the same company. They just can't get paid to do any work."

"Being fired actually is a form of banishment. People sometimes have to stay out of secure areas. Bank tellers, for example, can't go into bank vaults after they're fired or laid off. Even back in the seventeenth century, people were sometimes just banished from one house or one small area."

Mercy moved her eyes up toward Kate. "Banishment really is being kicked out of one area. Sometimes the area, though, is really big."

Patience said in a loud voice, "Even after being banished, Roger Williams was still arguing with John Cotton. They were debating each other in their books, pamphlets, and letters."

Kate shook her head in agreement. "Their debate was a very public one. They wanted everyone to think about their ideas." Kate opened up her backpack, reached inside, opened up her purse, and took out the book *Roger Williams, God's Apostle of Advocacy*. She then read a sentence from the book: "L. Raymond Camp claims that 'Cotton generally opposed Williams, but to encourage further negotiation with the defendant, he urged the court to defer a banishment decision until later.'"[51]

"Even if John Cotton was sometimes nice to Roger Williams, I still don't like some of Cotton's ideas," Patience said as she tore another page out of the book. She then put the page on the floor and set it on fire with a cigarette lighter.

"You shouldn't be starting a fire," Kate said.

"Why not?"

"What if the fire gets out of control?"

"A metal elevator won't burn up."

"Yes, it can. What if you burn a hole in the floor and then the fire starts burning up the plywood and other things near the elevator?"

"We're being careful." Patience was rubbing her hands together just a couple of inches from the tiny fire. She looked up at Kate while moving her left hand closer to the fire. Several sparks flew upward and hit her hand. Patience grabbed onto her left hand with her right hand as she jumped backward and away from the fire. She then licked one section of the palm of her left hand.

Kate asked, "Are you okay?"

"I'm fine. It's just a little burned spot on my hand."

Mercy said, "I have some stuff that should help." She moved over to the left corner of the elevator, opened up a purse, and took out a container of ointment and a bandage. She then covered the red spot on Patience's hand with some of the ointment and the bandage.

Patience said, "Thanks so much. It feels better already. I owe you one." She looked at Mercy before adding, "I'd love to give you some money for fixing my hand."

"No, thanks. You've already let me borrow some lip balm, so now we're even."

Patience smiled before walking up to the fire. She placed her right hand too close to the small flame. Her left hand with the bandage on its palm hung backward, refusing to get too close to the fire again.

Mercy stepped up to the fire, threw another page from the book onto the fire, and looked upward at Kate. "If you move over, you'll be closer to the fire. You could get warmed up."

Kate's voice was loud as she said, "It's not fair to hurt other people."

"We're not hurting anyone. If anything, we're helping other people by warming up this part of the building," Mercy shouted.

"A little while ago, I was talking to people in a different elevator. They smelled the smoke from your elevator and thought there was a fire somewhere in the building. They were really scared."

"So you're writing down everyone's names, running around to different elevators, and telling people what they should be doing," Freeborn said in a sarcastic way.

"Who made you the king of this falling-down building?" Patience yelled.

Freeborn and Patience stared angrily at Kate for a few seconds. Then Patience tore another page out of the book and threw it upward toward Kate's face. The paper hit the ceiling, barely missing her face. While the page was close to her eyes, Kate was able to read only a couple of phrases: "King Charles I" and "civil war." She then yelled back at Patience: "I'm not acting like a king! And I'm especially not acting like Charles I, the English king who was beheaded in 1649 after fighting with Parliament and persecuting Puritans, Separatists, and almost everyone else."

The paper floated down away from Kate's face and landed on the floor in the middle of the elevator. The tiny fire had disappeared. Only some ashes remained.

Freeborn moved her hands close to the ashes and rubbed them together. She then kicked the paper off the pile and said, "Yeah, I agree with you about King Charles I. He was forcing his personal idea of worship onto everyone."

Kate shook her head in agreement. "Puritans like John Cotton were at least trying to improve things, even if they messed up a lot."

"So how were they improving things?"

Kate thought for a few seconds before saying, "The Separatists were trying to separate themselves from the Church of England. The Puritans were trying to purify the way God was being worshipped. They became the founders of many great cities in our country. Purity and the creation of better cities helped everyone."

Freeborn frowned. "The Puritans did some really bad things too, like the Salem witch trials." She moved her foot forward, kicking the small pile of ashes, so they flew upward several inches.

"The witch trials were really bad, but they happened in many other places besides Salem." Kate looked at Freeborn's upraised eyebrows and added, "A lot of witch trials happened in Europe between the fifteenth and the eighteenth centuries."

"So the Puritans didn't start the witch trials, and they weren't the only ones doing some bad things back then."

Patience said, "Two wrongs don't make a right."

Freeborn shook her head in agreement before saying, "There were a lot more than two wrongs."

Looking at Kate, Freeborn, and Patience, Mercy said, "You all know a lot about history. Do any of you work in a museum?"

"I work at the New World Bank. I'm interested in Roger Williams because I'm one of his descendants."

"I'm a descendant of Roger Williams too." Patience smiled and then added, "I also work in a museum. This afternoon, I came over here to do a little bit of research for a museum project."

"I'm a descendant of Roger Williams too or should I say three?" Mercy looked at Kate and Patience; she then raised three fingers before adding, "I was named after Mercy Williams, who was one of Roger Williams and Mary Barnard's children."

"This is so, so, so, so interesting. I'm also a descendant of Roger and Mary. My ancestor, Freeborn Williams, was born in 1635."

"Are you trying to tell me your name? Is your real name Freeborn?"

"So maybe it is. Why should you care?"

"It's nice to know someone's name while we're talking to each other. However, if it'll make you happy, I'll try to forget your name."

"So please try to make me happy."

"Okay. I'll try."

Mercy said, "With all four of us being descendants of Roger Williams, we should be agreeing more with each other."

Kate sighed. "We're in different settings. I might be stuck inside this building, but a building is a lot larger than an elevator. I can also walk away into a warmer section of the building. Because you're stuck inside of a cold elevator, you're being very vocal about your freedom, especially as it relates to building a fire."

"That's a part of what was happening back in the seventeenth century." After pausing, Patience added, "People who felt they had no freedom got upset."

Kate said, "Back then, most people couldn't just move to a different place."

Freeborn asked, "Why not? The Pilgrims moved across an ocean."

"Back in the seventeenth century, transportation on a ship was expensive and dangerous. Many of the Pilgrims had to sell their homes and possessions to make the trip to New England." Kate thought for a few seconds and then added, "People also had to get legal paperwork—sort of like a passport—to leave England."

Patience said, "Moving across an ocean back then also meant that family members might be separated from each other for their whole lives."

Kate moved her flashlight's beam in several circles that connected together the three elevator people. "Communication was also more difficult. People could write letters to each other, but phones had not yet been invented."

Freeborn picked up the piece of paper off the floor, crinkled it up, and tossed it on top of the pile of ashes. "Even so, it must have been really nice for some of the Puritans to leave England."

Kate smiled. "You're right. I'm so going to love getting out of this building."

"So will all of us, but that doesn't mean we'll all start telling each other what to do."

"We'll still have to follow all the laws. We won't be able to start running through red lights, for example."

Freeborn laughed. "A lot of people these days speed up and go right through red lights and stop signs."

"They can get into a lot of trouble for doing that." Kate looked closely at Freeborn. "You wouldn't be one of those people, would you?"

"So why are you asking me that question? Are you a cop?"

"No, of course I'm not. However, cops aren't the only people who try to maintain peace in our society. We have a justice system."

Freeborn smiled sarcastically. "We also have neighbors who tell us to mow our lawns, to keep our dogs off their lawns, and to do all kinds of other things."

"Just like us, the Puritans had to do what different laws and people told them to do," Kate said.

"So in this elevator, what laws are we following?"

"We're not hitting each other, except with pieces of paper, right?" Kate asked.

"So I might have thrown a piece of paper, but I didn't hurt you with it."

"You're also still wearing the same kinds of clothing as when you weren't stuck in the elevator."

Freeborn laughed. "It's a little cold in here to change into a bathing suit and sandals."

"If it's so cold, you could take off your socks, leave just your boots on your feet, and put your socks on your hands."

"Okay, so I don't have any gloves on my hands. That doesn't mean I want to make my feet colder and my hands warmer."

"You're still acting like you're living in a democracy."

"So how am I doing that while stuck in this elevator?"

"You don't like the idea of kings, and you're debating things with me."

"Well, I guess I do like to have freedom of speech." Freeborn paused and then added, "So we can choose to say 'well' or 'so' at the beginning of a sentence."

"Are you changing the way that you're talking to people, Freeborn?"

"Well, I could change things. So then, people wouldn't get bored with how I'm talking."

"You can change some things, but you also have to follow some grammar rules."

"Well, why are you saying that, Kate?"

"If you don't follow some grammar rules, you'll be saying things that don't make any sense. For example, if you say, 'well-so' together like it's a single word, rather than 'well' and 'so' in separate sentences, you won't be making sense."

"Well, that's very interesting, Kate. You really seem so happy to be talking about rules and laws."

"I guess I am, but it's because I like my life to be organized, rather than messed up. The Puritans and Separatists, also, had to follow a bunch of rules and laws. For example, even though they were starting a new colony, they couldn't commit murder."

Patience said, "They also had to initiate some new rules and laws, like the 'Mayflower Compact.'"

Kate shook her head in agreement.

Patience said, "The people in the Massachusetts Bay Colony had to do what their charter from the king of England told them to."

Kate laughed. "Sometimes, they were just trying to look like they were following the charter because it was their legal document to set up their colony."

Patience said, "If the Massachusetts Bay Colony did things against the charter, like disrespecting the king of England, then their charter could be revoked. Also, many people were watching what the colony was doing. John Winthrop said, 'We shall be as a city upon a hill, the eyes of all people are upon us.'[52]"

"There's a Bible verse about a city on a hill: 'You are the light of the world. A city built on a hill cannot be hid' (Matt. 5:14, RSV)." Kate moved her flashlight's beam around the elevator and then added, "Being inside an elevator, you can still be seen by someone like me."

Freeborn covered her face before saying, "Well, even if the Puritans wanted to hide, they couldn't hide because so many other people were watching them."

Kate said, "They were creating a colony based on their own ideas about religion. They were thinking that having their own colony meant they could worship God in their own way."

Freeborn said, "Well, even now, not everyone in the world has full religious liberty."

Mercy said, "Being in an elevator, we really have no liberty to do anything at all."

Freeborn said, "We can talk."

A distant crashing noise made everyone in the elevator look up at Kate. She turned her flashlight in all directions, but she was unable to see anything. Looking back down inside the elevator, she sat on the roof again before saying, "I don't know what that noise was."

A few seconds later, several pieces of metal piping fell onto the elevator's roof and then bounced down into the shaft. When the metal pieces hit the bottom area of the elevator's shaft, soft crunching noises were heard.

"So are you okay up there?"

"I'm fine," Kate said. "How are all of you doing?"

Freeborn wiped some sweat off her forehead and said, "I think we're okay. After those scary noises, though, I need to pray for God's help. Being here in this elevator, I should at least have one freedom—prayer."

Mercy said, "I think we should have a moment of silence, so people of any religion can pray."

Patience said, "No, we should have a moment of silence, so we can be free to pray or not to pray."

"We could debate this issue for years." After pausing for a moment, Kate added, "In reality, people have been debating this issue for centuries."

Freeborn yelled out, "Why do we have to be silent while we're praying? We shouldn't have to hide our religion."

Kate suggested, "Some kind of rules should be made for praying and moments of silence."

Freeborn said, "Why do I have to follow your rules?"

"You don't, but you should follow the rules of the other people in your elevator."

"You're telling me what to do again!" Freeborn shook her hand at Kate and then added, "I'm feeling like Roger Williams probably did when people were telling him how to worship God."

"I'm not trying to tell you what to do." Kate paused before saying, "I'm a descendant of Roger Williams too."

Patience said, "I think Kate's just trying to help us. She knows that different rules apply to different places."

Freeborn looked angrily around at the metal walls of the elevator.

Patience touched Freeborn's shoulder. "I know you're super upset in here, Freeborn. Our settings really do affect our feelings and our actions."

Mercy shook her head in agreement. "I know I act differently at home, on the highway, at work, at church, and especially in this elevator."

Freeborn looked up at the ceiling. "So, Kate, does your setting above everyone else, up there on the top of the elevator, make you act like a king when you tell people what to do?"

Kate's face looked shocked. "I hope not. I think I'm acting more like a member of congress or parliament than like a king." Kate paused with a pensive look on her face before adding, "While I'm really just trying to get out of this building, I keep on running into different elevators with different people in them. I want to help people trapped in the elevators, but I'm incapable of helping very much. I'm mostly just selling and sharing items that are small enough to fit through the small holes that I've been making when I take out the light fixtures."

"So you're acting like a salesperson."

Kate blinked, looked at her backpack, and said, "Yeah, I think I am."

"So what are you selling and what are you sharing?"

"I have some cereal bars, candies, and celery sticks."

"Do you really have some food?" Patience asked in an excited voice.

"Yeah." Kate opened up her backpack. Her eyes fell upon the container of water; she took a sip and then returned it back into her pack. She next pulled out some Reese's Peanut Butter Cups. She waved the candy in front of the hole at the top of the elevator.

"I love chocolate," Patience said. She looked at the two other people in her elevator before adding, "We all love chocolate, especially when we're all hungry."

Mercy added, "The peanut butter in that candy even adds in a little protein."

Freeborn asked, "So how much money do you want for each piece of candy?"

Kate said, "I've only been charging a hundred dollars for each of these peanut butter cups." Her eyes shifted over toward the darkness of the elevator shaft. She cleared her throat and then looked back at the people inside the elevator.

Freeborn was glaring angrily upward before she yelled, "Are you crazy? Those are the tiny, bite-size ones."

"I had to move them across the inside of a partially fallen building. I should be charging a lot more than a hundred dollars for each piece of candy."

Mercy said, "Kate, you know we're all hungry. You're not being fair."

Patience asked, "Do you have any cheaper food?"

"I can sell celery sticks for fifty dollars each."

Freeborn hit the side of the elevator. Patience placed a hand on Freeborn's shoulder and said, "Kate only has a little bit of food. That's why she's charging so much money for it."

Kate shook her head in agreement. "The celery sticks are a good deal. There's a lot of liquid in them."

Patience said, "Being stuck in this elevator with no water, we do need liquid items more than sugary ones."

Mercy asked, "Will you take a check?"

Kate hesitated and then said, "No, I can't. You might cancel the check."

"I promise not to cancel it."

Kate shook her head from side to side before saying no.

"But you'll be getting out of here first. You'll be able to cash it before I can cancel it."

"You can still cancel a check after someone cashes it."

"Really?"

"Yeah."

"Even so, you would already have the money from the check."

"The bank could try to take the money back from me." Kate pulled her flashlight away from the hole in the elevator's roof and turned it off.

Patience said, "I have a great idea!"

Freeborn asked, "What?"

"Instead of paying Kate in money, how about if I trade my flashlight for some of her food?"

Kate turned her light back on, shined it into the hole in the roof, and asked, "Do you have a flashlight that's working?"

Patience reached into her purse and pulled out a three-inch long, red flashlight. She turned it on, pointed its beam up toward Kate, and then turned it back off again.

The beam from Kate's flashlight now moved toward Freeborn, who was stamping her foot. Freeborn said loudly, "I asked you before if you had a flashlight. You lied to me!" She grabbed the small red flashlight out of Patience's hand.

"You can't have that light! It's mine!"

"You lied to me and Mercy. You need to give us your flashlight as your punishment."

"I don't think any law says lying will result in having to give up a flashlight. If the law said anything, it would say to give back stolen items to their rightful owners." Patience cleared her throat and held out her hand.

Freeborn said, "It's mine, now."

"No, you stole it from me."

Freeborn and Patience both looked at Mercy as if they expected her to say something. She remained quiet. They then looked up at Kate. She said, "Federal and state laws still apply. However, being stuck inside of a building's elevator means people will have to come up with some of their own rules concerning correct behaviors."

Mercy shook her head in agreement.

Kate shined her flashlight around the elevator as she said, "Even now, you three have automatically positioned yourselves so that each one of you has a third of the elevator's space."

Patience said, "We could also use the Ten Commandments in the Bible." She looked at Freeborn before saying, "One of the commandments says, 'You shall not steal' (Exod. 20:15, RSV)."

Freeborn smirked. "Another of the Bible's commandments says, 'You shall not bear false witness against your neighbor' (Exod. 20:16, RSV)."

"My lie about not having a flashlight was intended to help us, Freeborn. I wanted to save the batteries in my flashlight until we actually needed the light."

"But your lying was falseness."

"The falseness wasn't turned against you, Freeborn."

"Yes, it was against me!" Freeborn turned on the flashlight and then jabbed the light toward her own heart. "Your lie kept me in darkness! You hurt me!"

Patience yelled, "That doesn't mean you can steal my flashlight." She took a step closer to Freeborn and tried to grab the flashlight from her right hand. Freeborn raised her right hand high above her head while extending her left hand outward toward Patience, stopping her from moving forward. Patience then swung her purse upward toward Freeborn's right hand; her purse struck the thumb that was pressed onto the flashlight. Freeborn's grip loosened slightly and then grabbed even more tightly onto the flashlight. When Patience swung her purse again, its metal zipper struck both Freeborn's hand and the flashlight.

Freeborn said loudly, "Stop it! You just hurt me. You're also going to break the flashlight."

"If I no longer own the flashlight, what difference does it make?"

Kate cleared her throat, but Patience and Freeborn didn't notice her. They were too busy glaring at each other. They also did not notice when Mercy walked around and stood behind Freeborn. Mercy then stood up on her toes and tried to grab the flashlight from Freeborn, who was still holding onto it very tightly. Freeborn lifted up her right foot and sent it backward, kicking Mercy's knee. Before Freeborn's foot could move again, Mercy jumped away and started to rub her knee.

Kate turned off her flashlight. Immersion into darkness only seemed to make the three elevator people noisier. Slapping noises and stomping feet joined in with growling voices. Kate turned her light back on again, opened up her backpack, took out three pieces of chocolate candy, and tossed them down into the elevator. Even though one of the pieces hit Freeborn on the head, none of the three elevator people noticed the candy. Kate then yelled out loudly, "I just threw some free candy into your elevator."

"So is it really free?" Freeborn turned on Patience's flashlight and shined its light onto the floor of the elevator. She then made circling motions with the light as she looked for the candies.

"Yes, it's really free. In order to find the candy, though, you have to stop fighting."

Freeborn smiled and changed the circling motions of the flashlight's beam into heart shapes.

Patience spotted a piece of candy near her foot and quickly picked it up. She then patiently waited for the others to find their own candy. Mercy picked up her piece of chocolate. Freeborn kept on moving the light on the floor, but no other candy was visible.

"So did you really throw down three pieces or just two?"

"There has to be another one. I was very careful and threw down three pieces."

"I think you're lying too, just like Patience did about her flashlight."

"No, I'm not lying." Kate paused and then asked, "Why would I lie? I'm up here, above your reach. There's no reason for me to lie."

"Yes, there is. You're siding with Patience about her flashlight, and you're trying to punish me for her lies."

Kate inhaled, exhaled, and then said, "Look, you're just upset because of being stuck in that elevator."

"Even so, I still need some food."

"Okay, here's one more free chocolate." Kate threw down a piece of chocolate; Patience immediately jumped forward, picked it up, and jumped backward again.

"No," Freeborn yelled out. She then started jumping up and down, making the elevator shake slightly.

Patience glared at her and then said, "You're going to kill us all with that jumping of yours."

"You deserve it."

"If you just give me my flashlight, I'll let you have your piece of candy. I'll also keep my flashlight here with us."

Freeborn looked at her sarcastically. "Really?"

"Yeah." Patience extended her right hand, which was holding onto the candy. Freeborn reached out to grab the candy, but Patience pulled her hand backward. "You need to give me the flashlight at the same time that I give you the candy."

Freeborn and Patience carefully traded the flashlight and the piece of the candy. The three elevator people all ate their candy at the same time.

Kate then negotiated with the three elevator women for some more food items. They finally decided on paying fifty dollars in cash for three sticks of celery, three cereal bars, and three more pieces of candy. To exchange the food items for the cash, Kate used two extension cords at the same time. As she pulled up one cord with the cash on it, the three elevator people took the food out of a plastic bag that had been attached to the second cord.

Patience said, "I guess you're really acting like a salesperson."

Kate said, "Right now, I feel more like a fisherman."

"So do you have any tuna fish?"

They all laughed as Kate put one extension cord around her waist and the other cord into her backpack. She then turned her light toward the walkway that was next to the elevator. "I'm going to try and get out of this building again, but I'll tell any first responders about what nice people you all are."

Freeborn asked, "After the way we were fighting, are you really going to say that we're nice?"

"Of course I am," Kate said, "There's freedom of speech in this country, so I can say whatever I want to say."

"So you're either going to lie to the first responders and tell them we're nice, or you're lying to us right now about what you'll be saying."

Kate laughed. "Either way, I guess I'll be lying."

Patience said, "You can always just avoid the truth and not describe us as *nice* or anything else."

"That sounds like a plan." Kate paused and then asked, "What about the fires you people were starting? Are you going to stop burning up that book?"

Mercy looked down at the ashes on the ground and then said in a high-pitched voice, "Since we were scaring other people, we'll try not to light too many fires. We'll also keep them small."

Patience said, "We do have to keep this elevator warm, or we'll all get hypothermia."

"You're right," Kate said in a depressed voice. "I know that it's cold over here, and I don't want you to get sick."

"This elevator is our own personal space, so we can do whatever we want to," Freeborn said in a too-loud voice.

"I understand," Kate said. "This elevator is like a newly established colony. If you want to, you can even act like the people in seventeenth-century Plymouth, Salem, Boston, or Providence. I just hope that, after I leave, you'll all get along okay." She waved good-bye, climbed down from the elevator, and moved along the metal walkway toward what appeared to be a wall.

After taking another twenty steps, Kate stopped in front of a light gray wall. She looked multiple times to her left and her right. Nothing was visible on either side. Finally, she decided to move toward her right. Five minutes later, she came up to an unpainted door with a partially rusted door handle. Slowly, she opened the door about an inch, peered inside, and then opened the door enough to walk through the doorway into a small utility closet.

On the walls of the closet were shelves made of rotting wood. On the shelves were some cleaning supplies, a pail, gloves, heavy rags, and some paint. A mop and a broom were standing in the far corner of the closet. Kate yawned, turned her flashlight toward her wrist, and looked at her watch. It was already after ten o'clock in the evening. She then opened up her backpack and pulled out a Roger Williams book, a cereal bar, and some water.

The dim light from her flashlight fell onto one of the pages in the book. The flashlight's beam lighted up the ending of a letter written by Roger Williams on December 18, 1675: "For we have now no passing by Elizabeths Spring without a strong foote. God will have it So....Oh let us make sure...to enter in that straight dore and narrow Way wch the Lo. [Lord] Jesus himself tells us, Few there be that find it. / Sir your unworthy / R.W."[53]

Kate read the letter again and then commented: "In this falling-down building, I have a lot of doors and narrow pathways to walk through too. The doorways and walkways throughout this building are really tough to get through. I'm so thankful to have two strong feet and the Lord's help, but I also have to be careful about what doors I enter into."

Kate looked down at her book again. A footnote on the same page explained that Roger Williams was talking about 'Matthew 7:14.'[54] She turned the pages of her Bible until she had found the Bible verse: "For the gate is narrow and the road is hard that leads to life, and there are few who find it" (Matt. 7:14, RSV). She shook her head in agreement before saying, "Running around inside this fallen-down building is like being lost and running around on a really tough road. Hopefully, I'll be one of the few who finds the right pathway leading to life." She sighed before continuing, "Even though I'm in a closet right now, I'm still able to run around inside a whole building. Those poor people stuck in the elevators are having a much tougher time."

Kate's eyes moved back to the closing section of Roger Williams's letter: "your unworthy/R.W." She then said, "Roger Williams, even though many people during your time thought you were a little crazy, you were still well-liked and really worthy of God's love. People like me are the unworthy ones."

Kate placed her Bible and Roger Williams's book into her backpack before lying down on the cold floor. She shivered and got back up again to put on the gloves. She moved the rags off the shelves and placed them beneath and on top of herself.

Before falling asleep, Kate folded her hands and said a prayer out loud: "Please help me, Lord, to move along the tough roads and to get through the narrow gates of this building and life in general. Please also help the people who are stuck in the elevators and anyone who has been hurt or killed in this terrible catastrophe. While my roadway is tough, I'm so thankful for having the freedom so that I can choose to follow you. I know that you will always be present and will always help me. Finally, please help me to enter through the correct doors and to do the right things to help other people. In Jesus's name I pray, Amen."

ROGER WILLIAMS IN
AN ELEVATOR

———————◉———————

A s soon as Kate fell asleep, she smelled smoke. She sat up and looked around for a fireplace, but only darkness was present. Then a small flame grew into a larger fire on a road in front of her; different shadows of burning objects were visible in the fire.

The first shadow that began to move around inside the fire was a December 1632 paper, which was signed by Roger Williams. The paper said that the king of England could not write out legal charters for Massachusetts and other places because the king was not the legal owner of the land. The natives were the rightful owners of their land. The year 1633 appeared in the fire. An image of Roger Williams then appeared and agreed to this tract of his being burned up. The 1632 paper's shadow disappeared inside the fire's flames.

Another image in the fire showed some natives who were in their winter home. Whoever woke up first in the morning was supposed to fix the fire. After one of them woke up and fixed the fire, groups of the natives cut down some trees and did some controlled burns of some of the area's plant life.

Another fire image showed Roger Williams on his way back to England and then moving around to different places. He met with different people during a civil war between King Charles I and the English Parliament. The date "July 1644" appeared in

197

the middle of the fiery war. Roger Williams published *The Bloody Tenent of Persecution for Cause of Conscience*. The date "August 1644" became another fire image; parliament then demanded that all copies of Williams's book be burned. Some, rather than all, of the copies were burned up inside the fire. When people started to look around for Roger Williams, they couldn't find him. He was already on a boat and headed back to New England with a charter for Providence Plantations. The charter gave the Providence colony the religious freedom that Williams had been pursuing.

Kate next noticed an image that showed Roger Williams himself inside the fire. Williams's "enemies called him a 'firebrand.' They feared the conflagration that free thought might ignite. They feared the chaos and uncertainty of freedom, and they feared the loneliness of it. Williams embraced all that. For he knew that was the price of freedom."[55]

Another image showed a part of what happened during King Phillips War: in March 1676, some natives burned Providence, including Williams's house and belongings. As Kate watched the house burn away, she slowly fell back into a dreamless sleep period.

About an hour later, Kate was dreaming again. She found herself inside an elevator. It was much larger than a normal elevator and had gold trim on the edges of its doors. She hit the "open door" button, but nothing happened.

"Am I locked up in here?" she asked. No one was there to respond to her question.

Kate looked at the interior of the elevator. On the wall opposite the control panel was a shelf with a coffeepot, mugs, and two doughnuts. She helped herself to a cup of coffee and a jelly doughnut; she then noticed a nice reclining chair to her right. She sat down, ate her breakfast, and stood back up again.

When Kate looked at the elevator's control panel, a computer screen and keypad appeared. A webcam grew above the panel. She turned the computer on. Its screen showed what was outside the elevator's doors. She touched the webcam, and a picture of her fingers appeared on the computer screen; her index finger and thumb acted like legs as they walked into the corridor outside the elevator. The computer then asked her, "Where do you want to go?"

"Somewhere safe would be nice."

The elevator moved upward, going faster and faster until it reached the top of the building. It then stopped, but the doors remained closed. Kate pressed the button that should have opened the doors, but the button would not work. She asked the computer, "Is this elevator broken?"

"No, it's just trying to show you a path to freedom."

"The elevator's closed doors are locking me in here. I don't think that's a path to freedom."

"No matter where you are, there are always choices. Even now, you can choose to press any one of many different buttons."

"You're right. I can also choose from a lot of buttons, like close, open, and different numbers." Kate thought for a few seconds and then added, "Even if the elevator car doesn't move to where I want it to go, I can still try to choose different paths when I press different buttons."

Kate looked again at the computer screen. It was now displaying a statue of Roger Williams. The statue stepped off the computer screen and into the center of the elevator; it then grew taller and taller until its head was nearly touching the elevator's ceiling. A United States flag grew up next to the statue.

"You look like the Roger Williams statue in the visitor center."

The statue was quiet as it held onto a book while staring pensively above Kate's head at one of the top corners of the elevator.

She said, "I'm talking about the visitor center that's across the street from the Roger Williams National Memorial." After waiting a few seconds, she added, "Are you the same as that statue, or are you a different one?"

The statue's eyes moved downward and focused on Kate's face.

She asked, "Are we back in the seventeenth century?"

The statue did not seem to know the answer.

"Do you know what time it is?" she asked. When the statue did not answer, she looked at her watch. It was five o'clock in the morning.

"You probably should have appeared in one of my earlier dreams, possibly right after I was reading about you in a book."

The statue reached over to the computer's screen, opened up an online version of a book, and pointed to some words: "They are punctuall in their promises of keeping time; and sometimes have charged mee with a lye for not punctually keeping time, though hindred."[56]

"Are you talking about the natives being on time and sometimes telling you that you were late?"

The statue shook its head affirmatively.

"This is really interesting. You're late in my dreams, just like you were in reality."

The statue smiled, resulting in the creation of a lifelike version of the Roger Williams statue.

Kate asked, "How can you tell time without a watch?"

Roger Williams pulled a seventeenth-century timepiece out his pocket and showed it at Kate.

"Oh, so you had a large watch, but you were still late sometimes."

He then pulled a compass out of his pocket.

"That compass must have been really helpful in the seventeenth century. You didn't have maps and streets with signs on them."

Williams pulled up a picture of a map on the computer screen.

"Oh, you did have some maps back then. That map of New England was created by Captain John Smith."

Roger Williams shook his head affirmatively.

"With your compass and map knowledge, maybe you can help me with something."

Roger Williams raised his chin, showing his desire to help. Kate asked, "Do you know how I can get out of this elevator?"

He pointed to the computer screen on the control panel. The New England map disappeared from the screen, and a diagram of the Pilgrim building appeared in its place.

Kate asked, "Is that a real map of this building? It looks similar to the one that Nancy gave to me."

Roger Williams shook his head up and down, telling Kate yes. He then pointed toward a place on the map with a large ventilation shaft. He moved his finger, showing how the ventilation shaft moved diagonally upward across a large section of the building, eventually ending at an opening on the roof of the building.

Kate said, "That shaft probably is a safe way out of this building. The thieves would have planted bombs near many of the doorways, but they probably wouldn't have bothered to put one in that shaft."

Roger Williams shook his head in agreement. Kate then asked, "Can I get a printout of that map?"

A paper version of the map immediately came out the bottom of the computer screen. The map floated in the air toward Kate. She asked, "Is there wind in here?"

Roger Williams responded by talking about the wind as a blessing: "God is wonderfully glorious in bringing the Winds out of his Treasure, and riding upon the wings of those Winds in the eyes of all the sonnes of men in all Coasts of the world."[57]

"I think you're saying that God made the wind—or possibly the air we're breathing—for everyone."

Williams shook his head affirmatively.

"I'm so glad God's making air for everyone. That means the people trapped in the elevators should all be able to breathe."

Roger Williams smiled at her.

The map softly landed on the floor near Kate's feet. She picked it up, put it into her purse, and said, "This map is wonderful! Thanks so much. You're helping me find a path to freedom, not just for myself, but for many other people who are stuck in elevators."

Roger Williams bowed down, showing his joy at being able to help someone.

Kate bowed lower than he had. She then said, "Please stand up. You are the most worthy one."

He smiled at Kate, but he still remained in a bowed-down position.

"Back in the seventeenth century, you helped a lot of people to lead more peaceful lives by letting them stay with you in Providence."

Roger Williams stood up straight and replied with a statement that was the same as the closing for a September 9, 1637, letter that he had written to Governor John Winthrop: "I know your owne heart studies peace, and their soules good: So your Wisedome may make use of it unto others who happily take some more pleasure in Warrs. The blessed God of Peace be pleased to give you peace within at home [and] ceround [surround] about you abroad. So prayes Your Worps [Worship's] unfainedly respective[,] Roger Williams."[58]

"Thanks for saying that I like peace, but you're still wiser and better than I am. Hundreds of years ago, you knew about some people having fun with war. In my century, a lot of people enjoy fighting over territory, even when they're in elevators together and have only a tiny territory to fight about. I didn't realize their enjoyment in fighting, though, until you told me right now about people taking pleasure in wars."

Roger Williams smiled at Kate and bowed down again.

"Your actions right now, as well as the closing to that letter, show that you're really courteous and humble." Kate looked down at the map within her hand and added, "I owe you some money too. Back in your century, paper was expensive because it was imported from England."

Roger Williams vehemently shook his head side to side, telling her no.

"How can I sleep if I know that I've taken paper away from someone like you?"

Roger Williams responded by quoting from one of his poems in *A Key into the Language of America:* "If debts of pounds cause restlesse nights / In trade with man and man, / How hard's that heart that millions owes / To God, and yet sleepe can?"[59]

Kate said, "You're right. Owing money to a person is different from owing to God. Only a really hard-hearted person would be able to sleep when owing anything to God."

Roger Williams smiled and waved his hand. The elevator doors opened. He stepped out into a hallway, which turned into a street that curved into an entrance to Prospect Terrace Park in Providence, Rhode Island. Roger Williams climbed up a small hill and stopped in front of his statue. He reached up, touched the statue's extended right hand, and was pulled upward until he was standing on the canoe. He then hugged the stone version of himself and merged into his stone self. As the Roger Williams statue looked out over the city of Providence, the trees behind him lost their snow and grew green leaves. Roger Williams had moved ahead into the spring, so his tough winter was now behind him as he stood in an elevated position, overlooking the city that he had founded in 1636.

Before Kate could walk out through the open elevator doors, they closed and locked her inside. She felt cold and realized that she was still living in the winter. While asleep within her dream, Kate pressed the elevator's button and then tried to manually open the modernized elevator's doors. Nothing happened, except for a few strange noises on the other side of the doors.

Roger Williams Statue at Prospect Terrace Park

FALLING ELEVATOR

ate woke up and realized that she was hearing the sounds of a metal axe striking into wood. The noises were coming from outside the utility closet. She picked up her hat and moved her right hand onto the flashlight that was still attached to its top flap. Her index finger moved in the direction of the flashlight's switch and then stopped. She put her hat on, but left the flashlight off. Still in darkness, she stood up and slowly moved toward her left. When she reached the door that she had entered last night, she placed one ear against the wood. As she listened, the axe's sounds became louder. The thieves were moving closer to the utility closet. Kate slid her backpack along the floor and placed it into a large pail on one of the shelves. She then rolled under one of the shelves and pulled rags on top of herself.

Suddenly, a loud sound against the closet's wall was made, followed by splinters of wood falling out of the wall and across the closet toward Kate. Her breathing became faster and louder as she tried not to move.

The axe tore through the wall again. Larry's voice asked, "What's this in here?"

After a pause, Henry said, "It looks like a little room with no door."

The axe made more noises as it tore out additional pieces of the wall. Larry said, "It's some kind of a closet. See? There's a door on the opposite end."

"It looks like it's only a closet."

"Before the new walls were added onto the old ones, this closet was probably open over here with a door on the opposite side."

"Another more logical possibility is that there used to be a door on this side of the closet, but it was just taken down when the wall was built. I'll check the map." The sound of some paper unfolding was heard.

"This closet isn't even on our map. Let's just move down to our next location."

"Do you think the police will try to get into the building again today?"

"They'll probably do what they did late yesterday—bring some bomb-sniffing dogs around. When they find more bombs, they probably won't try to dismantle any of them for at least another day."

"I think it'll be more than one day before they figure out how to rescue the elevator people."

"I don't know about multiple days, but I think we'll have at least one more day before anything happens." Larry paused and then added, "Once the police decide people will be dying from no food and no water, they'll definitely be entering the building."

"The doors will be used."

"They could also be opening up the large windows, but our escape route should be safe."

"Yeah, we should be okay, unless the ventilation system has too much junk in it from the bombs."

"That's why we have our backup plan."

Footsteps could be heard walking away from the utility closet. When the sounds of the footsteps could no longer be heard, Kate slowly pushed the rags off her body and rolled out from under the shelf. She turned on her flashlight, carefully pointing it toward the floor, rather than toward the hole in the wall. She retrieved her backpack before going over to the hole and carefully listened for a minute. No sounds were heard, so she shone her light out into the corridor where Larry and Henry had been standing. There were pieces of wood and glass all over the floor.

Because the hole in the wall was too high for Kate to easily climb through, she moved backward slightly and looked at the bottom half of the wall. She put down her backpack. Then she tried to pull a part of the wall toward herself and into the interior of the closet. The board she was pulling at curved downward and then broke. Kate saw something bright inside the wall. She shined her flashlight between the exterior and interior wooden pieces. There was definitely something inside, but she was unable to see far enough into the wall's interior to figure out what it was.

Sighing, Kate climbed through the now-larger hole in the wall. Several feet away was an office. The door had probably been locked, but axe marks on the door showed that Larry and Henry had possibly already unlocked the door.

Kate walked up to the door and turned the handle. The door opened, and she went inside. Pieces of wood and broken glass were lying all over the place, but she still found three bottles of water, a box of crackers, a jar of peanut butter, and some cookies. Next to the peanut butter was a small silver knife. Even though it was a sharp-edged knife, it had probably been used for the peanut butter. A large red flashlight was in one of the desk drawers. Kate wrote a message on a piece of paper, left it with one of her checking account checks, and put the food, knife, and flashlight into her backpack. She then walked back to the utility closet, climbed through its broken wall, and went out onto the narrow metal walkway. While pausing on the walkway, she pulled out a piece of paper and a pen from her purse and drew a picture of the map that Roger Williams had shown her in her dream. She then said to herself, "Because I actually saw a map of this building a few days ago, this map from my dream might be an accurate one."

She put the map into her purse and moved across the walkway until she arrived at a ladder. After slowly climbing up several levels, she began to hear music, feet stomping, and singing. She continued moving upward for another six levels; she then stepped out onto a walkway. She turned toward her left, which is where the sounds were originating.

207

When Kate's feet stepped forward on the walkway, they began to move to the rhythm of the music. "I hate this music," Kate said out loud. Her feet still were stepping forward in time to the song's rhythm. After a few more steps, Kate paused in her motions. Even though her flashlight was pointed toward the walkway, her eyes looked forward to an elevator about thirty feet in front of her. Its metal surface was mostly dark, but a few sections were slightly visible. From the floor and the roof areas, soft light beams were escaping between cracks in the elevator's surface; the escaping lights disappeared quickly as they moved out into the darkness of the shaft.

Kate walked up to where the walkway turned; it went around the shaft, encircling the silver metal. It looked like it was unsuccessfully trying to hide the noises coming from the elevator's interior. "So you hate this music too?" Kate asked the walkway.

The music inside the elevator stopped. The sound of several people whispering was followed by a female's strong voice saying, "No, we don't hate this music. If we did, why would we be playing it?"

"I'm sorry," Kate said. "I thought I was talking to myself."

"Well, you weren't."

"I'm really sorry." Kate paused before adding, "I don't like some kinds of music, but I like that song you were playing."

"Are you just lying to please us?" the same strong female voice asked.

"No, my feet were actually dancing to that song."

The whispering noises started up again. After a minute, a voice asked, "Who are you?"

"I'm Kate Odyssey."

"Do you work in this building?"

"Yes, I do. I work in the New World Bank, or at least I did until the bombings happened."

A different voice said, "You're the new person who just started working this week?"

"Yeah, I am. You sound like Joe, my new boss."

"You have a good memory."

"Do we still have our jobs?"

"Yes, you definitely do. We'll have to set up a new temporary office tomorrow morning, but you'll still have your job."

"What if we're still stuck in here tomorrow?" Kate asked. "How can we be in two places at the same time?"

"If necessary, one of the other bank branches will set up something temporary."

Kate was silent for a moment before saying, "That might be good, in a way."

"How so?"

"The laid-off people who were working in the Warwick office might get their jobs back again."

Silence came from inside the elevator; then the first female's voice said, "I think Joe is trying to avoid responding to your statement, Kate. He's looking down at the floor."

"He's probably just thinking about what to say." Kate's eyes squinted slightly, showing that she was just trying to sound nice. She obviously agreed with the first female and thought that Joe was trying to not respond to her statement about the laid-off employees.

Joe cleared his throat and then said in a low voice, "The truth of the matter is that I'm not the one who makes these decisions, so I really don't know what might or might not happen." After pausing for a few seconds, he added, "We'll also have to wait and make certain none of the laid-off employees were involved in the bombing of this building."

"None of the past employees were involved in the bombing. They were all good people and would not have ever done something like this."

"I hope you're right."

"I don't hope I'm right—I know I'm right." Kate paused and then said, "A couple of thieves did the bombings."

"We'll let the police figure things out."

209

Kate took a pen and her list of elevator people out of her purse. She then explained what she was doing and asked for their names. The lady's strong voice responded with "You already know Joe. I'm Debbie. The other two people in here are Fred and Tina." After they all spelled out their first and last names, Debbie asked, "Are you going to get us out of here?"

"I wish I could, but I'm stuck inside this building too." Kate sighed. "I can't find a door or even a window to escape from."

"If you go down to the bottom floor, you should be able to find some way out," Joe said.

"All kinds of things are blocking off different parts of this building."

"What kinds of things?"

"Giant pieces of wood, plaster, concrete, glass, broken pipes, electrical wires..."

Someone inside the elevator started to hiccup. Kate asked, "Is anyone in your elevator super-anxious about what has happened?"

Laughter from several people erupted from inside the metal walls. Then an angry male voice said, "We're stuck in a broken elevator. We're all super-anxious."

"You're Fred, right?"

"Yeah, I am. What difference does it make?"

"I'm just trying to figure out if everyone in the elevator is okay."

"We're all so fine," Fred's angry voice said with a touch of sarcasm in it.

Tina, who had a soft, hard-to-hear voice, asked, "What difference does it make to you, Kate, whether we're okay or not? You said you can't rescue us."

Fred yelled out, "She's probably lying. She probably can rescue us and is just trying to figure out who should be rescued first."

Joe said, "Kate, I'm your boss. You need to rescue me and the other people in this elevator. Right now, you need to do this."

"I really can't rescue you. I'll climb up to the top of the elevator and show you."

"Okay" was said at the same time by two of the voices in the elevator.

Kate started to climb up the side of the elevator to its roof. When she was nearly at the top, the elevator tilted slightly in her direction. She climbed back down to the walkway and then climbed up a ladder in the elevator shaft. When she was parallel to the elevator, she took one end of the extension cord that was tied to her waist and attached it to the ladder. She then carefully jumped from the ladder onto the roof of the elevator. The elevator shook a little bit and then was steady. Kate disconnected the elevator's light fixture and waved her backpack over the crack in the elevator's roof. "See? This is all that I have. I can take off the light fixture and do other little things, but I can't do much else."

"Have you been using a screwdriver to remove light fixtures?"

"Yeah, I've done that already for more than one elevator."

"Can't you use the screwdriver to pry open elevator doors?"

"Yesterday, I was able to open one set of elevator doors with the screwdriver, but the doors were already broken. There was a crack that was separating them." Kate shined her light down into the elevator. All four faces were sad as they looked up at her.

Joe asked, "Why are you trying to figure out if we're healthy or not?"

"I've been trying to decide if I should tell you the truth about this building. If anyone's likely to start screaming, I was going to keep quiet."

Fred's loud voice said, "After saying something like that, you have to tell us the truth now!"

Kate shined her flashlight fully onto his face. It was bright red. She asked, "Do you have high blood pressure?"

"It's none of your business." Fred looked down at the elevator's floor. After taking several deep breaths, he looked back up at Kate. "Especially when I'm trapped in an elevator, don't I have a right to privacy?"

"Yes, you do have some kind of right to privacy." Kate sighed before saying, "I'll tell you everything I know that's happening." She explained about Larry and Henry trying to find some jewelry in the walls of the building; then she mentioned other bombs hidden in places to stop the first responders from entering the building. She didn't mention the item or items that were lodged in the broken wall of the utility closet. However, she did take her map out of her purse and draw an *x* on the spot where the utility closet was located. She then added in some squares to show where different elevators that she had visited were located.

Joe said, "If you're trying to escape, you might set off one of the bombs by accident."

"I'm not trying to exit through any of the doors. I'm rather looking for a large ventilator shaft. It's supposed to open up onto the roof."

"Do you think the thieves left any bombs in that ventilator shaft?"

"No, I don't think so. It actually might be their escape route."

Tina walked into one of the corners of the elevator. She took a cigarette and lighter out of her purse, lit the cigarette, and quickly inhaled. She then tried to hide the cigarette by putting it partially inside the palm of her hand and moving her hand behind her back.

Fred looked at Tina and said, "Oh, no, you're not doing that again!"

She moved the cigarette forward and up to her lips quickly enough to inhale again. Rather than exhaling right away, for a few seconds, she kept the smoke static within her lungs. She then slowly let the smoke leave her lungs while she stared at Fred. The exhaled smoke hit him in the face. He coughed, directing his cough toward Tina. He then grabbed her hand, pried open her fingers, and removed the cigarette from her hand. Finally, he threw the cigarette onto the elevator's floor and stomped on it.

"I really need to smoke," Tina said in a whiny voice.

"We already talked about this," Fred said. "Secondhand smoke, especially in an elevator, is just wrong."

"It's not my fault that I have to smoke! I'm an addict. I'm addicted to smoking. If I don't smoke, I feel sick."

Kate looked downward at Tina and said, "I understand how you feel. I'm an ex-smoker myself."

Tina looked up at the hole in the ceiling and said, "Thanks." She lit another cigarette, put it into her mouth, inhaled, and exhaled.

Kate said, "It's too bad that you're stuck in this elevator. A different elevator might have been better for you. There's actually one that has some smoke from a fire."

"One of the elevators is on fire?"

"No, the people are just trying to stay warm by starting fires."

"Isn't that dangerous?" Tina inhaled deeply, coughed, and exhaled. Her hand shook as she immediately moved the cigarette back into her mouth again.

"So they won't burn themselves, the people in that elevator are trying to be careful. The fires are also very tiny."

Tina laughed. "Are you really calling the fires *tiny*? That's almost my name." She inhaled and exhaled before adding, "I'd probably fit right into that place."

Fred took a step toward Tina before saying, "Your secondhand smoke would also hurt the people in a fiery elevator. I don't think they'd want you in their elevator either."

"Yes, they would want me there. I could help by starting their fires with my cigarettes."

Debbie said in a strong voice, "Whether you think you belong somewhere else or not, it doesn't matter. You're in this elevator. Three of us are nonsmokers, and we need to breathe."

"If I stand in this corner, most of the smoke goes out through the crack."

Kate asked, "What crack?"

Tina pointed toward the upper half of the back right corner of the elevator. Where the side wall and the back wall were joined together, there was a two-foot long crack.

Joe said, "There are two other cracks in this elevator." He pointed to two places on the floor. "Our elevator is still safe though."

"If it weren't, it would've fallen before now," Debbie said. She looked over at Tina, who had tears in her eyes.

213

Joe also looked at Tina before asking Debbie, "Do we need some more music?"

"Definitely." Debbie turned on her iPod. "Fly Me to the Moon" by Frank Sinatra began to play. Fred started to dance the foxtrot with Tina. The elevator shook slightly, but they continued to dance.

Kate yelled out, "The elevator's shaking." However, no one listened to her. Joe and Debbie were busy watching Fred and Tina's steps. After a minute of trying to learn the correct movements, Joe moved closer to Debbie and began dancing with her. Their steps were uncertain and erratic; they were obviously less experienced than Fred and Tina. Both couples began to move clockwise around the small elevator. While the dance steps were almost too small, the dancers were still moving in time to the music. After the song ended, all four of the dancers stopped moving. At the same time, the elevator stopped its shaking.

Another song, "Get Down Tonight" by KC & the Sunshine Band, began playing on the iPod. Fred and Tina started to dance the cha-cha together. Joe then asked, "What are you dancing?"

Fred showed Joe and Debbie how to do a couple of basic cha-cha steps, and then all four elevator people were again dancing. The elevator tilted slightly to the left and then tilted at a bigger angle to the right side. Kate said loudly, "You're shaking the elevator again."

The four people inside the elevator completely ignored her and continued their dancing.

Kate yelled, "Please, stop! The other elevators weren't shaking like this one is."

Joe looked up at Kate, frowned at her, and shook his head. He then put one of his fingers in front of his lips. He obviously wanted her to be quiet.

The elevator tilted to the left again, but only Kate seemed to notice. She yelled out, "I have to run. Good-bye."

"You're just trying to stop us from dancing," Debbie yelled back.

"You can't dance in a shaking elevator. It's too dangerous."

Fred said, "This is our elevator! We can dance in here if we want to."

Kate responded, "You're just psyching out because you're stuck in an elevator."

Tina said, "You may be right, Kate. Perhaps we all just need to feel like we're free because we're not really free."

Fred yelled, "Of course we're free. We live in a democracy, which means someone like Kate can't tell us what to do."

"I'm just trying to help you—like Roger Williams was also trying to help people back in the seventeenth century."

"No, you're not like Roger Williams was. He was an advocate of freedom, not for people telling each other what to do."

Kate frowned. "Roger Williams did tell people what to do."

"No, he didn't."

"Yes, he did. He told people in the Massachusetts Bay Colony that they needed to separate religious activities from political ones, and he was completely correct. Separation of church and state became a part of our constitution."

"Separation of church and state is very different from separation of dancing and elevator activities."

"I'm not trying to tell you what to do. I'm just trying to help."

Fred jumped up and down several times. The elevator shook each time he jumped. Finally, he said, "Especially since your boss is in this elevator, you have to listen to us."

"No, you should listen to me. I also think Joe agrees with me. It makes no sense to jump around inside a shaking elevator."

Joe said, "I only partially agree with you, Kate. You're actually making Fred even more upset than he already is. Tina's also quite anxious. Please, get away from here, so they can calm down a little bit."

Fred laughed loudly. His angry face turned even redder. "You're banished!"

"It's the twenty-first century. You can't banish me like Roger Williams was."

"It's our elevator. We can do what we want to!" Fred reached into his pocket and took out a gun. When he pointed it upward toward Kate, she jumped away from the top of the shaking elevator over to the ladder. As she gripped one of the rusty metal rungs, she felt a rush of wind behind her. The sounds of screaming voices and scraping metal fell downward through the elevator shaft.

Kate gripped more tightly onto the ladder. After inhaling and exhaling a few times, she moved her flashlight toward the shaft. Its beam did not reach far enough for her to see the elevator. She disconnected her extension cord from the ladder, moved down onto the walkway, and wound the entire cord around her waist. She then started to climb down the ladder. She had only traveled down three stories when her foot could no longer step on a rung. She moved her foot around on the wall of the shaft, trying to find a partial or bent rung of the ladder. Nothing was there. She flashed the beam of her light onto the wall beneath her, but no rungs or other parts of a ladder were visible.

She yelled out, "Are you guys okay?"

A distant voice from inside the elevator shaft said, "I think so."

Kate yelled again, "Is that you, Joe?"

"Yeah, it is."

"Is everyone else okay, or just you?"

Joe said, "Well, my knees hurt, but I'm alive." After a pause, he added, "We're maybe okay, but Fred is only half conscious."

Debbie yelled, "We're all in pain! Call 9-1-1!"

Kate said, "I'll try to find a phone that's working."

"Oh, no, not again!"

"What's wrong?" Kate asked.

"The elevator's shaking, and no one's dancing or anything." Debbie's voice paused and then added, "I only stood up."

Joe's voice said loudly, "Okay, we'll all have to stay exactly where we're at. We can't move at all."

Debbie's voice said, "If Fred wakes up, there's no way he'll be able to stay still."

"Take off your scarf and his tie."

Debbie's voice asked, "Whatever for?"

"Here's my belt and tie. We'll tie him up, so he won't be able to move around too much."

"Okay. I'll take his gun out of his pocket too."

Kate yelled out, "I'm leaving now. I'll try to get you guys some help." By the time someone from the elevator replied, she had already started climbing up the ladder and could not hear well enough to understand any of the words. Then metal-against-metal scraping noises made her stop and shine her light into the elevator shaft. The elevator could not be seen, and no voices were heard.

Kate started to cry. With one of her hands, she rubbed at the tears in her eyes. However, her other hand that was still holding onto the ladder quickly became tired and weak. Both of her hands grasped onto the same rung of the narrow ladder. Several of her tears fell onto its rusty metal surface. She opened and closed her eyes multiple times, trying to see beyond the tears that were still there. Finally, she was able to see and began to slowly climb up the ladder. When she reached a higher level, she found a walkway and stepped out onto it.

After Kate put down her backpack next to her feet, she folded her hands and said a prayer: "Dear Lord, Please help the people in that elevator. Even though they were not behaving too well, I'm sure they're sorry now for the bad things they've done. If they're still alive, please help them to stay alive and to be rescued quickly. If they have died, please forgive them of their sins and take care of them. In Jesus's name I pray, Amen." She then picked up her backpack and began climbing up the ladder again.

SHARING ELEVATOR

───────────◉───────────

When Kate reached another metal walkway, she noticed a draft of cold air to her right. She moved her flashlight toward the draft, but all that was visible was a partially opened door. Stepping away from the elevator shaft's ladder, she moved through the doorway. Beyond the door was a corridor that was not too badly damaged. There were some broken bits of glasses, but no wood panels or boards were visible.

Kate walked into the corridor and paused, looking to her right and then to her left. The right side seemed to be cooler, so she turned that way and began walking. Within a minute, she was in front of an office. The door was locked, but the office had large windows on both sides of the door. Because of the closed shades on the interior of the windows, Kate could not see inside the office. However, a large crack was visible on one of the windows. She pushed at the largest section of the cracked window's glass. It curved slightly inward, but when she let it go, it just popped back into its original position. She took off her backpack and shoved it into the window. The glass broke into several pieces and fell into the office's interior; Kate's backpack fell through the window's large frame and landed in the office's front room.

Pulling up the now-partially broken shade, Kate climbed over the windowsill and stood up next to her backpack. She moved her flashlight around the room, examining its contents. As soon as the beam of light lit up a water machine, Kate walked over to it, grabbed the only paper cup, filled it with water, and sighed multiple times as she gulped down the water. After drinking three eight-ounce cups of water, she looked to the sides and back of the water machine. No more paper cups were visible.

Kate walked over to the nearest desk. On the far left side was a plastic water bottle. She grabbed the bottle, brought it over to the water machine, filled it up with water, and placed it in her backpack. She then went back to the same desk and looked inside all the drawers. She found a flashlight, some sugar-free candy, a box of cereal, and two protein energy drinks. After placing these items in her backpack, she left a note and one of her checks on the desktop.

Looking in the drawers of two more desks, Kate found no useful items. She then walked through a door in the back of the office and into a narrow hallway. She went into two more offices, but found no food. At the end of the hallway was a small room with a refrigerator, a microwave, several tables, and chairs. Because the electricity was still not working, the refrigerator items were not very cold. There was some melted ice cream, as well as a few cans of soda and beer. The canned beverages were quickly placed into Kate's backpack. She left a note and a check before going back through the hallway and into the main office.

After climbing through the broken window, Kate went back into the corridor. A draft of cold air ruffled her hair. She looked up and saw a small vent near the ceiling. Shivering, Kate turned around and walked back toward the door that led to the elevator. She moved past the door and walked to the opposite end of the corridor, where she opened an unlocked door. Another metal walkway led up to an elevator shaft. After shining her flashlight up and down the shaft, Kate started to climb up the ladder. Her backpack was heavier than before, so she had to stop climbing and rest after every ten or eleven steps.

Higher up in the shaft, Kate soon heard someone talking. She shined her light straight upward and saw the metal of another elevator. She kept climbing until she was only five or six steps from the top of the ladder. She paused for a moment and shifted her backpack more toward her left shoulder. When she moved her right foot upward to the next step, it made a noise by scraping against the rusty metal of the ladder.

A voice from inside the elevator asked, "Did you hear that?"

A second voice said, "No, I didn't." After a pause, the same voice said, "You must be hearing things."

"I'm not imagining things again. I really did hear something," the first voice said. "Didn't anyone else hear that noise?"

Multiple people inside the elevator said "no" at the same time.

Kate climbed upward to the last step on the ladder.

The first voice said, "Someone's really outside our elevator. I even saw a little bit of light in the bottom corner over there."

"You're only confused and maybe seeing things," the second voice said. "Remember? We talked about what will happen when the oxygen level in here goes down even more. People might get headaches and have hallucinations."

A third voice said, "I'm still feeling light-headed."

A fourth voice said, "I have numb, tingling fingers and toes."

The first voice said, "I'm not making things up! I really heard something."

Kate stepped onto a walkway next to the elevator and yelled out, "I'm really here, right outside your elevator."

For a few seconds, everyone was quiet. Then the first voice asked, "Who are you?"

"I'm Kate Odyssey. Who are you?"

"Mary Hart."

"Are you related to Thomas Hart, the firefighter?"

"Yeah, I'm his sister. How do you know him?"

"I met Tom yesterday at lunch."

Mary asked, "Were you two on a date?"

"We actually weren't on a date yesterday, but we had some good food together, and I gave Tom my phone number."

"Hopefully, you and I can meet and maybe also have lunch together sometime soon. I can tell you a lot of nice things about Tom. In fact, if the door to this elevator were open, we could have lunch together right now."

"Do you have some food in that elevator?"

"We only have a half of a candy bar left. However, we can break it up into small pieces, so you can have some too."

Before Kate could respond, a different voice said, "This elevator's air might not have enough oxygen in it. We probably shouldn't all be talking so much."

Kate asked, "Is everyone okay?"

"Some of us are feeling a little bit funny."

Kate said, "I'll try to help. I might be able to take the light off the top of your elevator. Then there will be a hole for some fresh air."

"Thanks" was said by a couple of voices at the same time.

Kate climbed up to the top of the elevator and took off the light fixture. She immediately coughed because of the smell. She then shone her flashlight through the hole in the elevator's roof. There were seven people looking up at her. One of them was lying down stretching out his arms; he was taking up nearly half of the elevator's space. The other six people were squeezed together in the right front part of the elevator. They were sitting down on the floor and leaning against one another. Pairs of people were facing each other with their legs stacked up onto each other's legs. A large backpack and three purses were in the right rear corner.

"We're okay," Mary said.

The man lying down in the left half of the elevator sighed. "With just that small hole in the ceiling, I already feel better."

"I think we all feel better," a familiar female voice said.

Kate shone her light toward the familiar voice before asking, "Are you Phebe Robinson?"

"Yeah, I am." She looked up at Kate. "I remember meeting you in an elevator on your first day at work."

"You were so nice to me."

"You were even nicer to me."

"The nicest part about us meeting was being able to hug a new friend."

Kate and Phebe both smiled at each other. Then one of the men in the elevator said, "Phebe is known as a hugger. She has been showing all of us different ways to hug."

"That's such a wonderful idea! What ways have you been showing everyone, Phebe?"

"Here's one way that works well in a crowded elevator." Phebe reached out both her hands to the elevator people who were closest to her. The other people also grabbed onto each other's hands, so they were all connected together. They then all squeezed their hands at the same time. Everyone laughed before slowly disconnecting their hands away from their neighbors.

Phebe said, "Here are a couple of more methods, but there really are hundreds of different ways to connect with other people." Phebe gave a high five to the woman in front of her and then intertwined her other arm with the arm of the man on her left side.

Kate smiled. "I can't believe how happy you all look."

One of the men said, "Having that hole in the ceiling has cheered us up. We now can breathe better, so we have a little bit more freedom than what we had before you got here." He looked around at the faces of the other elevator people, and they all shook their heads in agreement.

Kate opened up her backpack and took out her list of people's names. She added Mary's and Phebe's names to the listing. After Kate explained what she was doing, the other five people told her their names: Job Robinson, Waite Winsor, Obediah Angell, Resolved Tillinghast, and Paul Olney.

An alarm clock suddenly went off. Waite Winsor picked it up, turned off the alarm, and then reset it to go off in another fifteen minutes. All seven people then stood up and moved around.

Phebe was now stretched out in the left part of the elevator. She looked up at Kate, smiled, closed her eyes, and said, "I so love when it's my turn to have a lot of personal space."

Kate's facial expression showed her surprise. "I didn't realize that you were taking turns. I assumed the person in the biggest section was the richest person."

Job said, "You're thinking of our elevator like it's a part of a city. The biggest areas are usually the most expensive ones and are therefore bought by rich people."

Mary said, "The biggest homes are sometimes bought by the people who are trying to show everyone else that they're rich. They might just be really heavily in debt."

Kate laughed. "In the other broken-down elevators that I've visited, people divided up the elevator's space evenly among themselves. Their positions in the available space, though, were sometimes debated."

Phebe said, "That's sometimes what people do in normal elevators."

Job laughed. "At other times, in normal elevators, people don't share the available area correctly. There's often at least one person who refuses to move and then winds up getting some extra space."

"Our situation is a little bit different from normal," Phebe said. After looking around, she added, "I'm so glad everyone's sharing our space in the way that we voted on."

"Did you all really vote on how to split up the elevator's space?"

Job responded, "Yes, we did. What happened was everyone said yes to taking turns in a big section of the elevator."

Phebe, the current stretched-out lady, said. "After being crowded in with each other, stretching out over here is so nice. Even though I'm still inside this elevator, I now feel like I'm free." Phebe started to sing the song "Freedom Reigns," which is Jesus Culture music written by Michael Larson. After she sang the line "Freedom reigns in this place,"[60] Resolved coughed loudly.

Phebe stopped singing and asked, "Do you think we lack freedom in this elevator, Resolved?"

"Yes, we definitely are lacking our freedom here. I don't see how anyone could debate that point."

Phebe sang another part of Michael Larson's "Freedom Reigns" song: "Where the spirit of the Lord is / There is freedom."[61]

"Why do you think God's spirit means freedom?"

"He has the power to make us do whatever he wants us to do. He could make us walk, jump, sing, or do whatever. He could pick us up, carry us into a church, and make us stay there forever. However, he doesn't force us to do anything. He lets us choose to follow him or not."

"I think it's interesting that God gives us the freedom of choice," Resolved said.

"He knocks at the door, but we need to open it up and let him in." Phebe stretched her arms out, looking like she wanted to hug God.

Kate said, "I remember the actual Bible verse that says that idea: 'Look! I stand at the door and knock. If you hear my voice and open the door, I will come in, and we will share a meal together as friends' (Rev. 3:20, RSV)."

After stretching a few more times, Phebe sang the whole "Freedom Reigns" song. Everyone, included Resolved, was quiet as they listened to the entire song. After finishing the song, Phebe sat up and pointed to one of the elevator's walls. Kate flashed her light on the wall, where some clothing items had been strapped together.

Phebe stood up, went over to the wall, pulled on a group of sweaters and jackets, and stretched them out; the clothing was now dividing the elevator into two sections. She explained, "We took the straps off our purses and used some extra clothing to make this curtain. Each of us can have some private personal space by stretching out the clothing."

"That curtain's so neat. None of the other elevators had such a great divider or any kind of decorations."

"What other elevators are you talking about?" Phebe asked.

"There are some other broken-down elevators in this building."

"Is anyone hurt?"

"I don't know for sure, but I think one of the elevators might have some injured people inside." Kate moved her flashlight's beam back to the elevator's walls. In addition to the clothing, photos were visible on the side and back walls of the elevator. "Whose pictures are those?"

Phebe said, "They're everyone's. We took them out of our billfolds and purses. After someone hangs a picture on the wall, we have a rule."

"What's that?"

"We have to tell a story about the picture." Phebe hugged herself and smiled. "I've actually told a lot of stories about my two wonderful children."

Kate commented, "Telling stories is a great way of sharing experiences with each other."

Waite said, "It's also a great way to pass the time. We've been having more fun than watching television shows."

Kate said, "I enjoy watching crime shows and movies. Were there any stories about drunk drivers or other criminals?"

Resolved said, "No one in this elevator should be telling you about my son's misbehaviors. It just wouldn't be right."

"I understand. I'm not really a part of your group right now."

Phebe suggested, "If you stick around long enough, Resolved might decide that you're a friend, and he will then tell you all about his son."

"Hopefully, the son is not in jail right now."

Resolved sighed. "Okay, I'll tell you. He was a drug addict for a few years. He used to steal things to support his habit. He even stole money and belongings from me. He sold two of my laptops online and used the money for drugs. Then one day, he was in a car accident while he was intoxicated and on drugs. His best friend was in the car with him and nearly died. My son then realized that he was hurting other people, not just himself. We talked to

225

our minister, who helped to set up my son in a special program. Now, he's no longer an addict. Plus, he has helped at least three of his addicted friends to come clean." Resolved raised up his chin, showing how proud he was of his son. He then pointed to a photo on the wall. "There's his picture while he's singing in the choir at our church."

"He looks like a great son."

"He really is. I constantly thank God for helping him to recover."

"I'm really happy you shared that story about your son. I'm so glad that he's changed into a wonderful person."

"He now has a job and is a very caring, helpful son. For example, during that last snowstorm, he came over to my house at five in the morning and shoveled all the snow off my driveway and sidewalk. He then went off to work in cold, damp clothing." Resolved sighed. "If I had known about his clothing, I obviously would have given him the very clothing off my own back."

"It's so nice to have caring, sharing family members." Kate shined her light back onto one of the walls. "Do you have other photos of him over there?"

Resolved pointed to two of the photos. One photo just had his son in it; the other photo had his son with Resolved and other family members.

Kate said, "I love those pictures. They really make your elevator look great!"

Two of the elevator people said "thanks" at the same time.

Kate's eyes kept on staring at the elevator's wall. A necklace with a wooden cross was positioned in the middle of the photo section. "Whose cross is that?"

Phebe replied, "It used to belong to my grandmother, but it belongs to me now." After pausing for a few seconds, Phebe added, "Actually, I'm sharing the cross with everyone else in this elevator."

"That's wonderful!"

"Yeah, it really is. My grandmother gave me the cross as a present when I was baptized. Whenever I look at it, I remember that day."

"What happened?"

"The water was really cold, but when I was immersed in it, I felt warmer. It was like my heart and soul became more alive, which made me so very happy."

"That's so wonderful, Phebe!"

"In this elevator, sharing my faith with my newfound friends has been such a blessing! We've been reading the Bible and talking about a lot of positive things. We've also been praying for help, not just for ourselves, but for everyone else in this building."

"You're so nice, Phebe. Your positive reaction to this catastrophe is making me feel a lot better."

"I'm really glad to be able to help you, Kate. I just wish I could do more."

"You're already doing a lot."

The other people in the elevator with Phebe shook their heads in agreement. After pausing for a few seconds, Kate asked, "How did you attach the cross and the pictures onto the walls?"

Phebe responded, "I have some tape in my purse." She paused for a few seconds and then added, "If you need some scotch tape for anything, I can try to throw it up through that hole in the ceiling."

Kate smiled. "You're so generous, but I already have some duct tape and a pair of scissors."

Job said, "Those are the two most necessary tools to have in almost any environment."

Kate asked, "Would you like some of the duct tape?"

"No, thanks, we already have enough tape."

Kate moved her flashlight over each of the elevator's occupants. They all looked normal. She asked, "Is everyone okay? Does anyone have a headache and need some aspirin?"

Job said, "My fingers and toes were feeling sort of funny, but they're okay now."

"Are you sick?"

"No, I don't think so. Just being stuck in this elevator is making me upset, which is probably what's giving me strange physical symptoms."

Paul said, "Because there are seven of us in here, we might not have had enough air. I've been feeling a lot better since you opened up that hole in the roof."

Job shook his head in agreement and then stopped. He seemed to have changed his mind. "It could be insufficient air, Paul, that's making us feel funny, or it could be something else."

Kate twitched her nose, inhaled, and then paused before exhaling. She was unable to identify a smell.

Mary said, "Perhaps we're just all upset, and that's affecting how we feel physically."

Job asked, "Kate, can you please look around the outside of the elevator to see if there's a broken pipe or anything else strange?"

"Yes, I will right now." Kate moved her flashlight around her immediate area, but no pipes were visible. She left her backpack on top of the elevator, climbed down to the walkway, and moved in a large circle around the elevator. On the opposite side, she saw a door, followed a walkway over to it, and touched its handle. Its gold-colored metal was damp. Kate moved her hand away from the handle and shone her flashlight upward. Nothing was visible, but a drop of liquid fell down and landed on the door's handle. Kate shined her light on the handle and then bent over so that her nose was close to it. After inhaling deeply, she coughed several times. She then walked back to the elevator and climbed up onto its roof.

When Kate's flashlight was directed through the hole in the roof, seven faces looked upward at her. She said, "I think everything's okay. There's some kind of a leak with drops of liquid falling onto a door handle, but whatever the liquid is, there isn't enough of it to be dangerous."

"Where's the leak? What part of the elevator is it closest to?" Resolved asked.

"It's nearest to the elevator doors, but it's at least fifteen feet away."

"Could you smell what it was?"

Kate hesitated before saying, "I don't know for sure what it was, and I don't want to scare anyone by guessing about different possibilities."

Resolved said, "Because of how you said that, I know you're lying."

Phebe, who was now standing up in the crowded section of the elevator, said, "Kate is too nice. She would never lie."

Resolved looked at Phebe, made a face, and said, "Nice people sometimes lie when they're trying not to hurt anyone."

Mary, who was now lying down in the personal-space section of the elevator, said, "Even if the leak is a gas or oil leak, we'll probably still be okay."

Resolved asked, "Why would we be okay?"

Mary said, "My brother's a firefighter, so I know about these kinds of things. Even with a gas leak, we'll be okay for a while, unless we start a fire."

Kate cleared her throat and asked, "How about if I change the subject?" She looked down at the seven faces that were now looking up at her. Mary was holding onto a flashlight and pointed its light upward toward Kate.

"What else could be more important than a possible gas leak, especially for seven people trapped in an elevator?"

Kate smiled, lifted up her backpack, and said, "I have some food, so we can all eat a little bit more than just a half a candy bar."

Mary stood up before asking, "Did you say that you have some food?"

"Yeah, I have some bottled water too."

All seven faces were still staring upward at her. She opened her backpack and showed the elevator people some crackers, peanut butter, candy, and one of the bottled waters. "I need to hold onto a few items, in case I find another elevator with hungry people inside. However, there's enough food here for us to have a nice lunch together."

"Are you sharing the water too?" Job asked.

"Of course I am. I'll send down to you this one bottle of water and some food items."

"How much money would you like for those items?"

"I paid about twenty dollars for them, but you don't have to pay me anything."

"Twenty dollars is more than twice the money those items would cost at a grocery store," Job said.

"You're right. However, I already left a twenty-dollar check on someone's desk when I took these items."

"You overpaid someone for those things."

"I had no choice. No one was in the office, so I needed to be extra generous in paying for the stuff that I took."

Job took his billfold out of his pocket and looked around at the faces of the other people in the elevator. They all shook their heads up and down, showing their agreement in paying for the food and water. Several of the faces also had huge smiles on them. Job said, "I'm sorry if I've been sounding grouchy, Kate. We're really very happy to be able to buy some food from you."

Kate said, "I don't really want to take money from you, Job, especially since Mary offered to share her half of a candy bar with everyone."

Job said, "It's not right if we just take things away from you when we have money to pay for them. If we had no money, then I think the situation would be different."

Kate thought for a few seconds and then shook her head in agreement. She used an extension cord to collect twenty dollars. Inside the twenty-dollar bill was a piece of a candy bar.

Kate said, "Thanks so much, Mary. You're one of the nicest people I've ever met."

Mary said, "You're so welcome, but I think you're even nicer than I am."

Kate and Mary smiled at each other as Kate started to move some food and water downward on the extension cord. She put peanut butter between some of the crackers and then sent down crackers that were filled with lots of peanut butter.

Waite distributed the crackers and candy to everyone else before he held onto some of the food for himself. Before people started to eat, Obediah said a prayer: "We thank you, Lord, for this wonderful food and water. We're so thankful to be alive and to be sharing so much with one another. We also ask that you help all of us to be safely rescued from this elevator. In Jesus's name we pray, Amen."

Mary said, "I don't believe how good this cracker is." The other six people in the elevator shook their heads in agreement as they shared the peanut butter crackers, candies, and the single bottle of water. When the bottle was empty, Kate sent another bottle of water down to them. She then explained that it was the last one she could give them for right now.

The alarm clock went off. It was Waite's turn to relax in the personal-space section of the elevator; however, he waved his hand at Paul, indicating that Paul could take his turn now.

Paul's hands had been clamped tightly into fists. His hands relaxed as he moved over into the noncrowded section and said, "Thanks so much, Waite. You know how I get claustrophobic in that section."

"We all know about your problem," Phebe said. "I'm just so happy that we all have—at least once—given up our turns in that good section of the elevator."

Paul said, "I'm so thankful to all of you. After spending time with you guys in this elevator, my life is going to be so much better than it was before."

Kate asked, "Will you be doing anything differently?"

"I'm planning on doing some work for a volunteer agency. I want to help homeless people, so they can have better lives. I never knew before what it was like to live with so little food in such a small space."

Resolved said, "I'm planning on going to college. I want to become a politician now that I know more about informal rules and laws. I also love to debate ideas with other people."

Phebe said, "I've learned more about myself by being in this elevator."

Kate asked, "What have you learned?"

"I love to hug people and animals. Also, I've never really liked to be all by myself in my house. Now, I'm going to volunteer at an animal rescue center. I'm also going to offer to adopt some homeless cats. They can come into my house for a temporary home, and I'll have some wonderful pets to make me happier than I am now."

Mary said, "I've learned something too. I've always wanted to go into nursing. Now, I really want to go into that field."

Waite said, "I have never liked to wait for anything."

Kate asked, "Really? With your name, waiting for things should be interesting."

"I never thought waiting was good. When I was younger, I was always kidded about having to wait for my turn."

"Were you bullied?"

"Yeah, in a way, I was. Other kids always used to jump in front of me and then say, 'wait.'"

"From what I've been seeing, you've been able to wait for your turn in the good section of the elevator."

"I know. Spending time here with strangers has helped me to be a little more patient. I've also learned about other people and some of their problems." Waite looked around at the other elevator people, who were all smiling at him. "However, I think all of us can hardly wait until we're rescued and can leave this metal prison."

Job said, "What's interesting, Kate, is that we're all friends now. We've already decided that we'll often be seeing each other after we escape from this place."

Kate said, "Will you be friending each other on Facebook?"

"Yeah, we will," Job said. "We've already shared our names, phone numbers, and e-mail addresses. We'll be getting together once every month or two."

Obediah said, "I want to be a minister, just like my ancestor Roger Williams was."

Kate smiled at Obediah while saying, "I'm a descendant of Roger Williams too."

"That's so wonderful! Once we're all rescued, we'll definitely have to contact each other. Comparing our genealogies should be interesting."

After everyone in the sharing elevator had talked some more about how their future lives would be different because of the elevator experience, Kate said good-bye. "I'm going to try to get help. I'll tell the first responders where you all are."

"Thanks, Kate. Please tell my brother Thomas that I love him."

"You'll be able to tell him yourself."

"In case anything bad happens with that leaking pipe, please promise to tell him for me."

"Of course, I definitely will." Kate wrote down information from Mary, as well as from all the elevator people about their loved ones and what to tell them. She then waved good-bye and went back to the ladder on the wall of the elevator shaft. Sighing, she started to move up the ladder. "At least my backpack is a little bit lighter now," she said out loud as she climbed up the ladder.

Hidden Elevator

———————⬤———————

After climbing up two levels, Kate moved her right hand into an empty space; the ladder was missing at least one rung. She moved her head to shine her flashlight upward, but she was unable to see any parts of the ladder. Stepping out onto a walkway, Kate began to move to her left. After a few minutes, she found another elevator shaft. It had more dust in it than the other shafts did, but its ladder was similar to the other ones in the building.

Kate began to slowly climb the ladder. After going up three floors, she coughed several times because of the large amount of dust in the air. She stepped off the ladder onto a walkway and moved her flashlight to the left and then to the right. There was less dust to her right, so she moved in that direction. The walkway's debris got worse and worse, but Kate continued to walk carefully along the dirty, rusty metal pathway.

About forty feet away from the elevator shaft, there was a huge hill of wood, dust, jagged metal strips, plaster pieces, broken electrical cords, paper, and glass. Several pipes looked like they were trying to hide themselves while they were still partially sticking up out of the debris. Kate stopped walking and stared at the giant hill. As she stood quietly looking upward, a voice from inside the hill said, "Please help us, Lord, to be found and rescued. If this is the Apocalypse, please stay with us and keep us safe until it is time to join with you in heaven. In Jesus's name we pray, Amen."

Kate softly said "Amen" before walking up closer to the hill. She said loudly, "I liked that prayer."

Some murmuring from within the hill sounded like people were talking softly to themselves. No one said anything loud enough to be heard outside the hill.

Kate asked, "Did you create that prayer, or did you read it from a book?"

A voice on the other side of the hill said, "We weren't praying."

"Some of the words you said were 'Lord,' 'Jesus,' and 'Amen.' That sounds like a prayer."

"We're not in church, so we weren't praying."

"People can pray in different places. They don't have to pray in just one place at one specific time."

"I wasn't praying."

"Okay, I guess I just heard you wrong."

"Yes, you definitely heard us wrong."

After a pause, Kate asked, "Where are you?"

"We're stuck inside this elevator."

"I think you're actually inside a hill."

"No, we're in an elevator. Maybe there's a hill next to us."

"I'll look around some more." Kate looked at the walkway that she was standing on. It went straight through the bottom of the hill of debris. There were no additional metal walkways to the right or the left.

"Have you found our elevator yet?"

"No, I can't find it. I can't even find any metal walkways, except for the one that I'm standing on. Maybe your elevator is beneath the hill that's in front of me."

"I guess anything's possible."

"I'll try banging on the hill, and you can tell me if the noises are coming from just outside of your elevator or from somewhere else."

"Okay."

Kate took the screwdriver out of her backpack. She hit the hill five times. Each time, some of the debris fell off the hill and went downward. Several seconds elapsed before noises from the falling debris could be heard.

The voice inside the hill said, "Those sounds are coming from right outside our elevator. I even placed my hand where the noises were being made. I could feel some kind of vibration, like metal was hitting metal."

"Your elevator must be inside this giant hill of dirt and broken things."

"If we're really inside a giant hill, how come we can still breathe?"

Kate tried to look up at the top of the hill, but all she could see was the sloping wall of the debris hill. No roof area was visible. "Probably only a part of your elevator is hidden inside this hill. Either the top area or the other side is free from some of this debris."

"That makes sense."

Kate opened up her backpack and took out a pen and her list of names. "Can I have your name and the names of any other people in the elevator with you?"

"Do you also want our social security numbers, bank accounts, passwords, and credit card information?" the voice asked sarcastically.

"No, of course I don't." Kate sighed and then said, "I've been writing down the names of people in the elevators. That way, if I ever get out of this building, I can give the police a list of everyone who's still alive. I think most people will want to know if their loved ones are okay."

Soft murmuring came from inside the hill as its inhabitants talked softly for a minute. Kate could only hear some mumbling noises, rather than any specific words. Finally, the same lady's voice asked loudly, "What's your name?"

"I'm Kate Odyssey."

"Oh, I heard about you. On Monday, you just started working in the New World Bank."

"You're right. I used to work in a different branch of the bank, but it was closed down."

Murmuring was heard for another minute. Then the same voice said, "Okay, I think you can be trusted. I'm Heidi Dexter."

Kate wrote Heidi's name on her list before asking, "Is anyone else in your elevator?"

"There are two more people, but they don't want their names written down."

"Okay. I'll just write down the words 'two people.'"

Heidi said, "Someone told me, Kate, that you're a descendent of Roger Williams. Is that true?"

"Yeah, I am."

"It's so interesting that you're writing things down. Roger Williams used to write a lot, and one of my ancestors published some of his stuff."

"Are you a descendant of Gregory Dexter?"

"Yeah, I am. Roger Williams knew about Dexter's reputation and his movable press. This is why Williams chose Gregory Dexter 'to print both *A Key into the Language* (1643) and *The Bloody Tenent*, for Dexter was known for printing especially polemical pamphlets and would almost certainly have had occasion, like many printers before him, to use a movable press to escape detection.'[62]"

Kate smiled. "Dexter used a movable press, so he could hide out in different places and maybe even run away to different places, right?"

"Yeah, he did. Some of the pamphlets and books that he published didn't even have his name on them. He sometimes had to remain anonymous, or he would have been sent to prison."

"Today too people often remain anonymous." Kate looked down at her list of names.

One of the nameless people from the elevator said, "We sometimes have to be anonymous these days. There are too many people out there stealing identities. Hiding oneself is a way to stay safe." The voice had a low tone and sounded like a man's.

The other nameless person said, "You're right about that. I've had my credit card information stolen twice in the last year." This voice had a medium tone; it sounded like a young man's voice.

Heidi said, "If my credit card information is stolen, it won't really matter too much. Everything's already maxed out."

The low-tone voice said, "Hey you two, didn't we agree not to talk about this stuff?"

The other voices both apologized. Kate then asked, "Are you all okay?"

Heidi said, "We need something to drink and some food."

Kate asked, "Do you have a flashlight, by any chance?"

The low-tone voice asked, "Why do you care?"

"I'm just trying to help. If I can somehow get onto the roof of your elevator, I might be able to open up a part of it." Kate paused before adding, "If you can shine a flashlight on the walls and roof of your elevator, I might see the light going through one of the corners of the roof or some other place in your elevator."

Heidi asked, "Do you have any food, Kate?"

"Yes, I do. I have a bottle of water too."

Heidi said, "Okay, one of the men in here is holding onto our only flashlight." She paused and then asked, "Can you please shine that around?"

The low-tone voice said, "Here it is shining on the ceiling of our elevator right now. Can you see it, Kate?"

"No. I'll step backward a little bit." Kate moved a few steps away from the hill. "I still can't see anything. Can you try to light up the walls?"

"Okay. The flashlight is now going around the edges of the wall closest to you, Kate. Can you see anything?"

"No, I still can't."

"I'm turning this flashlight off and saving it for when we need it," the low-tone voice said. "If you figure out some way to get food or water inside to us, we have over two hundred dollars in cash that we can give to you."

Kate said, "Thanks, but there's no way for me to climb onto the roof. I'm sorry, but I won't be able to help with food or water. Perhaps I can help in some other way."

"How?"

"I don't know. I've already been praying for everyone who's stuck in the elevators."

Heidi started to cry.

After thinking for a minute, Kate said, "Things will work out."

Heidi was still crying.

"If you want to hear some interesting stories, I can tell you about the people in the other elevators."

The low-tone voice said, "I don't think Heidi wants to even think about elevators right now."

"Is that true, Heidi?" Kate asked.

Heidi suddenly stopped crying and asked in a jittery voice, "Do you know what happened? I heard explosions and then our elevator got stuck here."

The medium-tone younger man said, "We can't use our cell phones, and I can't get Internet access on my laptop."

Heidi said, "I'm worried that everything in our world is messed up. It could be the Apocalypse."

"You said something about the Apocalypse in your prayer."

"You're right. I did reference it."

"So when I first stood outside your elevator, you really were praying."

"I just feel funny talking about religion to a stranger."

"I'm religious too, Heidi."

"Even so, I don't want to talk about it."

"Especially if you think it's the Apocalypse, why are you trying to hide your faith?"

"I'm not hiding my faith. I prayed partially because these two men were as scared as I was. I was trying to help them, and I think the prayer made them feel a little better."

"So why did you tell me that you weren't praying when you really were?"

Heidi sounded upset as she said, "I'm a shy person who's maybe dying inside an elevator. You're a stranger who somehow is not stuck inside an elevator. I still don't completely trust you, so I don't want to tell you too much."

Kate's face showed her sorrow. "I'm sorry. I didn't mean to upset you. The truth is I don't think it's the Apocalypse, at least not yet. I heard two thieves saying that they had set off the bombs in this building."

"If the bombings happened only in our building, why can't we use our cell phones?" Heidi asked.

"There's also no Internet, which doesn't make sense for bombs in just one building," the medium-tone voice said.

"The thieves probably used some kind of electronic blocking devices," Kate said.

"I know about those devices," the low-tone voice said. "They're actually used more often in other countries."

Heidi said, "Okay, I think it's time to block out the bad smells again." A soft spraying sound came from inside the hill. After about ten seconds, Kate noticed a flowery smell.

"Did you just spray perfume in your elevator?"

"Yeah, I did. It helps to hide the dusty smell in here, at least for a little while."

"That's a great idea. If I get to another elevator, I'll see if anyone else has some perfume."

"A little while ago, you said something about telling me stories of people in other elevators. Have you found any other elevators yet?" Heidi asked.

"Yes, I've found people who are stuck in seven other elevators. I was able to give them all some food, water, or both."

"What are the other elevators like?"

"All the people are upset, and they're acting in different ways. Because of the different people, activities, and elevator locations, each elevator seems to have its own culture."

"That's interesting. What are people doing inside these elevators?"

"In one elevator, two people are kissing each other. Also, people who have books are reading a lot."

"Do you have a book to read too?"

"Yeah, I do. I've been reading it at night."

"What's happening in the other elevators?"

"In one elevator, the people are sharing photos and stories. They took photos from their billfolds and taped them to their elevator's walls. These photos made the silver metal walls look so much nicer than any of the other elevators' walls. The people also have been telling stories to each other about the pictures."

"Oh, we're really completely bored in here. That's something that we could do too if only we had some tape."

The low-tone voice said, "We don't have any tape."

Heidi said, "We could still show each other our photos and tell stories about them."

The low-tone voice said, "No, we can't do that. We'd have to keep our flashlight on for too long. You know we don't have any extra batteries."

"Maybe we could just tell stories, rather than even looking at pictures."

"You can tell us about your family, if you really want to, but I don't want to say anything about my family and my background."

Heidi cleared her throat, sounding as if she knew the real reason why he wanted to keep information about himself hidden.

Kate suggested, "You don't have to tell stories about yourselves. You could always tell stories about your neighbors and friends."

The people inside the hidden elevator were quiet, hiding their thoughts from Kate. She said, "Some people in other elevators were listening to music, dancing, and exercising."

241

"Physical activity sounds like fun," Heidi said.

Kate smiled. "You should just be careful not to jump around too much."

"Why must we be careful? Do you know something that we don't? Are there bombs near our elevator?"

"As far as I know, there aren't any nearby bombs, but the building has partially fallen down. You don't want to dislodge any essential parts of your elevator."

"How can we exercise without moving around?"

Kate said, "You could sit down and just move your arms around."

Heidi said, "I'd really prefer something more aerobic, like jumping jacks."

The low-tone voice sounded upset as it said, "No, Heidi, you're not going to jump around inside this place. It really wouldn't be safe. We can all wait until we're rescued for jumping up and down."

Heidi asked, "What if we can jump a little bit and make the hill fall off our elevator? Then Kate might be able to get inside and give us some food and water." A jumping sound escaped from the elevator and was heard by Kate.

The low-tone voice yelled, "Stop that!"

"No, I won't! We need some food and water. If we have to wait much longer to be rescued, we probably won't even be alive." Several more jumping sounds were heard.

"We need to stay safe until we're rescued. If you don't stop that, I'll make you stop it!"

"If we're under a hill, as well as being inside this elevator, how will first responders even find us?" Two more jumping sounds happened.

A punching sound was heard, followed by no more jumping sounds.

Kate asked, "Heidi, are you okay?"

Everyone was silent.

"Heidi?"

Some mumbling sounds came from inside the hidden elevator.

"Do you two gentlemen know if Heidi is okay?"

The low-tone voice said, "Of course she's okay. She's just trying to be quiet, so she doesn't upset us."

Kate asked, "Heidi, if you're really okay, please say something to me."

When no one said anything, Kate's facial expression and angry voice showed how upset she was. "Tell me the truth, you two men. Who hurt Heidi, and is she still alive?"

Murmurs within the hidden elevator were followed by the low-tone voice saying loudly, "We're all okay in here. Why don't you just leave us alone?"

"I'm trying to escape from this building. As soon as I get out, I'll tell the first responders where you are and what happened to Heidi."

"You don't have our names, but we have yours. We also know where you work, so it might be a good idea for you to just leave us alone." The low-tone voice sounded strong and threatening.

Kate took a step backward and sat down. She started softly crying.

"Are you still there?" the low-tone voice asked.

Kate inhaled, cleared her throat, and then said, "Yeah, I'm still here. I'm not going to be quiet about this though. You can threaten me all you want to, but I'll still be telling the first responders about your behaviors. Some things just shouldn't be hidden."

"There are two of us, plus Heidi, who will side with us. There's only one of you. We can sue you for wrongly accusing us of criminal activity."

Kate stood up. "Okay, I'm leaving."

"Are you going to behave yourself?"

Kate laughed. "What about you? Are you going to start behaving yourself? I'm guessing that you've done this kind of thing before."

"I'm not going to tell you—or anyone else—about my background."

Kate laughed again. "Now I know why you're trying to hide information about yourself. It's not because you're shy like Heidi. It's rather because you don't want anyone to call the cops."

"You should know enough then to leave me alone."

"No, I won't. Too many disasters have happened because people try to ignore or just hide from criminal activity. Look at what happened during the Holocaust. While some people acted correctly and helped Jewish families, too many other people just did nothing. I'm never going to be a person who will just do nothing." Kate's loud voice showed her anger.

"Good-bye to you in more ways than one," the low-tone voice said.

Kate picked up her backpack. "I'm leaving now. As soon as I can escape from this building, I'll be sending the police after you." She turned around and moved across the walkway. After passing by the elevator shaft with the broken ladder, she kept on walking. Finally, she found another shaft and started climbing up its ladder.

ELEVATING TO FREEDOM

O n the twenty-third floor, Kate paused, stepped out onto a walkway, and pulled out the map from her backpack. She drew in squares to show the locations for the last couple of elevators that she had visited. According to the map, the ventilation shaft began at the top of a closet that was just outside this elevator shaft. Kate looked around. There was a wooden door about six feet to her left. She moved horizontally across the walkway and looked above the door into a closet. A four-foot wide circular metal shaft was at the top of the closet. The hatch had its own door with a rusty handle.

Kate jumped upward and tried to push against the ventilation shaft's door. However, the shaft was more than seven feet above the ground, so she was unable to even touch its door. She looked around, trying to find something to stand on, but only her backpack was visible. Finally, she stared at the closet door and said, "Oh, maybe the closet has a chair or something else to stand on."

Kate's hand reached out and turned the handle. The door was unlocked, but its top was touching the ventilation shaft's metal. As Kate slowly opened the door, it made a loud scratching sound. Once the door was open enough for her to step inside, she paused for a few seconds while carefully looking around and listening for other noises. She then said sarcastically, "Thank you, thieves, for being more interested in stealing things than in following me around this building."

Inside the closet, Kate immediately saw a four-foot high ladder. It was a perfect size for helping her climb up into the ventilation shaft. She pulled the ladder out of the closet, closed the closet's door, and then set up the ladder beneath the ventilation shaft. Looking at her backpack, she almost picked it up and then just left it on the ground as she climbed up the ladder. When she reached the top step, she pulled at the metal door's rusty handle, but it would not open. She went back down the ladder, took out the small knife from her backpack, climbed back up to the metal handle, and chipped away some of its rust. It still would not open.

Kate went back down the ladder to the ground and threw her knife at the metal handle. After several tries, she was able to hit the shaft's handle with her knife. However, she still could not move the handle and open up the hatch.

Kate went into the closet and sat down on the floor before taking out some peanut butter and crackers from her backpack. After dipping one of the crackers into the peanut butter, her hand froze. She looked at the peanut butter, smiled, and put some onto the edge of her knife. After climbing up the ladder again, she rubbed the peanut butter on the hatch's handle. She waited for a minute and then wiped it off with a tissue. Pushing on the handle, she was finally able to open it up.

The interior of the ventilation shaft seemed even darker than the closet and other parts of the building. Kate shined her flashlight into the shaft; its silver metal inclined upward. At least in this section of the shaft, the incline was not too extreme, so most people would be able to easily crawl upward inside the shaft.

However, Kate was not like most people. She stood on top of the step ladder and just stared at the walls of the metal circular shaft. She shined her flashlight as far forward as the light would reach. She then said out loud, "These walls are not wide enough for me or anyone else. In the distance, they're just closing in on each other." The light from her flashlight moved backward until it was shining on the metal wall section right next to Kate. She ran her left hand along the left side of the shaft. "This metal is too cold and slippery."

Kate slowly moved down the step ladder, which was twitching slightly from her nervous motions. Finally, she was on the ground again, but her breathing was still speeded up. Her heart was racing, and her face was red. Sighing, she put the peanut butter, crackers, and knife into her backpack. Before she closed the zipper on her backpack, her eyes stared at her Bible. She then prayed, "Please help me, Lord. I need to go through that narrow metal doorway, so I can help other people. If I escape, I can tell the police about the other bombs. I can also help them find the people who are stuck in elevators. In Jesus's name I pray, Amen."

Kate spent the next few seconds slowing her fast breathing by deeply inhaling and exhaling. She then picked up her backpack, climbed up the ladder, and entered the ventilation shaft. After moving forward for only a minute, she stopped crawling and put her cold hands into the pockets of her slacks. She rested for a minute before pulling her hands out and starting to crawl again. However, the metal was still too cold. She stopped, opened up her backpack, took out some gloves from her purse, and put them on. She then continued to move along the silver metal of the ventilation shaft. After every fifteen or twenty feet, the inclining shaft was turning to the right. Its path was shaped like a hill that was circling around the center of the building.

After crawling through four of the turns, Kate found a secondary shaft that was connected to the main ventilation shaft. She shined her flashlight up into the smaller shaft. Its incline was at a bigger angle, and its metal was moving upward in a nearly vertical fashion. She took out her map, looked for this secondary shaft, and did not see it anywhere. She shined her light back into the main shaft and began crawling along its cold metal surface again. After moving for only a few feet, she again stopped. She had heard some noises coming from below her current position. They sounded like the scratching noises that she herself had made when opening and closing the closet door against the ventilation shaft's metal.

Someone was also talking, but she only heard the word "turn."

Kate's breathing speeded up. She slowly inhaled and exhaled, but her breathing was still too fast. She loudly sighed and then moved backward until she arrived at the secondary shaft. She stood up with her head and back inside the smaller, vertical shaft. She then pressed her back against the metal of the three-foot-wide shaft. Placing her hands and feet on the opposite side of the curving shaft, she pushed herself upward again and again until she was at least ten feet away from the primary shaft. She then turned off her flashlight and tried to slow down her fast breathing. Before she was able to breathe normally, she could hear the noise of a backpack or some other item being moved along the primary ventilation shaft.

The voice of Larry, one of the thieves, asked, "Why was that ladder out in front of the ventilation shaft?"

"Don't blame me for messing up. I know I put it into the closet, just like you told me to do."

"Who else would have been moving the ladder around, besides one of us?"

"Anything's possible in such a big building. Someone in one of the offices may have needed the ladder and then didn't bother to put it away."

Larry sighed. "You're probably right."

"I'm so sick of breaking the walls inside this building."

"So am I. Anyway, we'll be out of this place in about fifteen minutes."

"Hopefully, no one will see us leaving."

"I doubt people will be looking at the roof."

"I really wanted to find that jewelry."

"So did I," Larry said. "Well, at least we have some social security numbers and credit card information."

"How much money will we get when you sell them?"

"We might get around $10,000."

"That'll be a little bit nice."

"Yeah, we'll also be able to keep looking for that jewelry."

"Where will we be looking next?"

"The building across the street has new walls built over the old ones too. We should check out that one."

"Does that building have a jewelry store somewhere?"

"Yeah, it does."

Henry's voice sounded far away as he said, "Well, if we don't find the old jewelry again, we can at least get some nice saleable new items."

Kate could not hear Harry's response, probably because they both had maneuvered around the next turn in the primary ventilation shaft. She waited another ten minutes and then moved back down into the main ventilation shaft. She slowly moved forward, trying not to make any noise and being careful to point her flashlight down onto the floor immediately in front of herself.

After about five minutes, some cold air blew onto Kate's face. She said softly to herself, "Larry and Henry must have just left the ventilation shaft." She continued to move forward and upward through the shaft. When she reached the roof of the building, she saw a blue sky with clouds through the partially open door of the shaft. Holding her breath, she peeked through the opening. She could not see anyone. She pushed the door fully open, climbed out onto the roof, and blinked her eyes in the sunlight.

Kate's eyes soon became used to the light. She then noticed two men who were standing on one of the back corners of the building. They were too far away for Kate to see if they were Larry and Henry, but she slowly moved away from them. She stood behind a large triangular-shaped metal vent. After waiting for a few minutes, she peered around the edge of the vent. The two men were no longer on the roof. She walked over to where they had been standing. The lights from police vehicles partially lit up the outside of the building. A series of fire escape ladders and platforms were below her. As she watched, she noticed some motion on one of the platforms. Two men were using the fire escape ladders to climb down the back of the building. They were about halfway to the ground.

Kate went over to the right side of the building. Here, also, were some fire escape ladders. She began climbing down. After she had moved down several flights, she stopped on a metal platform and started screaming, "Help!"

At least ten police officers and firemen looked upward toward her voice. One of the firemen and two of the police officers began climbing upward on the ladders. She yelled, "Two thieves were climbing down over there." Her right hand waved toward the back of the building.

One of the police officers frowned as he watched her hand motions. He then put a device close to his mouth and talked into it. Kate was too far away to hear his actual words, but at least five police officers immediately started to run around to the back of the building.

As Kate waited for the fireman and police officers to get up to her platform, her eyes kept moving back and forth along the street in front of the building. Suddenly, her eyes froze on a minivan. It was several buildings away, but it looked like the same gray minivan that Larry and Henry had been standing next to while she was running away from them in Roger Williams Park. As she watched, two men got into the van, and it started to move down the road.

Kate yelled, "Stop that gray minivan! It's where the thieves are."

On the fire escape ladders, one of the police officers climbing upward toward her stopped moving and spoke into his two-way radio. On the street in front of the Pilgrim building, several police officers jumped into their cruisers and drove after the minivan. A moment later, Kate realized that the fireman who was climbing toward her was moving unusually quickly; he would be the first man to arrive on her platform. As she watched, she noticed the man was moving his shoulders like Thomas Hart did. The helmet was hiding his face, but Kate still yelled out, "Tom!"

He was several levels below her as he looked upward and smiled. His eyes remained on her face as he kept on jumping upward two steps at a time. When he had finally reached her level on the metal platform, he took three more steps forward before asking, "Kate, are you okay?"

"Yeah, I am. How are you?"

"Now that I've found you, I'm okay. I was so worried."

"I've been worried about you too, Tom. I assumed that you would be one of the first responders, and I was really worried about another bomb going off and hurting you."

"We've been using bomb-sniffing dogs, and I think we've found the locations for all the remaining bombs."

"There are still people alive in some of the elevators."

"Yeah, we've been assuming that a good number of people are still alive."

"Will you be rescuing people before or after the bombs are deactivated?"

"We're planning on searching for survivors and carefully rescuing everyone. Then the bombs will be removed for deactivation."

Kate extended her right hand out softly toward Tom's left arm. He took a step forward so that he was only a few inches away from her. Her hand moved upward and touched his left shoulder. Tom put his right hand behind her back, moved her closer, and softly kissed her forehead. She looked up into his eyes before kissing him softly on his lips.

Noises were being made by a couple of police officers who were climbing up the ladder's steps. When they were right below the platform where Kate and Tom were located, their noises increased; the officers sounded like they were trying to make some loud noises on purpose. As Kate and Tom kissed again, the two police officers stepped up onto the same level on the metal ladder. One of the officers cleared his throat. The other one sighed really loudly. Tom stopped kissing Kate, but he still held onto her hand.

The throat-clearing officer asked, "Are you okay, ma'am?"

"I'm fine," Kate said. She looked at the police officers who were now standing right in back of Tom and laughed.

"What's so funny?" the throat-clearing officer asked her.

"This platform is getting as crowded as an elevator."

All four of them laughed together. Then Kate said, "We should go up to the roof, so I can show you the ventilator shaft."

Tom said, "No, you have to climb back down to the ground with me. I'll be able to help you in case any problems happen."

"Why can't I help rescue people?"

Tom smiled. "I think it's so wonderful that you want to help others, but you've been through a lot."

"I'm okay. I go to exercise classes often, so I'm physically healthy."

"You might be dehydrated or have some other problem." Tom gently squeezed her right hand. "I want you to be safe."

"I can stay out of your way and still help. I know about the inside of the building."

"We have lots of diagrams of the Pilgrim building."

"Yeah, but I'm the only one who knows about how some of it has changed since the bombings."

Tom shook his head in a negative way. The two police officers whispered together; then the loud-sighing officer sent a text message to someone.

Kate asked Tom, "How about if I just show you the correct ventilation shaft to use?"

"Are you talking about a shaft on the roof?"

"Yeah."

"What exactly do you know about the building's safety?"

"The thieves said there are bombs set to go off if people enter some of the entrances, exits, and large windows."

Tom looked at the two police officers. Their expressions showed that they already knew this information.

Kate said, "They also said something about the bomb-sniffing dogs, so they know you're trying to get into the building."

"Do you know how many bombs there are?"

"I don't know that, but I do know which ventilation shaft is safe. I can also show you the places where I went in the building. These places did not blow up, at least not while I was there, so they will probably all be fairly safe." Kate paused for a moment before adding, "The hidden elevator though should be approached carefully."

"Where is it hidden?"

"It's under a hill of fallen debris. There were at least three people inside, and one of them, Heidi, was hurt or killed by one of the men in the elevator with her. The man also threatened me if I told anyone about what had happened."

"We'll have you file a police report."

"Also, the area near the fallen elevator might be unsafe."

"There's a fallen elevator?"

"Yeah, I think at least one person in that elevator was seriously injured."

"Do you know how many people were killed?"

"I don't know for sure if anyone died. However, I did see that one elevator fall down. There were four people in that elevator." Kate looked down at the ground as tears formed in her eyes.

Tom said, "Those people might all still be alive."

"I really hope they're okay. I've actually prayed for them multiple times."

Tom touched Kate's chin. She looked up into his caring eyes as he said, "Prayer works."

"Yes, I know that it does." Kate smiled and then added, "Jesus said, 'Truly I tell you, if you say to this mountain, "Be taken up and thrown into the sea," and if you do not doubt in your heart, but believe that what you say will come to pass, it will be done for you. So I tell you, whatever you ask for in prayer, believe that you have received it, and it will be yours' (Mark 11:23–24, RSV)."

"That's one of my favorite Bible verses."

"Actually, it's two Bible verses." Kate looked up toward the top of the building. "Besides praying, I can also help the trapped elevator people by showing you the safe ventilation shaft."

"Is that the one you used to get out of the building?"

"Yeah, I'm a little bit claustrophobic, but I crawled through multiple elevator shafts and two ventilation shafts okay."

Tom's eyes widened. "A lot of people are claustrophobic. I also know you really dislike elevators. Luckily, you weren't trapped inside one of them."

Kate smiled. "I think talking to the people who were stuck in elevators helped me to become less claustrophobic. I found out that people really can live—at least temporarily—in such a small space."

"Talking to people in elevators must have been interesting."

"It was. I also gave them food, water, and other items. The different elevators had some of the same activities, but also different activities and unique rules."

"Once we've rescued everyone, you'll have to tell me more about the elevator cultures that you encountered."

"I will, definitely." Kate looked at Tom's face and asked, "So can I show you the safe ventilation shaft—the one that I used?"

Tom turned around and looked at the two police officers. The cleared-throat officer said, "It should be okay if she just shows us which shaft she used."

Tom said, "By looking at a map of the building's interior, Kate, can you show us the safe ventilation shaft?"

"I might be able to help with some things by looking at a diagram; however, I don't know if I can figure out which of the two rooftop shafts is safe by just looking at a map. I think I need to actually be on the roof."

"Are you feeling well enough to climb back up onto the roof?"

"Yeah, I am." Kate turned around and grabbed onto one of the ladder's rungs.

Tom was still holding onto her hand. He said, "I'll go first. You can follow me, and the two officers will follow you."

"Okay." Kate followed Tom as he started to climb up the ladders. On every platform, they all stopped for a moment to make certain that Kate was okay. When they arrived at the roof, Tom helped Kate to climb up over the top edge. She immediately ran over to a ventilation shaft, opened it up, and jumped inside. Behind her, Tom yelled, "Kate, no, you can't go in there."

Kate did not stop, but instead kept on pushing herself down the slope of the ventilation shaft. When she reached the place where the smaller vent went upward, she said loudly, "There's a smaller vent right here, Tom. I actually hid in this vent for a while."

"Kate, please wait for me."

"I'll wait when I get to the opening of this vent."

"Where will it open up?"

"Not too much further, it'll open up right above a closet."

By the time Kate pushed open the ventilation shaft's door, Tom was right behind her. She looked down at the step ladder and said, "I think they knocked the ladder over."

"Who knocked over the ladder?"

"After I got into this ventilation shaft, the thieves escaped in the same way. I had to hide from them in that smaller vent. After they passed by me, then I escaped. As far as I know, those thieves were the last ones who stood on that ladder." Kate opened the shaft's metal door even wider and started to slide off the edge of the shaft.

Tom grabbed onto her arm, so she was unable to jump down. He said, "Just wait a minute, Kate. If something's different, we need to go back up onto the roof."

"I'm sure we'll be okay. The thieves didn't have enough time to do anything over here like set up another bomb." Kate turned her head around and smiled at Tom. When he loosened his grip on her arm, she pushed herself forward and jumped out of the shaft.

She landed on her feet and then fell down onto her hands and knees. After a few seconds, she stood up, turned around, and said, "I'm fine, Tom. Here, I'll set up the ladder for you."

"No, there's a bomb! Don't touch that ladder!" Tom's light was shining on one of the ladder's steps.

Kate took a step backward and moved the beam from her flashlight along the length of all the ladder's steps. "You're right. There is something funny here." Under the second step of the ladder was a small box with a wire.

"Okay, Kate, if you can move backward a few steps, I'll jump over to where you landed. First, I'll just need to send a text to the other responders about this step ladder." After he sent a text message, he jumped beyond the ladder and stood up next to Kate. He then took a few pictures of the box and texted them to some other people.

Suddenly, the ventilation shaft's door opened up, and the loud-sighing police officer jumped down from the shaft. He landed right next to the step ladder. Tom said, "Stay away from that ladder."

The officer looked closely at the ladder's box. He then took a folded-up container out of his backpack and placed it on top of the step ladder. "That should keep people off the ladder. I'll have someone bring down another one for us to use."

A minute after the officer sent a text message, the throat-clearing officer jumped out of the ventilation shaft and joined them in the area near the closet and the covered-up step ladder.

Tom turned to Kate and asked, "Exactly how many elevators did you find with people inside them?"

"I only found eight elevators with people. One of the elevators was hidden beneath debris, so it might be tough to find it again. There were also a few elevators with no one inside them."

"Did you see any people outside the elevators?"

"I only noticed the two thieves. I think most people had already left the building to go home for the day. Just the people leaving later than four o'clock were stuck in the elevators."

"How come you weren't in an elevator?"

"I'm a little bit nervous inside elevators, so I was trying to go down the stairs yesterday when the bombs went off." Kate paused for a moment before asking, "Some of the people near the bottom of the building probably used the stairs, instead of the elevators. Do you know if any of them were hurt?"

Tom said, "Because of the timing, it's possible that most of the people on the bottom floors had already exited the building."

The loud-sighing officer said, "About ten minutes after several bombs on upper floors exploded, a bomb went off in the building's lobby. It's possible the thieves tried to plan things so that people wouldn't be hurt."

Kate told the officers about the conversations that she had heard.

The throat-clearing police officer said, "It sounds like they were trying to kill at least one person. It's more likely the thieves planned on entering the building while other people were exiting."

Tom said to the throat-clearing officer, "I think you're right. The thieves would have timed things with their own needs in mind."

Kate said, "From the little I know about these thieves, they always try to please themselves. Plus, when I was in Roger Williams Park, they tried to kill me."

Tom said, "I was told about that incident. I'm so glad you managed to escape."

Kate started walking forward. Tom grabbed onto her hand and said, "Kate, you have to let me do my job."

She looked at Tom and asked, "How am I keeping you from doing your job?"

"I'm supposed to keep civilians like you safe."

"You are keeping me safe."

"No, I need to help you to get out of this building. Together, we can go through the ventilation shaft again."

"Who's going to rescue the elevator people?"

"These two police officers can start rescuing people." Tom took off his tool belt, helmet, and a backpack. He gave them to the two officers and then said, "These items should help."

The loud-sighing officer said, "You need your helmet."

"The extra light in my helmet will help you to rescue people more quickly."

The officer sighed loudly and then said, "Okay."

Kate said, "Tom and I should stay and help. More than two rescuers are needed."

Tom squeezed Kate's hand as he said to her, "If we go back to the roof, we can show some more police officers and firemen which ventilation shaft is the safe one. Then there will be more than two officers rescuing people."

"Okay. Let me first show you on a map where I think the elevator people are located." She took out her map; at the same time, Tom pulled a larger better map out of his pocket. They compared the maps and decided to use Tom's. Kate showed him where the elevators were located. While Tom put circles on his map to indicate possible locations of the elevators, the two police officers added circles to their own maps. Then he and Kate went back into the ventilator shaft, climbed through to the roof, and met some first responders. Kate climbed out of the vent and smiled at the brightness of the sunlight, despite the fact that her eyes were blinking in its brightness.

Tom explained what he knew about the interior of the building. Some of the other firemen looked at the circles on Tom's map and drew similar ones onto their own versions of the map. Tom and Kate then moved over to the side of the building as more than ten first responders entered the ventilation shaft.

Tom's cell phone rang. He answered it by saying "Hi." After listening for a moment, he said, "Okay." As he put his cell phone back into his pocket, Kate said, "Oh, your cell phone is working."

"Yeah." Tom inhaled and then said, "Your cell phone should work okay now too."

"Inside the building, no one's cell phone was working. I thought maybe someone had blown up some cell phone towers."

"The thieves placed a device that was blocking Internet access and cell phone usage, but the device was deactivated just a little while ago."

When Tom took a step toward the escape ladders and platforms on the side of the building, Kate said, "Before we go down the fire escape again, can I use my cell phone? I need to tell my mom that I'm okay."

"You should definitely call your mom, but try to keep the phone call short for right now. We should get off this rooftop." Tom paused and then added, "Here, you can use my cell phone."

"Thanks." Kate dialed her mom's number. It only rang one time before her mom said, "Hello."

"Hi, Mom. It's so wonderful to hear your voice."

"Kate! I was so worried about you."

"I'm fine, Mom. I'm not hurt or anything."

"I know you were inside the bombed building. Have you been rescued, so you're safe now?"

"Yeah, I'm outside the building with a really nice fireman." Kate smiled at Tom. She then continued, "I'll have to hang up right now, though, because I need to get further away from this building to be safer."

"Okay. You have to come over to where I'm at."

"Where are you, Mom?"

"I'm a couple of blocks away in the statehouse. The governor said that family members could meet here, if they wanted to."

"That was so nice of the governor."

"Yeah, it was. The police can bring you over here. Then we can eat here, or I can just drive you right over to my house for some food and rest."

"Okay, I'll get to the statehouse as soon as possible." Kate said good-bye to her mom. Tom then let her use his cell phone to call some of the people in the broken building's elevators. She told them about the first responders being on their way to rescue everyone. After giving Tom back his cell phone, she followed him down the series of ladders and platforms.

When they arrived on the sidewalk next to the building, a man walked up to them. "Hi, you're Kate Odyssey, right?"

"Yes, I am."

"I'll drive you over to see your mom."

Tom looked at the man and asked, "Who are you?"

"I'm Ted. I'm with Homeland Security." He showed his badge to Kate and Tom.

A lady's voice began to yell from the top of the Pilgrim building. Kate's eyes lifted toward the building's roof; a lady was standing near the edge, yelling, and waving her hands.

Kate said, "That voice sounds like the lady who was yelling inside of one of the elevators."

Tom's cell phone rang. After listening and saying "Okay," he looked over at Kate. "I need to help that screaming lady. I'll be back in just a few minutes." He then ran toward one of the fire engines and started to remove some equipment.

The Homeland Security man said, "I think he'll be more than a few minutes. Now might be a good time to go see your mom. I can drive you there."

Kate looked over at Tom, hesitated, and then smiled. "I'd love to see my mom. I can send Tom a text message."

Ted waved his hand toward the parking area. He led Kate to a black sedan with a police officer's push bumper on the front. He held open one of the doors, and she got into the backseat. After he sat down in the driver's seat, they both put on their seat belts. Kate sent a quick text message to Tom as Ted started up the car and pulled away from the curb.

Kate asked, "How many relatives are waiting in the statehouse?"

"Why are people in the statehouse?"

She stared at Ted intently before asking, "Why don't you know about people in the statehouse?"

Ted said, "I love this song." He then turned up the sound of "Get Me Out of Here" by Paul McCartney on the radio. He started humming along with the line "Feels like we're all involved in some kind of game."[63]

Her face looked surprised. "Can I see your badge again?"

Ted ignored her question. At the next intersection, there was a stop sign, but he drove right through without stopping. A couple of blocks later, he had to slow down for a red light and to avoid hitting other cars.

Kate grabbed onto the door handle with her left hand and tried to open it, but the door was locked. She looked in her purse for the small knife. It was no longer there. "Oh, it's in the backpack," she said loudly.

"What's in the backpack?"

"So you really can hear me."

"Yeah, I just turned down the sound of the radio."

"Oh, you're right. You actually did that." Kate paused and then asked, "Where are we going?"

"We'll be stopping in just a minute." A block later, an intersection was closed off by six patrol cars. Ted stopped the car, took off his seat belt, and said, "Let's get out."

Kate grabbed the door handle. It was working now. She got out of the car, and Ted stood behind her; something was resting on her back. "Is that your hand or a gun?"

He said, "Relax. You'll be okay. In a few minutes, you'll even be able to go and visit your mom."

A police officer came up to them and said, "This area is closed off."

Ted said, "Not to us, it isn't." He quickly waved his badge at the officer and then turned it around before Kate could see what kind of a badge it was. Then Ted pointed toward a police car with two people in the backseat. "We just need to talk to those persons of interest for a minute."

"Okay." The officer walked over to the car and opened up the backdoor. The two backseat occupants had handcuffs on. Ted asked the officer, "Did they have guns?"

"Yeah, they both did."

Ted looked at Kate and waved one of his hands toward the car. She slowly walked over to the police car. When she stopped to look inside, she recognized Larry and Henry. "Oh, it's you two."

The familiar voice of Larry asked her, "How did you escape?"

"I crawled through that giant vent."

"Were you following us?"

She shook her head sideways and tried to say no, but her voice only said the word after she had moved her lips a couple of times.

"You're lying," Larry said.

"Well, I did hear someone in the vent, but I didn't actually see you."

Larry squinted his eyes before asking, "How do you even know us?"

"I work in the New World Bank. We met there."

"Do you also like to run around Roger Williams Park?" Larry asked. He stared at Kate's face.

She glanced at the ground, cleared her throat, and said, "Sometimes."

"You really do like to lie, don't you?"

Kate looked angrily at Larry. "No, I don't like to lie. I also only lie when I have to. People like yourself are the ones who like to lie."

"I've never lied to you."

"Yes, you have."

"When did I lie?"

Kate thought for a few seconds and then said, "I forgot, but you've hidden the truth from me. That's lying."

"Speaking of hidden truths, did you find anything while running around the Pilgrim building?" Larry was staring at her face again. Henry, Ted, and three police officers also stared at Kate's face.

She swallowed a couple of times and then tried to make her facial expression appear angry as she said, "I found lots of people who were stuck in elevators." After pausing, she added, "One of the elevators even fell down into its shaft. The four people inside probably died."

Everyone was quiet for a moment. Larry then asked, "What else did you find?"

"There were closets, rooms, corridors, ventilation vents, and debris all over the place."

"So you didn't find any of the remaining bombs?"

"No, I was just trying to escape, but I heard you say something about a backup plan. Were you going to use your guns to kidnap or to kill people?"

Larry stared at her with a surprised look on his face. "How did you possibly know?"

Kate laughed. "I didn't know for sure. I was just guessing, but now the police officers here have heard of your intent to kidnap and/or murder innocent bystanders."

Larry asked, "How about what you were doing in that building? Did you find anything interesting, like missing jewelry?"

Kate tried to keep her face expressionless and to not look down at the ground. After thinking for a moment, she said, "I made some new friends. I also learned a lot about Roger Williams and the wonders of freedom."

"I think the people trapped in the elevators learned more about freedom than you did," Larry said.

Kate looked at Larry and Henry before laughing. "Freedom is one thing you two will not know about for a long time."

Larry frowned. "I'm not guilty until a court system has proven me guilty."

"There's more than enough evidence to prove you're guilty. A lawyer will probably even make you plead guilty, so you can try and avoid the death penalty."

Ted's cell phone rang. He listened for a minute and then said, "Okay." After putting his cell phone back into his pocket, he said to one of the police officers, "I have to leave. Can you take Kate to see her mom?"

"Where's her mom?"

Kate responded, "She's in the statehouse with some other relatives of people who were stuck in the elevators."

The police officer said, "Okay." Ted then got into his car, turned it around, and went back down the street.

Another police officer came up to Kate and asked, "Where's Ted?"

Kate pointed down the street. "He went that way and then turned right." The officer conveyed the information into his cell phone, got into a patrol car, and drove off in the same direction as Ted had gone.

Kate turned to Larry and asked, "Is Ted one of your crime buddies?"

"No, of course he's not."

"Maybe he actually does work for the Department of Homeland Security."

One of the police officers said, "He was checked out. He doesn't work there, but he does work for one of this country's federal agencies."

"Oh, so he was lying, but he's probably trustworthy," Kate said. After looking at the police officer's name tag, she asked, "Charles, could you take me to see my mom?"

"Yeah, I can right now." He closed the backdoor of the car containing Larry and Henry. He then explained, "If you want to talk to Larry and Henry some more, Kate, you can try to see them at their trial."

"I'd rather not talk to them anymore." Kate thought for a moment and then added, "If I have to be a witness at their trial, though, I'll definitely be there."

"That's so great! I wish everyone was like you and willing to help out with our justice system."

"Thanks."

Charles walked over to an empty patrol car, opened up the backdoor, and motioned for Kate to come over and sit down. Kate hesitated and then said, "Can I sit in the front seat?"

"Of course you can. Normally, it's safer in the backseat, but I know you're nervous after your experience with Ted." After Kate got into the car and it started moving, she called her mom to apologize for taking so long to get to the statehouse. "I'll be there soon, Mom."

Rhode Island State House, Providence, Rhode Island

Interior Marble Stairway in the Rhode Island State House

Wall and Rotunda in the Rhode Island State House

Elevators in the Rhode Island State House

An Elevated
Community

───────◉───────

A few minutes later, the police car pulled up in front of the Rhode Island State House. Charles and Kate got out and crossed the street. A lady was standing on the sidewalk and smoking a cigarette. As Kate walked up closer to her, the lady turned around. Kate smiled and said, "Hi, Tina."

Charles was watching Kate as he said, "I'm guessing you two know each other."

Tina shook their hands. "We met while I was stuck inside an elevator." Tina put the cigarette in her mouth, inhaled deeply, and exhaled noisily before adding, "Now, I'm free and can smoke as much as I want to."

Kate said, "You're a really nice person. You should try to quit, so you'll live longer."

Tina said, "Thanks for saying that I'm nice. People usually call me more negative things because I smoke."

Kate smiled. "No one's perfect. I think I told you before that I'm an ex-smoker."

"Yes, when I was in the elevator, you helped me to feel a little better by saying that." After pausing, Tina asked, "Are you really an ex-smoker?"

"Of course I am. There are also other ways that I've messed up my life."

Charles said, "I'm not perfect either. The Bible says, 'all have sinned and fall short of the glory of God' (Rom. 3:23, rsv)."

"Back when I was a smoker, I had a low opinion about myself. After I quit, my confidence became much higher."

Tina asked, "How did you quit?"

"I practiced quitting before actually quitting. That's how I figured out what behaviors I had to change in order to quit."

"Besides not smoking cigarettes, what other behaviors did you have to change?"

"I substituted different activities. For example, I always wanted to smoke after eating. Instead of sitting there at the dining room table and thinking about smoking, as soon as I finished eating a meal, I immediately jumped up and did some kind of physical activity. The exercise was very helpful."

"That might work for me too. Thanks, Kate."

"I think getting some practice is the best technique. Then you'll have the chance to experiment with different activities that will help you to quit."

"Being in that elevator gave me some practice. Especially after our elevator fell down, I really tried not to smoke. I didn't want to hurt people who were already hurt."

"How is everybody doing now?"

"I think everyone's okay, but I'll be going into the statehouse in a few minutes to find out for sure. After you left the roof of our elevator, but before we were rescued, I got to the point where I was getting a little bit used to not smoking. The practice in that elevator will help me when I try to quit again."

"Are you really going to quit smoking?"

"I'm going to try, and hopefully, I'll be successful this time."

"That's so great! If you need my help, please call me or send me an e-mail." Kate pulled out some paper and a pen from her purse. She and Tina traded information and promised to become friends on Facebook.

Tina said, "Having a friend to help me will be so wonderful. I'll really have to quit now."

After saying good-bye, Kate and Charles walked across to the stairs, climbed upward, and went into the statehouse. They passed through security and paused to look up the stairs and into the interior of the statehouse. Kate said, "I love these marble stairs and columns."

"The lights here are really great too."

Kate followed Charles as he walked up some stairs and into a conference room.

Several groups of people were present. Closest to the door were the five people from the watery elevator: Mike, Jim, Joyce, Josh, and Janet. They were arranged like when they were initially standing inside their elevator: Mike was standing in the center of the group, and the other four people formed a square shape around him. Each person was holding onto a can of soda or a glass of wine. When Kate walked up to them, the five people rearranged themselves into a circle around her and Charles. After everyone was introduced, Kate asked, "Are you all okay? Did drinking that elevator water make any of you sick?"

Mike said, "We're all fine. We even have a little more space here in this conference room than we did in our elevator."

Kate said, "This room is a little bit crowded."

Mike smiled. "Even so, we have all chosen to be here. It's not exactly the same as being stuck in an elevator again. We have the freedom to leave, if we want to."

Charles said, "There are a lot of other rooms we can go to in the statehouse."

Mike said, "I'm having fun talking to everyone here. I'm also happy to be out of that elevator."

Kate asked, "Are you too warm?"

"No, I'm fine."

"Why's your shirt unbuttoned?"

"I just wanted my lungs to feel the fresh air that we have now."

Janet lifted up her right foot. "I took off my shoes. The heels were too high, and the soles were still a little bit damp from the water in that elevator."

Joyce said, "I only took off my makeup, but I sort of want to stay warm by keeping all my clothes on."

Everyone laughed. Kate looked at Josh and Jim. They both had removed their ties and unbuttoned the top two buttons on their shirts. She asked them, "Did you use your ties to help the first responders to rescue you?"

"No, we threw our ties out." Josh pointed to a wastepaper basket up against the wall. Kate walked over and looked inside. At least twenty ties were in the basket. She came back to the watery elevator group and asked, "So have a lot of people here decided not to wear ties anymore?"

Josh said, "I don't know about other people, but I'll still be wearing suits and ties a lot of the time. I just won't be wearing that one tie because it will remind me of being stuck inside an elevator."

Charles said, "It's great to see everyone so happy about being free."

Kate kicked her shoes off and then said, "I'm planning on starting a blog, so people who were stuck in those elevators can all meet up together in a month or two. If you want to write your e-mails on this list, I'll let you know what we're doing."

All five watery elevator people laughed at the same time. Kate's eyes began to appear wet with tears as she turned away and looked down at the floor.

Mike asked, "You don't really want to write up a list of people again, do you?"

"Yes, I definitely do. This time, though, I'm creating a list of people who want to get together with each other, rather than people who are being forced to be together."

Mike looked pensive and then said, "I think that's really a good idea. I was just laughing at you a minute ago because it appears that you keep on making lists of people. It's almost as if you're trying to get some more friends on Facebook."

Kate looked at Mike. "I like having a lot of friends, but they don't have to be all in one place, like on Facebook."

Mike reached out and gave Kate a hug. She hugged him back. She then smiled as she said, "If someone else wants to do a blog instead, I'd also be really happy with that."

Mike said, "I don't think anyone else wants to do all that work." He looked around at the other four people in his group. They all shook their heads side to side in a negative way. Mike then said, "I guess the work is all yours, Kate."

Everyone wrote down their e-mail addresses. Then Janet took the list over to other groups of people in the conference room. There were people from the accounting elevator, the liberty elevator, the fiery elevator, the falling elevator, and the sharing elevator. Each group looked over at Kate, laughed, and wrote their e-mail addresses onto the list.

Kate walked over to the four people from the accounting elevator. They were standing on the far right side of the room. When Kate asked them how they had been rescued, John explained how the first responders had first talked to them and then pried open the elevator's doors. Next, their elevator group had been escorted to an exit door of the fallen building and driven over to the statehouse.

Ellen said, "We've been discussing whether or not to sue the architects of that building. If we decide to do a class-action lawsuit, we'll definitely contact you about your participation."

"Thanks, Ellen," Kate said. "The people in your elevator were very helpful and intelligent. I know you will do a great job of researching what happened and trying to figure out what to do about the situation."

Kate warned them about the thieves wanting to kill John and possibly other people in his law office. She also told them about the police having the thieves in custody. "Because they're in jail, you're safe for right now. However, you might need to testify at their trial."

John said, "Thanks for letting us know about what's happening. With our jobs, we're always careful about criminals who might be mad at us. In this case, though, after the bombings in the Pilgrim building, those criminals are not likely to get out of jail for a really long time."

Ellen shook her head in agreement. "I'd be really happy to testify at their trial, and I'd love to actually see them in prison. A prison cell might look bigger than an elevator, but criminals have a lot less freedom than people in elevators do."

Kate waved good-bye and walked over to a different part of the room. Two people from the falling elevator, Joe and Debbie, were standing near a table with soda, bottled water, and wine on it. Kate helped herself to some bottled water and then asked, "How are you two feeling?"

Joe, her boss, said, "We're both fine. My knees were a little bit achy, but they're feeling better now."

Kate said, "I met Tina outside the statehouse. She was smoking, but she's going to come inside and say 'hi' to everyone."

"That's great." Joe looked at Debbie. "We were worried that she'd be mad at us because we didn't want her to smoke."

"I don't think she's mad. She's just addicted to cigarettes and needs the nicotine right now."

Debbie asked, "Are you okay, Kate?"

"I'm fine, and just so very happy to be safely out of that building. Do you know how Fred is? I heard he was unconscious. Is he still sick?"

Joe said, "He's sort of fine. He only has a few minor injuries, but his blood pressure is high, so he's staying in the hospital for a day or two until his cardio system is evaluated and hopefully improved."

"I was worried that he was going to die."

Joe said, "We were worried about him too."

"How about going to work? Will the bank be in a temporary building, or should I just stay home tomorrow?"

"I'll call you tonight and let you know for sure, but we'll almost definitely be open tomorrow in a different building."

A moment later, one of Kate's other colleagues from work, Sue, walked through the door of the conference room. After Sue and Kate hugged each other, Kate asked, "Were you stuck in any of the elevators, Sue, or did you get out of the building before the explosions?"

"I got stuck in an elevator."

"I found some of the elevators with people inside them, but I didn't find yours. Are you okay?"

"I'm fine, Kate. Initially in that elevator, I was really upset. However, by the second morning, I was starting to get used to living in an elevator. Then, I became really, really happy when the best police officer in the whole world rescued me." Sue smiled at Charles, who had just walked into the conference room.

Charles smiled back at Sue. He then walked up to her, knelt down, and said, "Sue, from the moment when I first met you, I have been in love with you. Every day, I have fallen more and more in love with you." He took a box out of his shirt pocket, opened it up, and held out an engagement ring. "Will you marry me?"

A giant smile formed on Sue's face as she reached out her left hand and let him put the ring onto her finger. She then said, "Yes, I will love to marry you. I want nothing better than to marry you and to always be with you."

"When would you like to get married?"

"I'll be so happy to marry you whenever you want to get married. I'll also be happy to have whatever kind of wedding ceremony will make you happy."

Charles said, "Many women love exotic, romantic weddings."

"I just want to be with you for the rest of my life. In fact, I'd prefer a small, inexpensive ceremony, but it has to be in my church or yours."

Charles gave Sue a kiss. He then checked his buzzing cell phone before saying, "I'll need to get back to work, but I'll call you later tonight."

"I'll be waiting for that call." Charles kissed Sue again and then left the conference room.

Sue's eyes remained glued to the conference room's door for several minutes after Charles was no longer visible. She then turned around and asked Kate, "Did you hear the good news?"

"Yes, I did. You're getting married."

Sue smiled. "That is great news, but I was thinking about everyone in the Pilgrim building being alive."

"Is that really true?"

"Yes, it is. So far, the first responders have found no dead people in the building. They've also stopped some potential problems from happening by turning off the gas. At least one pipe was leaking gas, but it's not doing that anymore."

"That's so great. Only multiple miracles could have kept everyone alive in that place, especially with such things as gas pipe leaks."

"Miracles happen a lot in our world."

Kate's eyes suddenly widened as she looked at the door of the conference room. Walking into the room were the tellers that she had laid off from the New World Bank's closed-down office. Lisa was in the front of the group. When she spotted Kate, Lisa speeded up and walked quickly over to Kate's location. Other bank tellers were right behind her. Everyone hugged each other, and Kate introduced all her colleagues from the closed branch to Sue, who was one of the Providence New World Bank employees.

Lisa said, "We were all so upset about what happened, but we're now so glad that you're alive, Kate."

Another one of the tellers said, "We're also so glad that you helped us with our resumes. Every single one of us now has a new job!"

Kate's eyes filled with tears at the same time as her smile appeared on her face. She said, "I've never been so happy before! Can you all see the tears of joy in my eyes?"

The group of colleagues all smiled broadly. Several of them now also had happy faces that included tears of joy in their eyes. Lisa said, "We've all sent requests for you to be added again into our groups of Facebook friends."

Kate could no longer control her tears of joy. She began crying noisily and then said, "I really love you all. What would I do without my friends?"

The group of tellers closed in around Kate, and everyone took turns giving her a hug. After Kate told them about what had happened to her in the fallen building, they all told Kate about their new jobs. When they noticed that the conference room was getting really crowded, Lisa said to Kate, "We should leave now, so more of the relatives coming to see their loved ones will be able to fit into this room."

"Thanks for coming. You all really made my day into a joyful one."

Lisa said, "We'll be posting on Facebook about having lunch together somewhere this weekend. You have to promise to come and see us, Kate."

"Of course I'll come, and thanks for inviting me."

Everyone waved good-bye, and then the group of tellers followed Lisa out of the conference room. Before Kate had a chance to look away from the conference room's door, she saw her mom standing there. She waved at her mom, who came into the room, went over to Kate, and hugged her. Kate and her mom walked over to a table with some food on it, filled their plates, and then sat down next to each other in one of the corners of the room.

Kate's mom said, "One of the first responders told me about all the wonderful things you were doing."

"What did the person say I was doing?"

"You were helping people stuck in elevators by selling, trading, and giving away food and water items. Connecting to people in this way must be so wonderful! Roger Williams, also, sold items to many different people. He set up a trading post in North Kingston. By trading with the colonists and the natives, he helped the different groups of people to become connected to each other. A more peaceful existence was possible because of these connections."

"Thanks, Mom. You're always so supportive of me." Kate told her mom about some of the elevator people she had met during her ordeal. She also pointed to the people if they were present in the conference room.

For a few minutes, Kate and her mom watched as several families were reunited. In one of the families, the lady had been trapped in an elevator all by herself with no food and no water. After her husband and children came into the room, they all hugged and kissed each other. Then they all held hands as she told them about her experience. The youngest child, who looked about four years old, was completely fascinated by her story. His eyes were shiny as he stared with admiration at his mom's face. When she talked about being hungry and thirsty, he suddenly let go of her hand, ran over to a table, and brought back some food and soda for her. She looked at her son and said, "I already had some of this wonderful food, but I'm still hungry. Thanks so much, Danny."

"You're welcome, Mom."

The lady's family members then took turns helping her by placing pieces of food between her smiling lips.

Kate said to her mom, "That little boy really admires his mom."

"Yes, he really does. He also seems to be such a helpful kid."

"It's so nice seeing family members support each other."

Kate's mom gave her a hug. They then started talking about Kate getting married someday and having children. Suddenly, Thomas Hart came into the conference room. He immediately spotted Kate with her mom and walked over to them. Kate stood up and said to her mom, "This is Tom. He's the really great firefighter who helped me to think about elevators in a more positive way."

Kate and Tom sat down. Kate asked, "Has everyone been rescued yet?"

"All the elevators marked on your map were checked out, and everyone was rescued."

"A lot of those people are here right now in this room."

Tom looked around and smiled. "They all seem so happy."

"They are." Kate's eyes glanced briefly at a group of people who were dancing together, even though there was no music playing. Her eyes then went back to fasten more securely onto Tom's face. "I don't think the people who were in the hidden elevator are here. Do you know what happened to them?"

"The lady named Heidi was taken to the hospital, but she's expected to make a full recovery."

"That's wonderful! What about the two or more people who were with her?"

"There were two men with Heidi in that elevator. As soon as the elevator's doors were pried open, one of the men sprinted away."

"Was he caught, by any chance?"

"Yes, he was. He ran along a walkway and then fell into an elevator shaft."

"Was he hurt?"

"He broke both his legs, but he'll eventually be okay."

"It was so stupid of him to try to run away inside a fallen-down building."

"Criminals most often are stupid. That's why many of them are criminals in the first place."

"What about the other man in the hidden elevator?"

"He was fine physically, but upset emotionally. He was quite upset about the other man who hit Heidi multiple times, even after she prayed for God to help him."

"I heard at least a part of her prayer. She tried to hide the fact that she had been praying."

"I think she was scared of Al, the escaped criminal who sometimes was hitting her."

"That explains what was happening in the hidden elevator. Heidi wasn't hiding her faith on purpose; she was just trying to do what Al wanted, so he wouldn't do anything super extreme, like killing her."

"The other man in that elevator also told police officers about Al making threats against you."

"He did threaten me, but at least I didn't have to stay in an elevator with that weirdo."

"The police will be contacting you for more information. They'll probably need you to appear at one or more of that guy's court hearings."

"I would love to give testimony about someone like that. He should be put into prison for a long time."

"He will be. He's actually a convicted murderer who escaped from prison, which is partially why he tried to run away. He didn't want to spend the rest of his life in prison."

Mary Hart, who was Tom's sister, came up to Tom and hugged him. She then looked at Kate and said, "You and my brother seem to be getting along really well together."

"We are."

"I'm so glad." Mary looked at her brother and said, "Kate was so very helpful. When I met her and realized that someone was alive and trying to contact the police about everyone's location, my anxiety lessened. I felt like we would really be rescued sometime soon, which actually did happen."

Tom picked up Kate's hand and squeezed it. "We haven't even been out on a date yet, and I already feel very strongly about her."

Kate squeezed Tom's hand and said, "I also have feelings for you, Tom."

"Where would you like to go for our first date?"

"I'd love to go anywhere at all, even into an elevator, as long as you're there with me."

"I'll find us a restaurant in a building with a nice elevator."

"This building has really neat elevators."

Tom stood up and smiled. "I have about a half an hour before I have to head back to work. Are you okay with such a short first date?"

Kate shook her head affirmatively. She then looked at her mom, who said, "I'll stay right here, Kate, and help some of the families with any problems they might be having. After your date with Tom has concluded, call me on your cell phone. I want to go and visit the library here before I leave today."

Tom stood up and asked, "Would you like to go with me right now to the West Wing Café?"

"I'd love to." Kate followed Tom up to one of the elevators. As soon as the door closed, Tom put his right hand on Kate's shoulder. They stared at each other for several seconds before kissing. When the elevator door opened up again, a man in a green suit got onto the elevator with them. He cleared his throat and then said, "Are you two getting off on this floor?"

Tom glanced over at the green-suited man and said, "Yes, we are. Thanks for being so patient with us."

"You're welcome."

Tom held onto Kate's hand as they exited the elevator. She said, "I wonder if it's okay to kiss on the elevator in the statehouse."

"Kissing and hugging have to be okay. People often meet their loved ones here." Tom looked around and then laughed. "We're not in the basement. I must have pressed the wrong button."

"The Rhode Island Charter Museum is on this floor. Do you have enough time to go there too or just enough time for a cup of coffee?"

Tom looked at his watch. "I have almost thirty minutes left before I have to go back to work."

Kate and Tom walked over to the museum, opened the door, and stepped inside. The room was not too well lit. Tom said, "The lighting and document cases in here are designed to preserve the letters and other items."

A lady with a large camera on a tripod was taking a photo of one of the letters. Kate said, "I know people aren't supposed to use the flashes on their cameras in here, so using a tripod must help to make the photo less blurry."

The camera-tripod lady finished taking the picture before saying, "The tripod, along with a good camera, definitely helps."

Kate and Tom walked over to one of the document cases. Kate said, "Whenever I look at an original document written by Roger Williams, I always have problems trying to figure out his handwriting."

"So do I. At least we can also look at the typed versions of most of his documents."

"There are summaries too like on the plaque beneath this November 1655 letter." Kate read it out loud: "In this letter Roger Williams pointed out to his fellow town residents that the roads were still quite dangerous and that even after twenty years of habitation, the wolves were still a constant threat to human life."[64]

"This winter, our roads aren't that good either. There are so many potholes."

"I'd much rather be in my car and encounter a pothole, rather than be walking and encounter a wolf."

Tom said, "Williams's use of the word 'wolves' might have been a metaphor for something else."

"He did use a lot of metaphors in his writing. Maybe he meant wolves to mean real wolves, or maybe he meant wolves to mean people who were acting like wolves."

"Either way, his experiences of walking along seventeenth-century roads must have been difficult at times." Tom pointed to the exhibit of Roger Williams's compass and timepiece. "His compass would have helped."

281

"His belief in God would have helped the most."

"He didn't just believe in God. He knew there was a God."

"I think you're right about that." Kate walked over to another one of the charter museum's exhibits. "Here's *The Bloudy Tenent of Persecution* exhibit. I think the changes in some of the letter forms are interesting."

"The word 'bloody' is spelled out as 'Blovdy,' so there have been changes in the last few hundred years in spelling, as well as in how some of the letters are formed."

"I like this quote on the descriptive plaque: 'But the sovereign, original, and foundation of civil power lies in the People...'[65]"

"That's the true nature of a democracy: the power is with the people."

"I saw democracy really happening in the different elevator communities. The people in each elevator often would debate with other people in their elevator community. They would then vote to determine the rules to be followed."

Kate and Tom spent a few more minutes looking around the charter museum before leaving. When they walked out to the rotunda, Kate said, "This part of the statehouse is so beautiful."

She looked upward while Tom said, "That dome is the fourth largest, self-supporting, marble dome in the whole world."

"I love those paintings of Commercium, Educatio, Justitia, and Litera."

"I like the whole idea of religious freedom, but also freedom of commerce, education, justice, and literary items."

Tom held onto Kate's hand as they walked into one of the elevators, went down to the basement, and sauntered over to the West Wing Café. Tom ordered some coffee and doughnuts; they then sat down at one of the small round tables. They talked about their families and their hopes for the future. They both wanted to have children, a large house in a rural area, a garden, and possibly a swimming pool. They also were both thankful to be able to make donations to their churches every week. Kate said, "We have so much in common. I'm so glad that we met."

"I am too." Tom held onto Kate's hand as he added, "I especially loved rescuing you from that fallen-down building. I was so scared that I would not be able to find you, and then there you were, climbing down the series of fire escape ladders on the outside of that building."

"I was glad to see you too. Being on a fire escape ladder and seeing a great fireman like you was so wonderful. However, I was worried—and am still worried—that I might lose you while you rescue more people in that fallen-down building."

"I'm here with you now, and I know that God will watch over us both."

Tom's cell phone rang. He answered it and then said to Kate, "I have to head back to work, but I loved our first date. I'll be calling you later tonight about a second date."

Kate smiled. "Even though I was stuck in that building earlier today, just seeing you for a little while has made today one of the happiest days in my life."

Tom kissed Kate's hand. He then escorted her to the door of the library in the statehouse and waved good-bye. Kate called her mom. "I'm waiting for you right outside the library, Mom."

"I'll be there in just a minute, Kate."

When her mom arrived at the door leading into the library, Kate said, "This is such a beautiful room. I've been looking at the clock and the historic printers' seals."

Kate's mom looked up at the printers' seals above the clock. "I also love everything on the walls and ceiling of this room, but I love the books even more." Her eyes moved from the books near the ceiling to the books on their level. She then walked over to the left section of the library.

As Kate followed her mother, her mom said, "Around 1650, Roger Williams wrote a really nice letter to his wife. In 1652, the letter was published in a book by Roger Williams: *Experiments of Spiritual Life and Health, and their Preservatives in which the Weakest Child of God may get Assurance of his Spirituall Life and Blessednesse and the Strongest May Finde Proportionable Discoveries of his Christian Growth, and the Means of It.* The letter or excerpts from the book are probably here in one of these books." Kate's mom reached down to one of the lower shelves and picked up a couple of the books about Roger Williams.

Kate said, "I have another book here. If the letter's not in one of those books, it could be in this one." She took a book out of her purse and set it down beside the ones chosen by her mother.

"Is that your book, Kate?"

"No, I borrowed it from one of the librarians in my new office building."

After Kate's mom looked at the table of contents and index in each book, she found the letter and said, "Williams's wife had been seriously ill and then quickly got better. In the first paragraph of his letter, Williams attributed his wife's recovery to the Lord: 'Thy late sudden and dangerous Sickness, and the Lords most gracious and speedy raising thee up from the gates and jawes of Death.'[66]"

Kate said, "It's interesting that Williams uses the words 'raising thee up.' It's almost like his wife rode an elevator to a higher spot in her lifetime."

"I think difficult times can help us to become stronger, as long as we stay close to God and use his help."

"I'm sure some people will claim the elevation of Williams's wife was just her physical body getting better all by itself, but I think her recovery sounds more like a miracle."

"Having a physical body that can fix itself is actually a miracle all by itself, but I completely agree with you. A sudden recovery from a serious illness in the seventeenth century would not have happened because of antibiotics or other modern devices."

"I think everyone being alive and escaping from that building today is definitely a miracle."

"It really is a miracle, especially since someone like you who is scared of elevators was able to help so many elevator people. I think we should thank God for his help. There's a nice sentence here by Roger Williams that blesses the Lord. Reading a quote by Roger Williams in the statehouse library would be a really nice way of saying thank you to God."

Kate looked around the library. She and her mom were not alone. On the other side of the library were three other people: Phebe, Nancy, and Freeborn. Kate introduced them to her mom, who said, "I'm so glad you're all safe now."

Freeborn said, "So I'm so sorry, Kate, for acting so badly while I was so stuck in that elevator."

Kate said, "Everyone, including myself, was really scared and anxious. I'm sorry too if I upset you or anyone else."

Phebe and Nancy also apologized. They then walked up to stand close to Kate and her mom. Phebe asked, "Are you going to read that quote to us?"

"I'd love to." Kate's mom then said, "The quote's a really nice prayer."

Freeborn, who was still on the other side of the library, said, "So if the quote's a prayer, there might be a problem. I don't know if it's okay to pray in the statehouse. There's separation of church and state in this country."

Kate asked, "Would you prefer my mom to read this quote somewhere else?"

Phebe shook her head at Freeborn before saying, "No, you need to read that quote right here and right now. I really want to hear what Roger Williams said while we're in the library in the Rhode Island State House. Especially after being stuck in an elevator, I really want to hear a prayer from our country's historic advocate for religious freedom."

Freeborn frowned and then said, "Roger Williams was a Baptist and then a seeker. What if I'm Jewish? Should I have to listen to a Christian prayer?"

Phebe said, "You don't have to listen to anything. You're not stuck in an elevator anymore. You can even leave this room while the quote is read."

Kate's mom said, "You can stay right where you are, Freeborn. You're on the other side of the library, so if I read the quote softly enough, you won't even hear it."

Phebe said, "I think you should read the quote very, very loudly. It's from Roger Williams, who believed in religious freedom. He was not trying to hurt people of different faiths. He even helped some Jewish people to find homes in his colony. A prayer that he wrote would be one from his heart and soul. It will be a loving prayer, not some kind of attack on people of different faiths."

Freeborn's face looked thoughtful as she said, "Roger Williams did want people to have liberty of conscience and the freedom to love God in their own way."

Phebe said, "God is present everywhere in our world. Even if we're in the statehouse, God is still present. If someone were to say to God, 'You're banished from the statehouse,' God would never listen to that person. He instead would stay in the statehouse in order to be near those who loved him and wanted to talk with him through prayer."

Kate shook her head in agreement. "Separation of church and state does not mean that we've banished God from the statehouse or any other place. It only means that we have been making political laws—not church laws—in the statehouse."

Nancy said, "Roger Williams wanted people to have liberty of conscience and the freedom to love God in their own way." She paused and then added, "I think it's a really great idea for you to read a quote from Roger Williams in the Rhode Island State House. If people want to think of the quote as a prayer, they can. If people want to think of the quote as a part of an historic letter, they also can."

Phebe stared at Freeborn and then said, "We're not forcing anyone to pray and connect to God while the quote's being read.

We just really want to hear the words of Roger Williams here and now."

Freeborn smiled. "So you've all convinced me that you're right. We do have the freedom to pray, and we shouldn't banish God from our lives. After so many people were freed from elevators, we should definitely read a quote that's a prayer from Roger Williams." She walked over to stand next to the other people in the library. "So the quote should be read as loudly as possible, even if there's someone in the corridor outside of the library who might hear it."

Kate said, "I think Roger Williams would be happy if he knew what we're doing."

Kate's mom said, "Here's the prayer quote in Williams's letter to his wife. The prayer appears in a sentence after Williams mentions David and Psalm 103: "Blesse the Lord O my Soul, and all that is within me blesse his holy Name: Blesse the Lord, O my Soul, and forget not all his benefits, who forgiveth all thy sins, and healeth thine infirmities: who redeemeth thy life from destruction, and crowneth thee with mercy and loving Kindnesse.'[67]"

"Can you read that quoted prayer again, Mom?"

After her mom read the excerpt from the Williams letter two more times, Kate said, "God really has redeemed my life from destruction, and I'm so thankful for that."

Kate's mom hugged her daughter. Then all five people hugged each other.

A voice from the corridor said, "What were you just reading?"

"It was a quoted prayer from a Roger Williams letter."

"Can you read it again?"

Kate's mom said, "I'd love to read it again and again. In fact, I'm going to take a picture of it with my cell phone."

After Kate's mom took the picture, she looked up and saw a library filled with people. They were squeezed in tightly together, as if they were on a giant elevator. All the people were quietly waiting for Kate's mom to read the excerpt from the Roger Williams letter again. After she read the excerpt a few more times, everyone clapped their hands in joy. Some people then put their hands together and prayed silently. Others prayed out loud. Many different kinds of prayers were heard.

After saying "Amen" to each other's prayers, everyone began to talk. Happy connections were made by adults and children from different families, elevators, work places, and ethnicities. They expressed themselves with joyful words, gestures, and body language. Then many of the people took pictures of each other and posted them on different social media. Phebe, Nancy, Freeborn, and other people also took pictures of the Roger Williams prayer.

Freeborn then turned her iPad on. The song "Thrive" by the Christian band Casting Crowns, began to play loudly enough for everyone in the room and anyone in the corridor to enjoy it.

One of the people in the library went over to Kate and asked, "Is it appropriate to play music that loudly in a library?"

"I don't know what the rules are for behaviors in this library, but I think today is different from most days. Freeborn is now free after being stuck in an elevator and should be able to enjoy some music."

Kate and some other people in the room began to sing a few of the lines from the song: "Joy unspeakable, faith unsinkable, / Love unstoppable, anything is possible"[68]

After the ending of the song, some people left the library, and other people came inside. Freeborn read the Roger Williams prayer for the newcomers in the library. After listening again to the prayer, Kate and her mom left the library and walked over to the center of the statehouse, where the elevators were located. Metal copies of the seal of the state of Rhode Island were on the golden elevator doors. The word "hope" above the anchor made Kate smile. "I have a lot more hope now about my ability to ride on elevators."

Her mom said, "The statehouse has the seal in different places. I like the cloth version better because it has more details in it."

"I think I like the elevator version of the seal better, just because I've been so close to elevators lately."

"The state's website has some information about the seal." Kate's mom opened her purse, took out her smartphone, and quickly found the webpage. She said, "A statehouse seal containing the word 'hope' and an anchor were first approved by the Rhode Island General Assembly on May 4, 1664. According to the RI.gov website, some historical notes by Howard M. Chapin explain 'the words and emblems on the Seal were probably inspired by the biblical phrase "hope we have as an anchor of the soul", contained in Hebrews 6:18–19.'[69]"

"Can you pull up an electronic Bible on your phone? I'm curious about the exact wording of the Bible verses."

Kate's mom found an online Bible and said, "The first verse is saying that God is truthful in his promise of hope. I'll read it out loud: 'So that through two unchangeable things, in which it is impossible that God would prove false, we who have taken refuge might be strongly encouraged to seize the hope set before us' (Heb. 6:18, RSV)."

"God is steadfast. He would never change a promise."

"You're right about that." Kate's mom looked at her phone's screen and said, "Just verses 18 and 19 were mentioned on the state's website, but I'll be reading to you verses 19 and 20 right now. They both explain about the hope mentioned in verse 18: 'We have this hope, a sure and steadfast anchor of the soul, a hope that enters the inner shrine behind the curtain, where Jesus, a forerunner on our behalf, has entered, having become a high priest forever according to the order of Melchizedek' (Heb. 6:19–20, RSV)."

"Jesus is the hope and anchor of my soul." Kate smiled at her mom.

"You know that I feel the same way as you do." Kate's mom smiled back at her daughter.

"It's so neat to see these elevators with images of the state seal on them."

"I love the state seal too. It includes the ideal of hope and the strength of an anchor in a single spot."

Kate pressed the "up" button on the elevator before saying, "A couple of days ago, if I were only going up one flight, then I'd be taking the stairs. However, I now love riding in these elevators."

Kate's mom hugged her daughter. "I'm so glad that your experience in that falling-down building has elevated you to a higher level."

"Why do you think I'm at a higher level?"

"You're no longer scared of riding in an elevator that will carry you upward. You used to always want only the stairs, but now you have the freedom to choose either the stairs or an elevator."

As the elevator doors opened, Kate smiled. "I might sometimes still choose to take the stairs, but you're correct. I'm no longer afraid of being elevated upward by a power beyond my own."

The Bloudy Tenent of Persecution Exhibit in the Rhode Island Charter Museum at the Rhode Island State House

The bloudy tenent of persecution for cause of conscience discussed : and Mr. Cotton's letter examined and answered, 1644 — Roger Williams
[London: printed by Gregory Dexter, 1644.]
RHODE ISLAND HISTORICAL SOCIETY

This volume outlines Roger Williams's defense of the rights of individuals to what he called liberty of conscience, or the right to worship without interference by the government, and to form governments responsive to the will of the people. It was the framework for much of the ideology John Clarke used two decades later in the King Charles Charter of 1663.

"But the sovereign, original, and foundation of civil power lies in the People....And if so that a people may erect and establish what forms of Government seems to them most meet for their civil condition, it is evident that such governments as are by them erected and established have no more power, nor for longer time, than the civil power, or people consenting and agreeing, shall betrust them with."

Descriptive Plaque of the Bloudy Tenent of Persecution in the Rhode Island Charter Museum at the Rhode Island State House

Painting of Commercium in the Rhode Island State House

Painting of Educatio in the Rhode Island State House

Painting of Justitia in the Rhode Island State House

Painting of Litera in the Rhode Island State House

Library in the Rhode Island State House

Seal of the State of Rhode Island and Providence Plantations

Elevator Version of the Seal of the State of Rhode Island and Providence Plantations

ENDNOTES

1. Jill Rodrigues, "The Renaissance of Roger Williams," *Roger Williams University Magazine*, no. 9 (Fall 2013): 23, http://rwu.edu/sites/default/files/flipbooks/rwumagazine/rwufall2013/index.html#58 (accessed May 19, 2015).

2. Climax Blues Band, "Couldn't Get It Right," *songlyrics.com*, accessed June 17, 2015, http://www.songlyrics.com/climax-blues-band/couldn-t-get-it-right-lyrics/.

3. Ibid.

4. Daniel Erlacher, quoted in Shirley S. Wang, "The Benefits of Lucid Dreaming," *The Wall Street Journal* (Aug. 12, 2014): 1, http://www.wsj.com/articles/the-benefits-of-lucid-dreaming-1407772779?mod=e2tw (accessed Aug. 12, 2014).

5. Tadas Stumbrys et al., "The Phenomenology of Lucid Dreaming: An Online Survey," *The American Journal of Psychology*, Vol. 127, No. 2 (Summer 2014): 192, University of Illinois Press, *jstor.org*, http://0-ww.jstor.org.helin.uri.edu/stable/10.5406/amerjpsyc.127.2.0191 (accessed January 12, 2015).

6. Jessica Hamzelou, "The Secret of Consciousness: Reinterpreting Dreams," *New Scientist* 206, no. 2764 (June 12, 2010): 36-39, in *Academic Search Complete*, EBSCO*host*, http://0-search.ebscohost.com.helin.uri.

edu/login.aspx?direct=true&db=a9h&AN=51475659&si te=ehost-live (accessed January 12, 2015).

7. "Hahn Memorial," Roger Williams National Memorial, National Park Service, last modified May 3, 2015, http://www.nps.gov/rowi/learn/historyculture/hahnmemorial.htm.

8. Roger Williams, *The Bloudy Tenent of Persecution for Cause of Conscience Discussed; and Mr. Cotton's Letter Examined and Answered*, ed. Edward Bean Underhill. (London: J. Haddon, 1848), 2, in Internet Archive, *archive.org*, https://ia600401.us.archive.org/18/items/thebloudytenento00willuoft/thebloudytenento00willuoft.pdf (accessed January 16, 2015).

9. "Liberty for the Soul," *American History* 42, no. 1 (April 2007): 24-29. *Academic Search Complete*, EBSCO*host* (accessed January 21, 2015).

10. Roger Williams, "Introduction," to *A Key into the Language of America*, quoted in Edwin S. Gaustad, *Roger Williams: Lives and Legacies* (Oxford: Oxford University Press, 2005), 47.

11. Roger Williams, *A Key into the Language of America: or, An help to the Language of the Natives in that part of America, called New-England*, vol.: copy 1 (1643): 78, in Internet Archive, *archive.org*, https://archive.org/details/keyintolanguageo02will (accessed January 16, 2015), 9.

12. Roger Williams, *A Key into the Language of America: or, An help to the Language of the Natives in that part of America, called New-England*, vol.: copy 1 (1643): 78, in Internet Archive, *archive.org*, https://archive.org/details/keyintolanguageo02will (accessed January 16, 2015), 1.

13. Perry Miller, *Roger Williams: His Contribution to the American Tradition* (New York: Atheneum, 1966), 52.

14. Ibid.

15. Roger Williams Family Association, "Roger Williams ... A Brief Biography," *rogerwilliams.org*, http://www. rogerwilliams.org/biography.htm (accessed Jan. 21, 2105).

16. Larry Shannon-Missal, "Americans' Belief in God, Miracles and Heaven Declines," *Harris Interactive*, Harris Poll #97, (Dec. 16, 2013), http://www.harrisinteractive.com/ NewsRoom/HarrisPolls/tabid/447/ctl/ReadCustom%20 Default/mid/1508/ArticleId/1353/Default.aspx (accessed Jan. 28, 2015).

17. Roger Williams, "To Major John Mason and Governor Thomas Prence, 22 June 1670." *The Correspondence of Roger Williams*, volume 2, 1654-1682, ed. Glenn W. LaFantasie. (Hanover: Brown University Press/University Press of New England, 1988.), 611.

18. Roger Williams, *A Key into the Language of America: or, An help to the Language of the Natives in that part of America, called New-England*, vol.: copy 1 (1643): 78, in Internet Archive, *archive.org*, https://archive.org/details/ keyintolanguageo02will (accessed January 16, 2015).

19. Ibid.

20. Roger Williams, qtd. in Perry Miller, *Roger Williams His Contribution to the American Tradition*, College Edition, (New York: Atheneum, 1966), 139.

21. Edwin S. Gaustad, *Roger Williams: Lives and Legacies.* (Oxford: Oxford University Press, 2005), 26.

22. William Bradford, *Of Plymouth Plantation*, ed. Harold Paget. (Mineola, New York: Dover Publications, Inc. 2006), 164.

23. William G. McLoughlin, *Rhode Island A History* (New York: W.W. Norton & Co., Inc., 1978), 12.

24. *American History*, s.v. "Roger Williams," accessed January 23, 2015. http://0-americanhistory2.abc-clio.com.helin.uri.edu/.

25. Edwin S. Gaustad, *Roger Williams: Lives and Legacies.* (Oxford: Oxford University Press, 2005), 122.

26. Abraham Lincoln (1863), quoted in Karen Petit, *Mayflower Dreams.* (Mustang, Oklahoma: Tate Publishing and Enterprises, LLC, 2014), 343.

27. James P. Byrd, Jr., *The Challenges of Roger Williams: Religious Liberty, Violent Persecution, and the Bible.* (Macon, Georgia: Mercer University Press, 2002), 183.

28. Edwin S. Gaustad, *Roger Williams: Lives and Legacies.* (Oxford: Oxford University Press, 2005), 97.

29. Roger Williams, "To Governor John Winthrop, Jr., 18 December 1675." in *The Correspondence of Roger Williams,* volume 2, 1654-1682, ed. Glenn W. LaFantasie. (Hanover: Brown University Press/University Press of New England, 1988.) 709.

30. *American History*, s.v. "Roger Williams: *Bloudy Tenent of Persecution* (1644)," accessed January 23, 2015. http://0-americanhistory2.abc-clio.com.helin.uri.edu/.

31. Linford D. Fisher, J. Stanley Lemons, and Lucas Mason-Brown, *Decoding Roger Williams: The Lost Essay of Rhode Island's Founding Father* (Waco, Texas: Baylor University Press, 2014), footnote 13 on page 73.

32. "Roger Williams," *Issues & Controversies in American History,* Infobase Publishing, (Jan. 23, 2007), accessed June 13, 2014, http://icah.infobaselearning.com/icahspotlight.aspx?ID=111630.

33. "Roger Williams: Liberty of Conscience letter (1655)," *American History,* accessed June 13, 2014, http://0-americanhistory2.abc-clio.com.helin.uri.edu/.

34. Ibid.

35. Jonathan Beecher Field, "A Key for the Gate: Roger Williams, Parliament, and Providence," *The New England Quarterly*, vol. 80, no. 3 (Sept., 2007): 354, in JSTOR, *jstor.org*, http://www.jstor.org/stable/20474553 (accessed May 8, 2015).

36. *American History*, s.v. "Roger Williams: *Bloudy Tenent of Persecution* (1644)," http://0-americanhistory2.abc-clio.com.helin.uri.edu/ (accessed January 23, 2015).

37. State of Rhode Island–Division of Taxation, "Sales and Use Tax Regulation SU 99-143, Tax Exemption of Sales by Writers, Composers and Artists," *Sales Tax Regulations*, January 1, 1999, http://www.tax.ri.gov/regulations/salestax/99-143.php.

38. Roger Williams, "To Governor John Winthrop, 20 August 1637," *The Correspondence of Roger Williams*, vol. 1, 1629-1653, ed. by Glenn W. LaFantasie (Hanover: Brown University Press/University Press of New England, 1988), 114.

39. Roger Williams, "A Key into the Language of America," ed. by J. Hammond Trumbull, in *The Complete Writings of Roger Williams*, vol. 1. (New York: Russell & Russell, Inc., 1963), 181.

40. Quahog.org, "Roger Williams's Landing Place Monument," http://www.quahog.org/attractions/index.php?id=68, (accessed May 9, 2015).

41. Linford D. Fisher, J. Stanley Lemons, and Lucas Mason-Brown, *Decoding Roger Williams: The Lost Essay of Rhode Island's Founding Father* (Waco, Texas: Baylor University Press, 2014), 7.

42. Linford D. Fisher, J. Stanley Lemons, and Lucas Mason-Brown, *Decoding Roger Williams: The Lost Essay of Rhode*

Island's Founding Father (Waco, Texas: Baylor University Press, 2014), 17.

43. ri.gov, *Rhode Island Royal Charter of 1663*, http://sos. ri.gov/library/history/charter/, (accessed June 15, 2015).

44. Ibid.

45. ri.gov, "The Rhode Island Charter Museum," *State House Online Tour*, http://sos.ri.gov/StateHouseTour/ secondfloor/, (accessed June 11, 2015).

46. *American History*, s.v. "Roger Williams: Liberty of Conscience letter (1655)," accessed June 13, 2014. http://0-americanhistory2.abc-clio.com.helin.uri.edu/.

47. J. Stanley Lemons, "The Charter of 1663, Major Milestone on the Road to Religious Liberty," *A Lively Experiment: Reflections on the Charter of 1663*, Rhode Island Council for the Humanities, https://livelyexperiment.files.wordpress.com /2013/11/charter-essays.pdf, (accessed June 13, 2015).

48. James Calvin Davis, "A Return to Civility: Roger Williams and Public Discourse in America," *Journal of Church & State* 43, no. 4 (September 2001): 695, in *America: History & Life*, EBSCO*host* (accessed January 23, 2015).

49. Nan Goodman, "Banishment, Jurisdiction, and Identity in Seventeenth-Century New England: The Case of Roger Williams," *Early American Studies, An Interdisciplinary Journal* 7, no. 1 (Spring 2009): 118, in *America: History & Life*, EBSCO*host* (accessed January 23, 2015).

50. John M. Barry, *Roger Williams and the Creation of the American Soul: Church, State, and the Birth of Liberty* (New York: Viking, 2012), 174.

51. L. Raymond Camp, *Roger Williams, God's Apostle of Advocacy: Biography and Rhetoric* (Lewiston, NY: Edwin Mellen Press, 1989), 140-41.

52. ushistory.org, "Massachusetts Bay—'The City Upon a Hill,'" *U.S. History Online Textbook,* http://www.ushistory.org/us/3c.asp (accessed May 22, 2015).

53. Roger Williams, "To Governor John Winthrop, Jr., 18 December 1675." in *The Correspondence of Roger Williams,* volume 2, 1654-1682, ed. Glenn W. LaFantasie. (Hanover: Brown University Press/University Press of New England, 1988.) 709.

54. Glenn W. LaFantasie, ed. *The Correspondence of Roger Williams,* volume 2, 1654-1682. (Hanover: Brown University Press/University Press of New England, 1988.) 709.

55. John M. Barry, "God, Government and Roger Williams' Big Idea," *Smithsonian.com,* January 2012, http://www.smithsonianmag.com/history/god-government-and-roger-williams-big-idea-6291280/?no-ist.

56. Roger Williams, "A Key into the Language of America," ed. by J. Hammond Trumbull, in *The Complete Writings of Roger Williams,* vol. 1. (New York: Russell & Russell, Inc., 1963), 90.

57. Roger Williams, "A Key into the Language of America," ed. by J. Hammond Trumbull, in *The Complete Writings of Roger Williams,* vol. 1. (New York: Russell & Russell, Inc., 1963), 112.

58. Roger Williams, "To Governor John Winthrop, ca. 9 September 1637," in *The Correspondence of Roger Williams,* vol. 1, 1629-1653, ed. Glenn W. LaFantasie. (Hanover and London: Brown University Press/University Press of New England, 1988), 119.

59. Roger Williams, *A Key into the Language of America: or, An help to the Language of the Natives in that part of America, called New-England,* vol.: copy 1 (1643): 162, in

Internet Archive, *archive.org,* https://archive.org/details/keyintolanguageo02will (accessed January 16, 2015).

60. Michael Larson, Jesus Culture, "Freedom Reigns, *SongLyrics,* accessed March 27, 2015, http://www.songlyrics.com/jesus-culture/freedom-reigns-lyrics/.

61. Ibid.

62. Nan Goodman, "Banishment, Jurisdiction, and Identity in Seventeenth-Century New England: The Case of Roger Williams," *Early American Studies, An Interdisciplinary Journal* 7, no. 1 (Spring 2009): 136, in *America: History & Life,* EBSCO*host* (accessed January 23, 2015).

63. Paul McCartney, "Get Me Out Of Here." *Oldielyrics,* accessed March 27, 2015, http://www.oldielyrics.com/lyrics/paul_mccartney/get_me_out_of_here.html.

64. Rhode Island Historical Society, Plaque beneath the "Letter to the Town of Providence, ca. 1 November 1655," Rhode Island Charter Museum, Rhode Island State House, accessed on March 17, 2015.

65. Roger Williams, quote from *The Bloudy Tenent of Persecution for Cause of Conscience Discussed : and Mr. Cotton's Letter Examined and Answered,* 1644, on Rhode Island Historical Society Plaque, Rhode Island Charter Museum, Rhode Island State House, accessed on March 17, 2015.

66. Roger Williams, "The Letter which the Author sent with this Discourse to his Wife M.W. upon her recovery from a dangerous sickness," in *The Complete Writings of Roger Williams,* 7th ed., ed. Perry Miller. (New York: Russell & Russell, Inc., 1963), 55.

67. Ibid.

68. Casting Crowns, "Thrive," *lyrics.net,* accessed February 3, 2015, http://www.lyrics.net/lyric/30409046.

69. ri.gov, "Origins of the Seal of the State of Rhode Island and Providence Plantations," *State Symbols,* https://www. ri.gov/facts/factsfigures.php, accessed May 26, 2015.

CPSIA information can be obtained
at www.ICGtesting.com
Printed in the USA
BVOW11s1114080716

454881BV00008B/26/P